6 BLOCKS HOME

TARA J. STONE

ISBN: 1-7349142-4-6
ISBN-13: 978-1-7349142-4-5

For my family.

August 2015

A friend loves at all times,
and a brother is born for adversity.

Proverbs 17:17

ONE

𝄞

For a boy who took everything so seriously, Tobias Howard was always running late, and Sam was always waiting on him.

It was the first day of school, and Samantha Josephine Ingram was thrilled that her mom and Tobias's mom had arranged for them to walk to school together now that they both attended junior high. How proud she would be, a measly seventh grader being escorted by the handsomest eighth grader in town. But now that Tobias was running late — again — she wondered about the prudence of the idea. Maybe she should just start walking.

Sam hummed to herself, kicked at a pebble, and watched it skitter across the pavement. She huffed impatiently. Her insides started to squirm. If he made her late on her first day of junior high...

Behind her, she heard the Howards' front door open. She whirled to see Tobias hurry out, his mom standing in the doorway behind him. Tobias wore a scowl, as usual, but his mom smiled and waved at Sam.

"Enjoy your first day!" Tobias's mom called.

Unsure whom she was addressing, Sam nevertheless waved back and said, "Thanks, Mrs. Howard!"

Tobias didn't even look at Sam as he marched right past her toward the alley that cut between houses. Sam scurried to keep up and fall in step beside him. His legs were so much longer than hers.

"Good morning!" Sam tried to sound cheerful, but it came out rather breathless as she worked to keep up with Tobias's long and impossibly fast strides.

"Sorry I'm late," he muttered. He still wouldn't look at her.

"That's okay. I was getting pretty nervous, though. I almost started

5

walking without you, but then I didn't think I could find the school by myself." It was a lie. She had a precise map in her head.

Tobias didn't respond.

He was like that sometimes, but Sam didn't mind. She figured it was because he had such a large family, and he had probably grown used to just listening while everyone else did the talking.

Thinking he needed encouragement to participate in the conversation, she decided to ask him a question: "Are you excited? About being an eighth grader, I mean?"

"I don't know."

She waited for him to elaborate. He didn't.

"Well, I'm excited," Sam said, deciding that Tobias might feel more comfortable opening up if she did first. "To be in junior high, I mean. Not about being in eighth grade. I mean, how could I be excited about being in eighth grade when I'm only starting seventh grade?"

Still nothing.

Sam tried a new tack: silence. Maybe he would grow uncomfortable with the silence if she said nothing at all. And that's how the rest of the walk to school passed.

In silence.

$$| \text{\textbackslash} \quad \flat \quad \sharp \quad \flat \quad |$$

Sam had lied.

Even though she was more than pleased to walk to school with Tobias, she was not at all excited about the prospect of school itself. She was brilliant — so brilliant, in fact, that she had started to pretend that she was a terrible student. Well, maybe not terrible. Average. Or maybe just a tiny bit above average. She couldn't hide her brains altogether.

The teachers deemed brilliance reason to assign extra work. And the other students... Not that Sam cared what the other students thought. She had no interest in being well liked among the masses. But the bullying at previous schools had been inconvenient at best, painful at worst.

And so, ever since they had moved to this school district three years ago, she had played dumb. Sort of. She still wasn't well liked among the masses, but at least she could fly under the radar this way.

Starting a new school year meant re-establishing herself as just an average student. It took effort — more effort than one would think — but teachers and bullies alike were all about first impressions. Sam really only had to sell her average-ness for a week or two to be left in peace for the whole term.

Tobias reminded Sam which direction to go to reach the seventh grade wing when they arrived at the school, but he said nothing else before heading toward the eighth grade wing. Sam, happy to get any words out of him, let him believe that she was lost and overwhelmed. He didn't know about her big brains either. In fact, Sam had memorized the entire layout of the school months ago when sixth graders had been invited to follow a junior high student for a day.

Sam was a little sorry about hiding her brains from Tobias, but she knew some boys were intimidated by girls with big brains. She figured she would reveal the truth someday, but by then he would be madly in love with her and would be delighted to find that his ladylove was, in fact, a genius.

Sam smirked at the ridiculous thought. As if Tobias would ever fall in love with her. Ha!

But a girl could dream, couldn't she?

$$| \natural \; \downarrow \; \flat \; \downarrow \; |$$

Sam didn't hate her first day of junior high. But she didn't love it either.

Of all her classes, Sam felt sure she would like band the best. Most of the time, her parents left her to her own devices, but one thing they insisted on doing as a family no matter where they lived (and they hadn't always lived in nice neighborhoods like they did now) was music. Although neither of her parents played an instrument, they took Sam to symphony and chamber and jazz concerts two or three times a month. They had even gone to a handful of operas last season, which were enjoyable if not a little indulgent.

Sam had taken piano lessons as long as she could remember, and the opportunity to learn a new instrument excited her. She had chosen to learn the trumpet. It was hard — much harder than she had anticipated — but the challenge of it made her feel that band would be the only class worth her time and effort.

She successfully flew under the radar in all her academic classes except one: English. All because of that stupid icebreaker. Mrs. Gordon asked to go around the room, everyone saying their name and their favorite book. Sam, trying to be honest, declared that her favorite book was *Jane Eyre* by Charlotte Brontë. Mrs. Gordon's face lit up like Times Square, and Sam knew she should've said something about that boy wizard instead. Mrs. Gordon spent the remainder of the class throwing winks and *Jane Eyre* references Sam's way. She even started to call her *Adèle*, which Sam found more than a little insulting.

But the nickname wasn't the worst of it. By the end of class, Sam pegged the greasy-haired meathead in the back row as the primary threat to her desire for anonymity. Mrs. Gordon had unwittingly put a target on Sam's back, and she practically felt the meathead — Jason was his name, and he'd named a porn magazine as his favorite book — zeroing in. His height and bulk and sporadic patches of facial hair made Sam wonder if he'd been held back a grade or two, and he smelled like day-old sweat and onions. The thought of Jason cornering her in some dark alley made Sam shudder, and she thanked her lucky stars that Tobias would be walking her to and from school everyday.

Speaking of which… He was running late again.

Sam waited outside the front doors of the school and watched as the steady stream of kids spilling out turned to a trickle. Finally, Tobias emerged with another eighth grade boy Sam recognized as a frequent visitor to the Howard house. They laughed and joked together, and seeing Tobias smile immediately brightened Sam's mood.

"Hey, Tobias!" she called and waved as she skipped up to them.

"Oh, hey, Sam," Tobias said. "Ready to go?"

"Been ready for, like, ten minutes." She meant it as a joke, but it didn't come out right.

"I know. I'm sorry. I had to talk to one of my teachers."

"There's my mom. See you tomorrow, Toby," the other boy said as he trotted off toward a car parked at the curb.

"See ya." Tobias turned to Sam and raised his eyebrows as if saying the words *Are you ready* out loud would be too much effort.

"Toby?"

"Only my friends call me that." Tobias's scowl returned.

Oh. Did that mean he didn't consider her a friend? Ouch.

Sam bobbed her head as if it didn't bother her, and they started the walk toward home.

"So," she began, determined not to let him see her bruised feelings, "how was your first day?"

Tobias shrugged. "Okay, I guess."

Sam waited. This time her patience was rewarded.

"Yours?"

She shrugged and tried to mimic his tone. "Okay, I guess."

Tobias gave her a sidelong look and grinned.

She grinned back.

And they walked the rest of the way in silence.

|♩ ♩. ♪ ♩ |

"Samantha, is that you, honey?"

Sam's mom always asked this question when she came home from school. Sam had almost forgotten about this daily ritual over the summer. Now it struck her as curious, and she wondered if her mom expected someone else to come barging through their front door from time to time.

"No, it's the FBI," Sam called out blandly.

Her mom appeared from her hobby room. Sam had no idea what her mom did in her hobby room. Every time Sam went in there, she failed to find any trace of any kind of hobby. Nothing but an empty desk, a chair, and a locked file cabinet. What she wouldn't give to find out what that cabinet contained.

Sam's father had an office in the basement instead of a hobby room, but he was equally private about it. More, actually. Sam never understood what her father did for work — he was what they called a *businessman*, but like her mother's hobby, her father's business was a mystery to her. Whenever he left for work or traveled for business, which was often, he locked the door to his home office. Even when her father was in his office, Sam dared not enter. She'd learned that lesson early on, having walked in without knocking once. It was the only time her father had ever laid a hand on her. It was the last time she'd given him reason to.

"That's not funny, Samantha."

Sam shrugged and dropped her backpack by the door.

"That doesn't belong there," her mom reprimanded before she disappeared again into her hobby room and shut the door.

Sam rolled her eyes, picked up her backpack, and trudged toward her room. She mimicked her mom's voice: "How was your first day of school, honey?" In her own voice: "It sucked, thanks for caring."

The door to the hobby room whipped open as she was passing it, startling her.

"Mrs. Howard called to invite you to Tobias's birthday party on Saturday."

"Really?" Sam was genuinely shocked. And pleased. Maybe he did think of her as a friend after all.

"It starts at four. He's having some boys over, too, that are going to stay the night, but obviously you're only invited for dinner and cake and presents and all that."

"Well, right."

"Do you have homework?"

"On the first day? Please."

Sam's mom rolled her eyes (Sam thought at least she came by it honestly) and huffed indignantly. She muttered to herself as she turned away and closed the door once more. "Twelve years old and already giving me teenage attitude."

Sam shrugged at her mother's antics. She could never make up her mind whether she truly got on her mother's nerves or if it were all for show. If she'd had any siblings, Sam would've had some other Ingram kid's experience to compare with her own. But she was her parents' only child.

Sam sometimes imagined having a big family like Tobias's. He was the youngest of four — one girl at the top followed by three boys. Tobias's mom only rolled her eyes at her children in good fun, and an *Oh, brother* and a laugh always followed. Truthfully, Sam kind of wished her mom were more like Tobias's mom. More relaxed and happy and wanting to hear all about Sam's day.

The door opened again. Sam hadn't moved.

"Don't forget to practice for your piano lesson." The door shut.

Sam sighed and went to her room.

She didn't practice.

And her mom didn't notice.

TWO
𝄢:

"You did what?!" Tobias exclaimed, incredulous.

"Don't you like Sam?" his mom asked. She bustled around the kitchen preparing dinner.

"What? No. I mean... No. Mom. She's a seventh grader." Did he really need to say more than that?

"That's not what I meant, and you know it." Did he? "She just doesn't seem to have many other friends, and I thought you and your friends could sort of — I don't know — take her under your wing."

Tobias stared at his mom. She was always meddling. And she liked Sam way too much.

"She hums to herself all the time. And she wears socks with her sandals. And she's a *seventh grader*."

"An adorable and delightful seventh grader." She wagged her eyebrows.

"Mom."

"Tobias."

He exhaled in frustration, and his mom grinned. She knew she'd won.

"I don't know what you're so worried about," she said. "She'll probably spend more time in here with me anyway."

"She's a seventh grade *girl*." Why didn't his mom get it? He would never hear the end of it from his friends if a *seventh grade girl* came to his birthday party.

Frustratingly, his mom feigned shock. "A girl? You don't say. I never noticed." And she went back to peeling potatoes.

Tobias threw up his hands and left the kitchen.

THREE

&

Sam arrived for the party before anyone else.

When she rang the doorbell, she could hear Tobias's mom call out and Tobias answer. She waited. And hummed. And waited.

After a while, Tobias's mom called out again. Sam imagined the rumbling sound she heard next was Tobias hustling down the stairs to answer the door. Her imagination lined up with reality when the door yanked open, and Tobias stood there with a scowl on his face.

"Happy birthday, Tobias!" Sam said brightly, hoping his scowl had nothing to do with her.

She handed him a small gift bag. She had made him a keychain with a craft set she'd received several birthdays ago and never bothered to use until now. She was terrible at crafts, but she didn't have any money or time to buy anything.

Tobias stepped aside to let her in. "Hey, Sam. Thanks for coming." He didn't sound all that grateful, though.

"Thanks for inviting me," she replied as she entered.

Before Tobias even had a chance to shut the door, the next guest arrived: the boy she had seen laughing and joking with Tobias on the first day of school.

"Hey, Toby!" he said, a little out of breath. A car honked from the driveway, and he waved to dismiss them.

Tobias's scowl eased a bit. "Hey, Luke."

Luke didn't even glance at Sam. As if she were invisible.

The two boys chatted and punched each other's shoulders and ambled toward the stairs to the basement, where Sam knew the Howards had a huge game room with a pool table and the latest video gaming console.

She followed them, her eyes lingering on the family pictures cleverly arranged on the hallway wall as she went. In the center of the arrangement was an elegant decorative quote: *As for me and my house, we will serve the LORD.*

The walls in Sam's house were mostly bare, perhaps because her parents had long ago decided that wall decor was too much trouble to move from house to house every few years. But Sam decided that family pictures made a house feel more alive and welcoming, and she made a mental note to ask her mom later if they could have a professional family picture taken so they could hang it in their hallway.

In the basement, once Tobias had deposited Sam's gift on the pool table and Luke set his next to it, the boys went straight for the video games. Luke settled into one of the swivel floor chairs as if he'd been there a million times, and Tobias passed him one of the player controls. He looked up at Sam as if just now remembering her existence.

"Oh, sorry, Sam." Tobias shrugged. "It's only a two-player game."

Sam was a little mad at herself for having hurt feelings, but hurt they were. She swallowed and replied, "Oh, that's okay. I'll just watch."

But she didn't watch for long before the doorbell rang again and another boy shoved past her to join Tobias and Luke in front of the giant screen. And then another boy. And another. One of them did a double-take when he saw her, but none of them said a word to her.

Finally, realizing the awful truth that it probably hadn't been Tobias's idea to invite her at all, she headed back upstairs to find the one who *had* invited her: Tobias's mom. Sam found her in the kitchen pouring a bag of chips into a bowl.

"Hi, Sam!" Tobias's mom always seemed happy to see her, and it eased the sting of Tobias's repudiation a bit.

"Hi, Mrs. Howard."

"Lydia, remember?"

"But—"

"No buts. You and I are friends, Sam. And my friends call me Lydia."

Sam smiled. "Okay."

"Would you like to get a bowl out of that cupboard for the salsa?" Lydia nodded to a cabinet near Sam.

Eager to feel helpful, Sam did as Lydia asked. She pulled a bowl out of the cabinet and poured the nearby jar of salsa into it.

"Thank you, dear," Lydia said.

Somehow, even though Sam hadn't spent much time here, Lydia's kitchen felt more like home than her own house across the street. Sam attributed it to Lydia herself — she treated Sam with a familiarity and kindness that made her feel she belonged — but the decor, like the family pictures in the hallway, also gave the kitchen a comfortable, lived-in feeling.

A disparate collection of magnets held candid photos, greeting cards, and handwritten reminders on the fridge. The stove backsplash was a collage of old wine corks with a cluster of grapes painted across it. A rack on the counter held coffee mugs — some from places the Howards had traveled, others with inspirational quotes and doves or angels, all of them worn with use. The most colorful mug featured a beautiful painting of a young family — a man, a woman, and a baby — all with halos around their heads.

"Do you want to take these back down with you?" Lydia held out the bowl of chips and the bowl of salsa to Sam.

"Tobias didn't actually want me here, did he?" Sam wasn't afraid to ask the question so frankly. She was afraid of the answer, though.

"Why do you say that?" There was an odd twinkle in Lydia's eye. Like a smile that didn't involve her mouth. "Is he being rude?"

Sam shrugged. He was being rude, but she didn't want to say that.

"You know what I think?" Lydia said. "I think Tobias does want you here, but he thinks his friends will tease him about having a girlfriend."

Sam's eyebrows shot so high she thought they might fly off her forehead. "Girlfriend?"

"Sure. You're a girl. And his friend. Right?" Lydia winked and held out the bowls of chips and salsa.

Sam grinned and took them. She headed back downstairs, determined to squirm her way into the boys' conversation somehow. But when she went back downstairs, they were so raucous and rowdy, wrestling and shouting and teasing, she immediately changed her mind. She left the chips and salsa on the pool table and retreated upstairs once more.

"No luck?"

Sam shook her head. "Boys are weird."

Lydia laughed. Not one of those courtesy laughs people use when they know you're trying to be funny but don't quite pull it off. A real laugh, full of warmth and humor.

"Then I guess you're stuck with me again. Help me with the cake?"

Sam smiled and nodded. It disappointed her that Tobias had been so rude, and being ignored by him and his friends did sting; but she had to admit that she thoroughly enjoyed spending time with Lydia.

Her own mother never invited her to help in the kitchen. Heck, her own mother hardly ever went into the kitchen — her parents usually just microwaved frozen dinners or ordered delivery.

It seemed a traitorous thought, but Sam felt that the more time she spent with Lydia, the more she learned about the kind of woman she wanted to be when she grew up.

♩ ♪ ♩

When the pizza arrived, Tobias and his friends snagged all but one box and disappeared downstairs again. Sam ate with Lydia, Tobias's dad, and Tobias's brother, Bear.

Sam knew Bear wasn't his real name, but she'd never heard him called anything else. It fit. Built like a bear, he played on the high school varsity football team. But Sam secretly thought he was more like a teddy bear than a real bear. In fact, he reminded her of Lydia — always laughing and giving Tobias a hard time, and never anything but kind and gentle with Sam. She liked Bear.

Tobias's dad she didn't know as well. He worked at an engineering firm, and on the occasions Sam had been around him, he didn't say much. He smiled at Lydia's jokes and gazed at her the way Sam imagined all husbands should gaze at their wives. But he was quiet. She thought maybe he was like Tobias, opting to let Lydia and Bear do all the talking.

Tobias's other two siblings — his sister and another brother — were old enough to be out of the house by now. Sam had never met his other brother — Jake, she thought his name was — but she had met his sister, Liz, a couple times. Liz was talkative like Lydia and Bear, but she didn't pull off the good humor quite so well.

Sam enjoyed eating with Lydia and Bear and Tobias's dad. It made her feel like part of the family. She and her parents rarely ate all together. Once the frozen meals had been microwaved to the proper temperature, her mom would take hers to the couch to eat while she watched cable news, and her dad disappeared into his office — working dinners, he called them. Sam most often ate at the table alone.

After dinner, Sam helped Lydia clear the table and get the cake and candles ready.

"Way to make the guest do all the work, Mom," Bear teased as Sam brought over a stack of paper plates and a handful of plastic forks.

"I like helping," Sam assured him.

Bear's voice dropped to a whisper so only Sam could hear. "I think she secretly wants to adopt you and give Tobias back."

Sam snorted.

"What lies are you telling her?" Lydia called from the kitchen.

"Oh, I'm just telling her about your army of slave children hidden in the attic." Bear winked at Sam.

Sam smiled.

"You see what I have to put up with, Sam?" Lydia came from the kitchen with the cake and set it on the table. She looked at Sam. "You wanna call the boys up?"

Sam hesitated.

"I'll get them," Bear offered. He jumped up and left before anyone could object.

Lydia struck a match and lit fourteen candles while they waited. They could hear Bear's voice carry up the stairs, but they couldn't hear his words. The herd rumbled up the stairs, Bear bringing up the rear like a cowboy driving cattle.

The boys jostled and shoved Tobias, teasing him about the frosting hearts Lydia had painstakingly drawn on the cake. They thought the hearts were Sam's doing.

"Ooh, look what your girlfriend made for ya, Toby."

"Hearts? That's so girly."

"Of course it's girly. They were made by a girl."

"I think she loves you, Tobias."

Tobias blushed deeply and seemed to look at everyone but Sam. Even though her feelings were still hurt, she thought he was adorable when he blushed. She might have enjoyed it except that his friends' insinuations made her blush, too. She sent a pleading look Lydia's way, hoping Tobias's mom would claim her own artwork.

"You're right, Luke, she loves Tobias very much because *she* is his mother," Lydia said. "Now let's get on with it or you'll be eating more wax than frosting."

With that, the singing started. Bear sang more loudly than everyone else combined, and most of Tobias's friends giggled their way through the song, adding ridiculous lyrics and purposely singing off key. Halfway through the song, the doorbell rang. Tobias's dad left to answer it.

When the song finished, Tobias blew out the candles in one breath.

Before Lydia had a chance to start cutting the cake, Tobias's dad came back in and whispered something in her ear. Lydia gasped. Her face went from happiness to horror in an instant, and her hand flew to her mouth.

Then she looked right at Sam.

|: ♩. ♪ ♩ |

Lydia's reaction made Sam's world start to tilt.

Her life was about to change in a fundamental and devastating way. She knew it with absolute certainty. A shiver ran up her spine. Her hands started to tingle. She felt like one of those old movie blimps or hot air balloons that come unanchored and begin floating away unnoticed.

Lydia handed the cake knife to Bear and told him in a low voice to take care of the cake. Then she came up to Sam.

Sam held her breath.

Lydia bent close to her ear so the boys wouldn't hear. "Come into the living room, sweetheart."

She'd never called Sam *sweetheart* before. Sam knew instinctually what it meant, as if Lydia were preemptively comforting her.

Lydia ushered Sam into the living room, Tobias's dad just behind them.

Two men in suits stood in the middle of the room. Their eyes flicked from Lydia to Sam. One of them bent before Sam with his hands on his knees to come eye level with her. Lydia kept a firm hand on Sam's shoulder.

"Are you Samantha Ingram?" the man asked.

Sam nodded. "Yes."

"My name is Detective Ferguson," he said, "and that's my partner, Detective Ramon." The other man nodded. "Are your parents John and Renee Ingram?"

Sam swallowed and nodded again. "Yes."

"Samantha, I'm sorry to say, your parents have been in a terrible car accident."

Sam didn't know how to react. Scenes from movies flitted through her head, and she tried to grab onto one of them to understand how normal people would react. Her feelings were no help at all — it was as if they had disappeared altogether, leaving nothing for her to reference but celluloid images of other people's grief.

17

Was she supposed to cry? Gasp and cover her mouth? Scream?

"They're both in critical condition," Detective Ferguson continued.

Lydia squeezed Sam's shoulder. "Which hospital?"

"Saint Raphael." Detective Ferguson straightened.

"I'll get the keys," Tobias's dad said and left the room.

"It might be a while before she'll be able to see them," Detective Ferguson warned. He crouched to bring his face even with Sam's again. "Samantha, is there any other family you'd like us to contact for you?"

Sam frowned.

Until now, it had never struck her as odd that she had no family other than her parents. No siblings. No grandparents. No aunts or uncles or cousins. She'd compared her experience of being an only child to Tobias's family enough times, but she'd never thought about extended family. Did she really not have grandparents and aunts and uncles? Or did she just not know about them? It made her feel guilty somehow.

She shook her head. "I don't have any other family."

Detective Ferguson looked mildly surprised. "None at all?"

"No."

Detective Ferguson looked up at Lydia and straightened once more. He opened his mouth to speak, but Lydia cut him off.

"She can stay with us. It's not a problem."

FOUR
𝄢

Tobias sensed that something bad was happening in the next room.

It made his stomach tight with nerves, and he wanted nothing more than to tell all his friends to go home.

Bear dutifully took over as master of ceremonies and dished out the cake when their parents and Sam disappeared. Tobias was grateful that his brother kept up the pretense — a brief look exchanged between the brothers told him Bear's good humor and wide smile were just an act for the sake of his friends — but it also annoyed him. Part of him wished Bear would volunteer to start calling parents to tell them the party was over. Instead, he was stuck with all these insensitive idiots until morning.

Tobias's eyes constantly wandered to the wall, as if he could see through it into the next room. He didn't even realize someone had shoved a plate of cake into his hands.

"Hurry up, Toby," Luke said, flicking him. "Or are you scared I'll beat you again?"

It took a second for Tobias to register that Luke was talking about the video game they'd left on pause. "Right." As he shoveled bites into his mouth, his friends headed toward the basement stairs. By the time he finished, only Luke and Bear remained.

Tobias turned to his brother. "What do you think's going on?"

Bear shrugged. "I'll let you know if it's something you need to worry about."

"Thanks."

As Tobias and Luke walked toward the stairs, Luke asked, "What was that all about?"

Tobias shrugged. "Hopefully nothing."

Maybe he had imagined it. Maybe it had just been Sam's parents at the door telling her it was time for her to come home.

But he couldn't erase the look his mom had given Sam.

No. He hadn't imagined that.

Something bad was definitely happening.

FIVE

♭

In the car ride to the hospital, every one of Sam's physical senses was on high alert.

She noticed things she had never noticed before, and they all seemed unnaturally sharp and clear: the hum of the tires on the road, the whoosh of each car they passed, the steady rhythm of street lights wiping across the seat, the smell of the lavender-scented air freshener hanging on the rearview mirror and the way it swung and spun, the sensation of the seatbelt digging into her neck.

All these things Sam noticed and catalogued in her memory bank. But her inside feelings, her emotions, hadn't activated yet. It made her feel like a robot, and all she could think was that she must be a terrible daughter.

A good daughter would feel sad or angry or scared... or anything at all. A good daughter would have asked that detective questions, like where the accident had happened, whether other people were involved, what kind of injuries her parents had suffered.

A good daughter wouldn't have spent the afternoon wishing she were part of someone else's family.

|𝄾 𝅘𝅥𝅭 𝅘𝅥𝅮 𝅘𝅥 |

She never did get to see her parents at the hospital that night.

Tobias's parents waited with her for hours while her parents were in surgery. Around midnight, Lydia told Tobias's dad, whom she called Paul, to go on home and that she would stay with Sam. Sam would have rather gone with Paul than sit in that waiting room any longer, but she didn't want to feel any guiltier — and she knew she'd feel

21

horribly guilty if she left before her parents came out of surgery.

So she and Lydia waited. And waited. And waited.

In the wee hours of the morning, a man in scrubs — Sam didn't catch his name, and she didn't know if he was the surgeon or someone else — came to the waiting room to give them an update.

Her father had made it through his surgery but was not awake. The man in scrubs made it sound like he might not wake up for a long, long time.

They were still operating on her mother. Even if she made it through her surgery, the man in scrubs warned, she wasn't likely to wake up anytime soon either.

Both, it seemed, had gruesome head injuries — severe TBIs, the man called them.

When Lydia asked if they could see Sam's father, the man in scrubs shook his head. Although he had made it out of the initial surgery, they were still working to drain fluid away from his brain or some such thing.

Sam had never thought of herself as squeamish before, but the more the man in scrubs talked, the more she wanted to hurl. Part of her was relieved that they wouldn't let her see her father. She didn't want to see him that way.

But that sense of relief also made her feel guilty again.

Sam hadn't shed a tear all night. She wanted to. She knew she was supposed to. But tears just wouldn't come.

Until Lydia finally suggested they go home to wait for any further news.

Why that should be the remark that broke the dam, Sam didn't know. But as soon as she agreed to Lydia's suggestion, the tears overwhelmed her. Lydia wrapped Sam in a hug that quickly turned her tears into heaving sobs. She was simultaneously glad that her emotions were finally working and embarrassed that she was losing control.

"I'm sorry," Sam managed to squeak between sobs.

"No, honey," Lydia soothed and rubbed her back. "You have nothing to be sorry for. We can stay if you want to. I didn't mean to rush you."

Sam pulled away, shaking her head. "No, I want to leave. Please. I don't want to be here anymore."

Lydia pulled her close again and rocked her ever so gently. "Okay. That's okay. We'll go. We'll go."

SIX

⚓

Lydia was exhausted.

It was still dark, but the first birds of the morning were starting to chirp, beckoning the sun to rise.

They took a cab home.

Lydia gave Sam some of Liz's old pajamas and set her up in the guest room at the top of the stairs. Later today, they'd have to find a way into the Ingram house — did Sam even carry a key? — and pack up enough of Sam's belongings to make her feel at home here.

Paul still didn't know what she'd done, that she'd volunteered their family to take Sam in for the foreseeable future. Lydia was sure he wouldn't be angry and that he would've made the same offer had he been in the room, but that didn't mean she looked forward to telling him. For now, praise the Lord, he was sound asleep in their bed.

Lydia was exhausted, yes, but her mind and her heart were too full to sleep. Instead, she started her usual morning routine by making coffee.

She ached for Sam — not only because of what had happened to her parents, but because the poor thing had no family to support her at such a dreadful time. Before now, she'd never realized how truly alone the girl was.

The Ingrams were an intensely private family. John and Renee were, anyway. In the three years since the Ingrams moved into the house across the street, Lydia had had more conversations with Sam than with either of her parents. And an offhand comment here and there during those conversations led Lydia to believe John and Renee employed a wildly different parenting style than the one she and Paul had honed over the last two decades. That was the charitable way to put it. In her heart of hearts, Lydia wondered if Sam received even a fraction of the affection and attention she deserved.

Still, no matter what kind of parents the Ingrams were, their accident must be traumatizing for Sam. All the more because they represented the entirety of her family.

Lydia struggled to wrap her mind around that. She and Paul both came from fairly large families, and their own brood was nothing to sniff at. How was it possible that Sam had no other family at all besides her parents? Lydia couldn't even fathom such a thing.

She heard someone enter the kitchen behind her, and she turned.

Tobias.

She had expected Paul, naturally an early riser, but she wasn't all that surprised to see her youngest son. Tobias took after Paul in so many ways. If she had to guess, she'd bet he had been worried about them all night and had jumped at the first opportunity to ask what had happened.

"Coffee?" she offered.

Tobias nodded and came over to stand next to her.

"Your friends all still asleep?" she asked as she pulled two mugs from the rack next to the coffee maker.

Tobias shook his head. "They all went home last night."

Lydia nearly dropped the mug she was filling. She looked at him, waiting for an explanation.

"I told all my friends I was getting sick so they would call their parents and go home."

"Why? Weren't you having fun?"

"Not after you guys left. I didn't know what happened, but I knew it was bad. I couldn't have fun after that."

Lydia led the way to the breakfast table, and they both sat with steaming mugs of coffee. There was something precious to her about sharing an early morning cup of coffee with her fourteen-year-old son. It soothed the ache in her heart.

"Do you know what happened? Did you talk to your dad when he came home?"

"Sam's parents were in an accident, and you went to the hospital with her."

"Yes."

"Is she okay?"

She. Not *they.* His concern for Sam made Lydia melt inside, but she didn't show it — she didn't want to embarrass him. "She's going to stay with us for the time being."

Tobias looked up sharply. "She's here?"

Lydia nodded. "In the guest room. She doesn't have any other family. Not that she knows of anyway. So she's going to stay here until her parents..." Lydia had been about to say *until her parents recover,* but what if they didn't?

"It's that bad, huh?"

Fourteen. Tobias was only fourteen, but he could read people like books. Better than books actually. Reading had never been his best subject. Nor had any other subject, for that matter. Tobias's genius was in his heart, not his head.

Lydia nodded reluctantly. "It's bad."

SEVEN

♪

Sam didn't recognize anything when she woke up, and it took a moment to remember where she was and what had happened.

Her eyes felt crusty and dry, and her nose was stuffed up from crying so hard the night before. Her mouth was like cotton. She hated the taste of crying.

Sam lay in a strange bed in a strange room in a strange house. She didn't want to stay in bed any longer, but she didn't know what to do if she got up. What did the Howards normally do on Sunday mornings? What routines would her presence disrupt? Would they be eating breakfast together? Would she be expected to get her own breakfast as she would have at home? Should she shower before she went downstairs? Or at least change out of Liz's pajamas? But all she had were her clothes from yesterday, and she didn't relish the idea of putting them back on.

Sam's eyes roamed the room, looking for clues, trying to piece together a plan for her next step. It might help to know the time. She searched for a clock and spotted a small analog one on a shelf across the room: 11:23.

She had never slept that late in her life. Of course, she'd never stayed up all night before either.

Sam's gaze settled on the bathroom door. She thanked her lucky stars that the guest room at least had its own bathroom. It was absurd, she knew, but asking where the restroom was in other people's houses had always felt humiliating somehow.

As she finished washing her hands and admired the plushness of the sea foam green hand towel, she heard a knock on her door. What was she supposed to say? *Who's there?* Or, *come in?*

"Yes?"

"It's Lydia. May I come in?"

"Yes."

Lydia opened the door just enough to poke her head in. "I didn't wake you, did I?"

"No. I was up."

"Would you like to join us for brunch?"

"Sure."

"The boys just got back from Mass."

Sam didn't know what that meant. Had Tobias and Bear gone to a symphony concert? On a Sunday morning? She couldn't picture it. *Mass* must have meant something else to the Howards besides a great work of classical music. "Should I change first?"

"Only if you want to. I'm still in my pajamas. See?" Lydia opened the door a little wider to show off her sweatpants and worn t-shirt.

Sam couldn't help but smile. Lydia had a way of making her feel like she belonged. And Sam needed that this morning, more than she'd ever needed it.

"I hope you like pancakes," Lydia said.

"Very much."

"Well, come on, then!"

Sam followed Lydia to the dining room, where Tobias and Bear and Paul were already seated. All three wore button-up shirts and nice slacks, and despite Lydia's assurances, Sam felt self-conscious in her borrowed pajamas.

"There they are!" Bear said.

Sam took the empty seat next to Tobias. He avoided her gaze, and she avoided his. He must be embarrassed for her, showing up in borrowed pajamas.

"Good morning, Sam," Paul said.

"Good morning."

And then the strangest thing happened. There was no cue, no signal, nothing. But somehow they all knew to start moving as one in a perfectly choreographed ritual. They touched their forehead, then their chest, then each shoulder.

"In the name of the Father and of the Son and of the Holy Spirit," Paul intoned.

"Amen," the rest responded.

Sam didn't know what to make of it. She'd never experienced

anything like it.

Then, all together, they recited some gibberish:

"BlessusOLordandtheseThygiftswhichweareabouttoreceivefromThy bountythroughChristourLordAmen."

And then they touched their forehead and chest and each shoulder again.

"FatherSonandHolySpiritAmen."

They started to dish up and pass food around.

"What was that?" Sam asked no one in particular. She didn't mean to be rude, but the ritual had freaked her out a little bit. Did the Howards belong to some secret cult?

Everyone stopped and stared at her.

"The prayer?" Lydia asked. "We always pray before a meal. To ask God to bless us and the food we're about to eat."

"No, whatever you did just now," Sam clarified. "All together."

"Yeah, that was a prayer," Bear insisted, chuckling.

"But you didn't do that last night," Sam countered. "When we ate dinner."

"Well," Lydia started, "last night was sort of an exception because of the party. When we all sit down to eat a meal together as a family, we pray together. Otherwise, we pray on our own."

Sam looked around at Tobias and Bear and suspected that they hadn't prayed on their own last night. They started passing the food around again.

The whole thing still confused her, but she thought it best to drop the subject. Except she needed to know: "Do you want me to pray, too? Since I'm staying here, I mean."

Everyone stopped again.

"Do you pray when you're at home, Sam?" Paul asked.

Sam shook her head. "We don't believe in God."

Even as the words left her mouth, she wondered if it were true. She couldn't actually recall having heard her parents talk about God at all, but did that mean they didn't believe in him? Maybe they just didn't like him. As for herself, it wasn't so much that she didn't believe in God; it was more that the question of belief had never even crossed her mind. But now that the question had presented itself, she felt like it ought to be settled: did she believe or didn't she?

"I don't suppose it would make much sense for you to pray to someone you don't believe in, would it?" Paul reasoned.

"I guess not," Sam answered.

"But we do believe. And we do pray. And we'll continue to pray together before meals while you're here," Paul said. He was firm but not unkind. "Whether you choose to pray along is entirely up to you."

♩ ♪ ♩

After brunch, Lydia accompanied Sam to her house to help her pack.

Sam hadn't thought much of it at the time, but her mom had insisted she take a house key when she left for Tobias's party. It was fortuitous, perhaps, but thinking about it now gave Sam a queasy, odd feeling. She didn't usually carry a key. She never needed to. Her father often traveled on business, but her mom was always home. Always. The only exception, of course, was when they went out as a family to a concert. But she'd never known her parents to have date nights or to do anything as a couple, really. Having had some rest and a few hours to reflect, Sam now found it downright bizarre that her parents had been out driving somewhere together. And that her mom had made her take a key.

Those puzzling thoughts made entering the empty house more than a little creepy, and Sam was glad Lydia was with her. The bare walls and austere furniture seemed especially lifeless, and the contrast to the Howard house felt especially jarring. It embarrassed Sam somehow.

At first, Sam did little more than stand in the middle of her room and stare at all her belongings. The task of packing felt overwhelming.

Lydia watched from the bedroom doorway, and she must have sensed that the enormity of it all had paralyzed Sam.

"How about this," she started. "Grab what you think you'll want or need for the next week. We'll start there. If you need more, we'll come back."

Guidelines. That's what Sam needed. One week. She could figure out what she required to get through one week.

Slowly, methodically, Sam worked her way around her bedroom, checking off each item on her mental checklist: underwear, socks, shirts, pants and skirts, pajamas... Would she need more than the sandals she wore?

"What about your toothbrush?" Lydia prompted.

Yes. Of course. Toothbrush. She should've thought of that first.

Lydia continued to make gentle suggestions until Sam had even more than a week's worth of stuff packed. The clothes and the toothbrush had been easy — packing those had made it feel like she was going on vacation. But then Lydia asked about schoolbooks and favorite stuffed animals and games and knickknacks.

That's when it started to sink in.

When her bedroom started to feel as empty as the rest of the house.

|𝄾 𝅘𝅥 𝅘𝅥𝅮 𝅘𝅥 |

"Any news yet?"

Sam was getting settled in the guest room — *her* room for who-knew-how-long — putting her clothes in the dresser drawers and making the bed cozy with stuffed animals. She had long thought herself too old for stuffed animals, but their presence gave her a sense of security. Something familiar.

She turned when she heard Tobias's voice in the doorway.

"About your parents?"

There had been news, but Sam didn't know what to make of it.

She shrugged. "They're both in a coma. Nobody knows how long it'll be before they wake up. They said it might even be months."

Tobias bobbed his head in understanding. He opened his mouth to say something, but closed it again. He did it several times. Finally, he asked, "Are you allowed to see them?"

She was, but she didn't want to. The thought of seeing them mangled and hooked up to machines scared her. "Your mom is taking me later, when she gets back from..."

"From Mass?"

"Yeah." Sam still didn't know what that meant. And she was too embarrassed to ask.

Tobias bobbed his head again. "Well, um. Anyway. I just wanted to... I wanted to say I'm sorry about your parents. It's awful, what happened to them. And what you're going through. So. Yeah."

He turned to leave, but Sam called out, "I'm sorry, too." Tobias turned back to her. "About your birthday, I mean. I ruined your party."

He looked at her in a way she couldn't interpret and shook his head. "You didn't ruin my party, Sam." He waited a beat, as if debating whether to say more. But he didn't.

He left.

Clearly, Sam's emotions still weren't functioning properly. She was upset about her parents — she really was — but her stomach wouldn't stop doing flip-flops of delight. Tobias had come to check on her, to ask about her parents, to express his sympathy.

It was the most inappropriate time to swoon over her crush, but she couldn't help it.

Sam was in love with Tobias Howard.

A faithful friend is a sturdy shelter:
he that has found one has found a treasure.
There is nothing so precious as a faithful friend,
and no scales can measure his excellence.
A faithful friend is an elixir of life;
and those who fear the Lord will find him.
Whoever fears the Lord directs his friendship aright,
for as he is, so is his neighbor also.

Sirach 6:14-17

EIGHT
𝄢

"So what happened to your girlfriend, Toby?" Luke asked.

Tobias nearly choked on his ham and cheese sandwich. Luke smirked, and their other friends snickered. Even worse, Emma and Ceci and Fiona sat at the same lunch table with them today. He didn't look at the girls, but he could feel their eyes on him.

"What girlfriend?" Tobias knew Luke meant Sam, but he couldn't answer without making it sound like Sam *was* his girlfriend, which she definitely *was not*.

"You know. What's-her-name, from your party," Luke pushed, and Tobias immediately realized the error in his play-dumb strategy. Now Emma and Ceci and Fiona knew he'd had a party without inviting them, but another girl had been invited. "After she left, you made the rest of us go home. Thought maybe something happened to her."

Tobias felt his neck and face and ears getting hot, and he knew he was turning red. He hated how easily his friends made him blush. It wasn't manly at all.

"Oh, her." Tobias did his best to sound nonchalant. "She's just my neighbor. My mom feels bad for her because she doesn't have any friends—"

"No kidding. She's a weirdo."

Tobias ignored the interruption. "So my mom invited her to the party. She's definitely not my girlfriend."

Tobias risked a glance at Emma, but he couldn't tell anything from her expression.

"So what happened to her?" Luke pressed.

"Um." Tobias didn't know how much he should say, but he decided

35

that they'd all find out sooner or later anyway. If Sam's parents were as bad off as his mom made it sound, she'd be staying with them for a long time. "Her parents were in a bad accident. She's actually... She's staying with my family until they get out of the hospital."

The mood at the table flipped like a switch. Tobias could almost hear his mom saying, *Open mouth, insert foot.* Everyone suddenly became preoccupied with their food and avoided eye contact with him.

Except Luke. He could be such an ass sometimes, and Tobias could tell this was going to be one of those times. He'd made Luke feel like an idiot, and now the payback was only seconds away.

"She's staying in your house?" Luke smirked. "That's convenient."

His other friends and the girls gasped, shocked by Luke's crass train of thought.

Tobias wanted to punch that stupid smirk off Luke's face. Instead, he spoke through his teeth, "I told you, she's not my girlfriend."

Luke shrugged. "Whatever."

The conversation moved on, but Tobias had a hard time following any of it. He felt ashamed without understanding why. Sam *wasn't* his girlfriend, so it wasn't like he had lied.

But some part of his conscience told him he should have been more chivalrous somehow, perhaps defended Sam's reputation more insistently. So what if Sam wore socks with her sandals and hummed to herself? Tragedy had struck her life, and she didn't deserve people making lewd insinuations about her. Especially because she was only a seventh grader.

Practically a child.

NINE

𝄞

Sam hummed absently as she waited for Tobias at the front of the school.

Lydia had walked to school with them that morning so that she could explain the situation to Sam's teachers. All her teachers had offered their sympathy and promised to let her off easy for the next week or two if she felt she needed extra time to get her work done. She didn't. In fact, she thought she'd probably get her homework done in record time — it kept her mind off of what she'd seen last night at the hospital.

Sam had been right in not wanting to see her parents. She'd managed to hold herself together at the hospital, but she'd puked her guts out as soon as she'd made it to the bathroom in her temporary quarters (that's how she'd begun to think of the guest bedroom — she'd read the term in dozens of books, and it made her feel as if she were living some fictional tale that was bound to have a happy ending eventually).

It wasn't gory exactly. But if no one had told her those were her parents, she wouldn't have recognized them. Seeing them that way had disturbed her way down deep — not just in her stomach, but in the very core of who she was. And if she didn't keep her thoughts occupied, those images would creep up on her and attack her brain all over again.

So for the first time in her life, Sam didn't mind homework at all. She almost craved it.

Jason the Meathead exited the building, interrupting her musings. Sam followed him with her eyes. Others might try to avoid eye contact

37

with their bullies, but Sam thought keeping him in her sights at all times a better tactic for self-preservation. He couldn't sneak up on her then. She had also read somewhere that eye contact made it less likely that a perp would attack because they knew their victim would be able to identify them later.

Jason the Meathead wasn't that smart, though. He caught her watching him and shouted, "What are you staring at, you freak?"

Sam's heart jammed into her throat. Was he going to come after her? Now she wanted to look away but couldn't. She was frozen.

"Hey, sandal-socks." Another boy's voice, a slightly deeper one, set reality in motion again. She turned her head to see Tobias's friend, Luke.

Out of the corner of her eye, she noted Jason walking away.

"Lover boy will be along soon. Don't worry," Luke sneered as he passed her.

The remark caught Sam so off guard that she couldn't think of a way to respond until Luke was too far away.

Lover boy? Did he mean Tobias? Did that mean Luke knew about her crush on Tobias? Or that Tobias had a crush on her? No, that was impossible. Wasn't it?

The thoughts Luke had set off in her brain made her nervous waiting for Tobias. How should she act when she saw him?

When Tobias finally appeared, she smiled and waved at him.

He scowled. He didn't even stop. He just muttered, "Let's go," and kept walking.

Sam trotted to catch up. She had her trumpet with her today — practicing would be a good distraction — and its heavy weight made it hard to keep up with Tobias's fast pace.

"Hey, can we slow down?" she requested a block later.

Tobias stopped to let her catch up but didn't bother to turn around.

"Bad day?" she ventured.

"Yeah."

He started walking again, more slowly than before, but still more quickly than was comfortable for Sam lugging her trumpet.

"Do you want to talk about it?" Sam asked.

"No."

So that was it then. He knew. Tobias knew Sam had a crush on him, and he didn't like her back. He had probably laughed about it with his friends: a dumb little seventh grader with a crush on an eighth grader, how adorable.

Feeling sorry for herself, she lashed out: "Must have sucked even more than my weekend for you to act like such a jerk."

He stopped and stared at her, his mouth hanging open in shock.

Before she could think long enough to take it back, she continued: "Do you know how long I waited for you? How long I always wait for you? And then you just walk right past me like I don't even exist. I'm carrying this stupid trumpet around, and it's really freaking heavy, and I can't walk that fast, but you don't care, you just keep going and expect me to keep up even though your legs are longer and you're bigger and stronger and faster, and you don't even notice or offer to carry it for me, but I don't want you to carry it for me, but it would be nice if you offered or at least noticed or slowed down—"

Tobias grabbed the trumpet out of her hand. Gently. He started walking again, at a comfortable pace this time.

They walked the rest of the way in silence. Again.

It surprised Sam how easily she fell into a rhythm with the Howard family that week.

In the first couple days after the accident, she had felt like her life was one of those snow globes, and someone had turned it upside down and shaken it all up. But by the end of the week, the flakes of her snow globe life had begun to settle. The Howards went on in their normal routine (at least she assumed it was their normal routine — she hoped they hadn't changed too much for her sake), and she slipped herself into it as if things had always been that way.

Every morning she woke up to her alarm, took a shower, got dressed, and went to the kitchen, where Lydia fixed her a bowl of cereal and packed her a sack lunch (her own mother had never packed her a sack lunch except when it was required for a school field trip). Then Sam would stuff her books and sack lunch into her backpack and wait by the door for Tobias, who spent so long getting ready that he never had time to eat breakfast.

Sam and Tobias walked to school together as they had planned to do anyway before the accident. The morning after she had blown up at him for being a jerk, she felt awkward. He carried her trumpet for her that morning even though she told him he didn't have to. He didn't say much. But then again, he never said much. That afternoon, Sam decided she didn't want to feel awkward anymore, so she went on chattering at him as if she hadn't unloaded on him the day before. And

Tobias let her. By Friday, they had settled into a comfortable companionship on their walks to and from school.

Sam's teachers didn't give her much homework that week, and the other students noticed. Most gave her resentful looks, a few ignored her, and Jason the Meathead razzed her for being a teacher's pet. None of the other students knew why the teachers gave her special treatment, and none of them bothered to ask her, so she didn't bother to tell them. She had never had many friends in the first place, and she didn't want anyone to become her friend now out of pity.

Her evenings proved most different from life before the accident, and yet Sam quickly grew accustomed to this routine, too. The Howards ate together as a family as soon as Bear came home from football practice. Tobias was expected to have finished his homework before dinner, but he almost never did. Sam would have finished her homework before dinner except that she never had any. So she spent that time with Lydia.

Whatever Lydia did, she welcomed Sam's company. When she did chores, she asked Sam if she wanted to help. When she watched TV, she patted the spot on the couch next to her and invited Sam to join her. Sometimes she brought out paper and colored pencils and they just sat at the table and drew and talked and laughed together (at first Sam felt guilty about laughing, like she was only supposed to be sad while her parents were in the hospital, but she couldn't help herself — Lydia's laugh was infectious).

Eventually, Lydia would announce that it was time to make dinner so that it would be ready by the time Paul and Bear got home. Sam had heard that women who stayed home and cooked all the meals were oppressed by a patriarchal society, whatever that meant (her own mother had stayed home, but she didn't cook, so Sam couldn't be sure whether the standard applied to her or not). But Lydia seemed to find nothing but joy in cooking for her husband and her children. And the more Sam helped her cook, the more Sam understood the appeal.

Sam was endlessly fascinated by the myriad ways to prepare food, and there was something indescribably satisfying in watching the boys devour and ask for seconds of a meal she had helped make. Bear or Paul would compliment the chef, thinking it had been all Lydia's doing, and Lydia would look over at Sam and wink. It never failed to make Sam's insides buzz with pleasure.

After dinner each night, the Howards had another strange prayer custom that Sam only stuck around for once before deciding it made her too uncomfortable. Each of them had a type of beaded necklace — at least Sam thought it was a necklace, but none of them ever wore it around their neck — that they ran through their fingers as they chanted in unison. They called it a *rosary*. It creeped Sam out the first time she witnessed it, and thereafter she excused herself as soon as the meal concluded, before the beads came out.

After the rosary ritual, Tobias and Bear retreated to the video game console in the basement. Sam wondered if Bear ever had homework because he never seemed to do any, and Lydia and Paul never scolded him about it.

Sam used the time after dinner to practice her trumpet. Lydia gave her a cozy room in the basement so she could practice without disturbing the rest of the household. The room had already been soundproofed because Jake — the brother Sam had never met — had been in a rock band when he was in high school, and they had rehearsed there regularly. A deep, squishy sofa lined one side of the room, and two huge foam bean bag chairs bulged from the opposite corner. Plush pillows adorned all three. An eclectic but oddly attractive assortment of various-sized rugs and tapestries hung on the walls.

Lydia told her that no one had used the room since Jake had moved out.

"It's your room now," Lydia had said. "Use it any way you want."

It was this room, more than anything else, that made Sam feel the permanence of her situation. Even putting away her clothes in her temporary quarters had only made her feel as if she were on a long vacation. But having her own room — a second room, like her mom's hobby room — made the Howard house more like a new *home*.

The thought was both comforting and deeply unsettling.

TEN
𝄢

Things had changed between Tobias and Luke.

Tobias couldn't tell if the rest of their friends were aware of the tension. He just knew that Luke hardly included him in their group conversations anymore, and when he did, it was only to make some snide remark about Sam. By Friday, Tobias couldn't stand it any longer.

He caught Luke at his locker just before their last class of the day, pre-algebra, which they shared.

"Hey, Luke, wait up," Tobias called.

Luke turned at the sound of his name. He looked mildly surprised, but he waited. When Tobias caught up to him, they fell into step together.

"How's your little playmate?" Luke taunted.

"Sam. Her name is Sam."

Luke shrugged.

"Anyway, I don't how she is. We hardly ever see each other."

It was mostly true. At home, Sam constantly followed his mom around or shut herself in Jake's old practice room. They really only acknowledged each other's existence at dinner. But, he had to admit to himself, they did spend quite a bit of time walking to and from school together, which meant he'd had plenty of opportunity to find out how she was doing. He couldn't make up his mind whether he lacked the courage to ask or the compassion.

"Sure," Luke said caustically.

Tobias dragged Luke to a halt just outside their classroom.

"What's with you? Why do you keep doing that?" Tobias demanded.

42

"Doing what?"

"Making comments like that. Like there's something going on between me and a puny seventh grader when you know"—Tobias stopped himself before he said it too loudly and continued in a near whisper—"when you know I like Emma."

Luke shook off Tobias's grip without answering and entered the classroom. Tobias followed him, and they took their usual seats at the back.

The bell hadn't rung yet, and the din of students coming in covered their conversation.

"You're acting like an ass," Tobias jabbed.

It had the intended effect. Tobias never swore out loud, and doing it now got a reaction from Luke.

"I'm acting like an ass?" Luke snapped. "How about you, Mr.—"

The bell rang, saving Tobias from whatever epithet Luke intended to give him. As their teacher starting collecting homework assignments, they continued their squabble in whispers.

"You pretend that your friends are so important to you and that you like Emma so much, but it's obvious that dumb weirdo is all you really care about. As soon as she was in trouble, it's like the rest of us didn't exist," Luke spat.

"That's not true."

"No? Do you think it was convenient for our parents to come pick us up early just because you were worried about your precious little girlfriend?"

"I told you, she's not—"

"Tobias. Luke." It was their teacher, Mrs. Yates. "Care to share with the rest of the class?"

Tobias blushed and cursed himself for blushing.

"Tobias was just telling me about his girl problems, Mrs. Yates."

Tobias wished he could shrink into non-existence.

"Fascinating. But this is a math class, not drama. If you two can't focus, I'll separate you," Mrs. Yates warned.

As soon as she turned back to the whiteboard, Tobias scribbled a note:

> She's not my GF. I don't care about her at all. I just knew whatever was going on was an emergency and didn't want everyone around for it.

He looked it over and inwardly cringed at the claim he didn't care at all, but passed it to Luke anyway.

Luke read it and started to scribble back. It didn't take him long. It was only two letters:

BS

Tobias scribbled some more:

Sorry ur feelings are so fragile. Didn't know I had to ask permission to think about someone besides u.

He shoved the note back to Luke.

Luke read it. He didn't answer for several minutes, but Tobias, glancing at him out of the corner of his eye, could tell by the way his jaw worked that he had more to say. Finally, Luke wrote something brief and passed it back:

Just let Emma down easy. She really likes you.

It wasn't what Tobias had expected at all. Luke was jealous on Emma's behalf? That didn't make sense. Unless... Did Luke like Emma, too? He had never said anything, but that didn't make it impossible.

They didn't speak or pass notes for the rest of class. When the bell rang at the end of the period, Luke jumped up and practically ran for the door.

Tobias took his time packing his notes and textbook into his backpack. Just before he crumpled the scrap of paper with their conversation on it, he read it over again. He cringed once more when he saw what he had written: *I don't care about her at all.*

He didn't like Sam that way, but it wasn't totally honest to say he didn't care about her at all. Although he'd never say it out loud, he could at least admit to himself that something like friendship had developed between him and Sam. She was nice. Smart (he suspected that she was, in fact, way smarter than she wanted most people to know). Easy to talk to. Easy to listen to. Quick to laugh. Sincere. Cute.

Tobias stopped himself.

He cursed Luke. Luke had put that thought in his head. If Luke hadn't teased him so much this week, the word *cute* would've never crossed his mind.

He was sure of it.

ELEVEN

𝄞

Tobias seldom had much to say during their walks to and from school, but Sam thought he seemed especially quiet today.

No, more than quiet. Mad.

They walked side-by-side, and he ignored her. He didn't even offer to carry her trumpet. She figured he must have had another bad day.

"I'm excited for Bear's game tonight. I've never been to a football game," Sam announced, hoping to distract Tobias from whatever bothered him. "Are they fun?"

"Yeah, I guess."

"My mom used to watch football, but my dad hated it so much he made her stop." It was the first time she'd mentioned anything about what things had been like before the accident. It had slipped out before she really thought about it. Now that it was out, she regretted it. Thinking about her parents made her sad. She didn't want to be sad. Not when Tobias needed cheering up. "Do you like watching football?"

"Yeah."

A beat.

"But you don't like playing it, I guess?"

"It's all right. I like basketball better, though."

"I've never watched basketball."

Tobias stopped and gawked at her like she'd grown two extra heads. Was it *that* strange that she'd never watched basketball?

"You mean live."

Sam shook her head. "I mean ever. I never watched it on TV either."

"That's crazy."

Sam shrugged. She didn't want to talk about her parents again, but she felt like she had to explain. "My dad never wanted to watch it, so we never watched it."

She hated that she kept talking about her father in the past tense. Her dad wasn't dead.

Tobias studied her for a moment, and it made her self-conscious. She felt heat in her cheeks and ears.

He did that thing again, where he opened his mouth to speak a bunch of times but never said anything. Finally: "After Bear's game tonight, we're gonna look up videos of classic basketball games. And then you can say you've officially watched basketball."

With that, Tobias turned to continue walking. Sam, smiling, caught up and fell into step with him.

"Thank you, Tobias."

"For what?"

"I was trying to cheer you up, but you cheered me up."

He glanced sidelong at her. "You were trying to cheer me up?"

Sam shrugged. "Yeah. You seemed like you needed it."

Tobias snorted softly and smiled to himself.

"What?"

"Nothing."

| ♪ ♩ ♪ ♩ |

Since Sam and her parents had moved around so many times, they'd never connected with a community enough to become invested in local sports.

Sam very much looked forward to Bear's game, the high school's first football game of the season. In her mind's eye, she saw bleachers full of fans decked out in the school's colors, chanting cheers together, and screaming their heads off for their favorite players. She couldn't wait to be part of it.

The high school wasn't much farther from the house than Sam and Tobias's school, and so the Howards decided to walk to the game. Lydia gave Sam a foam finger to wear on her hand, and Paul carried a large tote bag with blankets and extra jackets for everyone. Tobias rolled his eyes when Lydia told him to pack his jacket in the tote, but she insisted that he would regret it if he didn't take it.

Tobias and Sam walked behind Lydia and Paul, who strolled hand-in-hand. Sam had never seen her own parents hold hands, and it surprised her how affecting it was to see Lydia and Paul walk that way.

Without realizing it, she had somehow formed the idea that holding hands was a thing only young couples did — couples who weren't married and used to each other yet. But watching Lydia and Paul hold hands put a longing in Sam's heart that she couldn't even begin to comprehend or describe.

Sam snuck a glance at Tobias and wondered if he would ever hold her hand that way.

Trudging with his hands in his pockets, Tobias seemed lost in his own thoughts.

Sam couldn't hear what Lydia and Paul talked about, but she did hear Lydia laugh every now and then. Every time she did, Paul would give Lydia a sidelong look and smile in a manner that reminded Sam of the way Tobias sometimes tilted his head to look at her. *Like father, like son*, she thought.

She snuck another glance at Tobias.

This time he caught her. He raised his eyebrows as if asking a question, but he didn't say anything.

Sam looked straight ahead and resolved not to sneak any more glances the rest of the way.

TWELVE
𝄢

Tobias was nervous.

He knew he shouldn't care so much what other people thought, but he couldn't help it. Even though Luke was obviously motivated by his interest in Emma, Tobias worried that his other friends felt the same way Luke did about Sam — that she was a weirdo and that Tobias had given her priority over his friends. No doubt he would run into at least one of those friends at this game. He only prayed that when he did, Sam was nowhere near him.

His luck ran out almost immediately.

As soon as they stepped inside the gates, Tobias's parents gave him cash and instructed him to take Sam to the concession stand to get drinks for the four of them while they went to snag seats. Tobias and Sam had just turned toward the concession stand, and Sam had already started humming, when he spotted Emma and Fiona.

"Oh." It came out of his mouth without his permission.

"What?" Sam asked.

"Um. It's nothing."

Emma and Fiona hadn't seen him yet, and he shuffled with his head down, hoping they wouldn't notice him. He moved faster than necessary.

"Are we gonna be late?" Sam asked.

"Huh?"

"Why are we in such a hurry?" She panted next to him, half-running, half-skipping.

"Hey, Tobias!"

Tobias winced. It was Emma.

48

He and Sam slowed as Emma and Fiona approached.

"Hey, Emma, Fiona," he greeted, trying to play it cool. "What's up?"

"Hi, I'm Sam." Sam stuck out her hand.

"Emma." Emma shook Sam's hand uncertainly, but she offered a friendly smile.

"Fiona." Fiona regarded Sam's hand but didn't move to shake it.

Tobias noted the rapid flicker of emotions in Sam's face, but she quickly settled into a neutral expression.

"Um. Sam's my neighbor, the one I told you guys about the other day. She's staying with us for a while," Tobias reminded them, hoping Sam wouldn't mind that they knew about her situation. He couldn't change it now if she did.

"I'm sorry about your parents," Emma said.

Sam blinked. "Thanks."

"Come on, Em." Fiona pulled on her arm. "I see Luke over there. I told him to save us seats."

"Well, it was nice to meet you, Sam. See ya, Tobias." Emma smiled and waved as Fiona dragged her away.

Tobias's gaze followed them until they connected with Luke. He waited for Luke to look over at them, but he never did. It hurt.

Luke had been his best friend since first grade. Maybe once upon a time, they could have worked this out — whatever *this* was, Tobias still wasn't entirely sure — and repaired their friendship. But Tobias had a sinking feeling that whatever damage had been done was irreparable. If only he'd realized sooner that they both had a crush on the same girl...

"Is she your girlfriend?" Sam asked quietly. It snapped him out of his reverie so fast he thought he might have whiplash.

"What?"

"Emma."

"No."

"But you want her to be."

Tobias opened his mouth to deny it, but he didn't want to lie to Sam. But would it be a lie, really? Now that he suspected Luke's interest in her, he didn't know how he felt about Emma. He still liked her. A lot. But he couldn't honestly say he wanted her to be his girlfriend when he knew it would cause his friend pain — even if that friend wasn't really acting like a friend at the moment.

"I don't know."

Sam swallowed and nodded. She turned away and headed toward

the concession stand.

Tobias followed her, feeling for some stupid reason like he'd done something wrong.

THIRTEEN

𝄞

Sam didn't bother to see if Tobias followed her.

She should. He had the money. But she didn't want him to see her flushed cheeks.

No matter how smart she was when it came to schoolwork, when it came to Tobias — or living life in general — Sam felt like a prize idiot. Why should his crush on a girl in his own class upset her so much? Of course he would prefer someone his own age. He would never be interested in Sam, and she simply had to stop entertaining fancies that he might one day. It infuriated her that her emotions had chosen this moment to run wildly out of control.

By the time Sam reached the concession stand, Tobias stood next to her again. She wouldn't look at him, though. Tobias ordered the drinks and paid for them. He handed two of them to her to carry back.

They didn't speak until they reached the stands. She had spotted Lydia and Paul halfway up the bleachers, but Tobias stopped her before she could start up the steps.

"Hey," he said. "I'm sorry Fiona was so rude to you."

Sam narrowed her eyes. He thought she was upset because of Fiona? "It's okay." She turned toward the stairs again.

"Sam." Tobias stopped her again, and she peered into his face. Tobias's eyes darted around the growing crowd of fans. "Can we talk? At home?"

Talk? About what? She didn't want him to tell her about Emma.

"Sure."

FOURTEEN
𝄢:

What was Tobias thinking, asking Sam if they could talk when they got home?

Was he crazy? He didn't need to explain himself to Sam.

Tobias couldn't even concentrate on the football game. He just gaped at the field, not absorbing the action at all, only thinking about what to tell Sam when they got home. She would be expecting him to tell her something important — he had made such a big deal about it at the bottom of the stairs. But even as he'd said it — *Can we talk at home?* — he hadn't been quite sure what it was he wanted her to know. He just knew something had upset her, and it was somehow his fault.

It was none of Sam's business what was going on between him and Luke and Emma. None of her business what was going on inside of him. Why should she care anyway? A silly seventh grader. If she thought she had a horse in this race, she was wrong. Tobias didn't owe her an explanation. If she had hurt feelings, it was her own fault.

By the second quarter, Tobias decided he would say nothing at all when they got home.

He would just pretend he'd forgotten about it and hope Sam wasn't brave enough to ask.

FIFTEEN

♭

Sam decided by the end of the second quarter that she really, really didn't want to talk about Emma.

So she made plans that when they got back to the house, she would go straight to bed. Hopefully by morning, Tobias wouldn't remember that they had anything to talk about.

She did her best to follow the game, but the most she managed was to spot Bear's number every time their team had the ball. Paul patiently explained the action to her throughout, but she only half paid attention.

At halftime, Tobias left to meet up with his friends. Lydia suggested he take Sam along with him, but both Tobias and Sam immediately and rather vehemently rejected the idea. Lydia raised her eyebrows in a knowing way and said, "Uh-huh."

Then Paul offered to take Sam to the booth where they controlled the scoreboard and announced the game. Eager to think about something else — anything else — Sam agreed.

The booth sat at the top of the stands with huge windows looking out over the field. Sam could see inside the windows as they approached. A handful of people milled about inside.

"See, that's the microphone for the announcer that we hear in the stands," Paul explained and pointed as they approached, "and that one's for the radio broadcaster."

"You can listen to the high school games on the radio?" Sam asked.

"Well, not on the regular radio. But they stream it on the school's website," Paul replied.

He knocked on the booth door, and a man Paul's age opened it.

"Paul Howard!" the man exclaimed. "What are you doing here? Come on in."

"Randy, I'd like you to meet a friend of mine. This is Samantha," Paul introduced.

The man smiled and shook her hand. "It's nice to meet you, Miss Samantha."

"It's nice to meet you, too." She smiled back.

"Randy and I both went to school here," Paul explained. "Played football together."

"Got into a lot of trouble together," Randy added and wagged his eyebrows.

Sam couldn't imagine Paul getting into trouble ever. He was such a quiet, gentle man.

"I thought you could show Sam how the scoreboard works," Paul said.

"Sure thing. Come on over here, Sam." Randy led them to a chair that sat in front of a panel of buttons.

He invited Sam to sit in the chair as he described the function of each button. Sam quickly understood the basics of working the scoreboard, but she had little context for what it meant to score a touchdown versus a field goal versus a safety. The words rolled off of Randy's tongue as if she should know exactly what they meant, and she resolved to pay more attention to the game during the second half.

When they returned to their seats for the start of the third quarter, Lydia chatted with another player's mom in the row behind them. Tobias was nowhere in sight.

As Lydia continued her conversation with the other woman, Paul leaned over to Sam and asked, "Are you enjoying yourself?"

Sam nodded. "Thank you for taking me to see the booth. Your friend, Randy, is very nice."

"Yes, he is."

"What kind of trouble did you guys get in when you were in high school?" Sam inquired. She thought it might be a rude question, but Randy had mentioned it in such a good-natured way, she hoped Paul wouldn't mind talking about it.

Paul chuckled. "Oh, just pranks, mostly. Nothing too serious."

"Like what?"

"Well, let's see." Paul tilted his head back as if trying to see his past in the night sky. "Once, we took apart our coach's car and put it back together again in the school cafeteria. A yellow, 1985 Chevy Camaro."

Sam's eyes went wide. That was a much bigger prank than she had expected.

Paul laughed at her expression. "He thought his car had been stolen when he couldn't find it in the parking lot, and he was about to call the police. We had to stop him and show him where his car was. Oh, was he mad. It took us until two o'clock in the morning to take it apart and put it back together again so he could drive home."

Paul laughed again, and Sam laughed with him.

The third quarter started, and Sam paid more attention to all of Paul's explanations. She even allowed herself to go crazy when their team scored or recovered a fumble or sacked the other team's quarterback. She learned that the position Bear played was called *center*.

Sam got so into the game that she forgot about Tobias's absence until he returned with two minutes left in the fourth quarter. He wore an intense scowl and would only respond to Lydia in grunts and eye rolls.

Lydia grunted back at him and nudged him with her elbow. Then she whispered something in his ear and tussled his hair. His scowl eased a bit, but something obviously still bothered him.

When the game ended (their team had won, which put everyone around them in a celebratory mood), they followed the crowd to the exit. The gate created a bottleneck, forcing everyone to press in together in a giant herd of swaying bodies. Sam found herself squished between Lydia in front and Tobias behind.

"Hold onto each other so we don't get separated," Lydia commanded over her shoulder. She grabbed Sam's hand. "Tobias?"

Sam felt Tobias's hand grip hers. His hand was much bigger than her own. But not uncomfortably so. On the contrary, the way his fingers enveloped her hand felt like a natural fit to Sam. She was grateful for the noise of the crowd, otherwise she was sure everyone would hear her heart pounding against her ribcage.

Progress toward the gate was slow, and because of her short stature, Sam had a hard time telling how much farther they had to go. At last, they spilled past the gate, and the crowd around them dispersed in a hundred different directions.

Sam had expected they would only hold hands until they'd made it outside the gate, but both Lydia and Tobias kept a tight grip on her. It only took a moment to realize why. Paul, holding Lydia's hand at the head of their small train, weaved through people, dodging this way and that at a rapid clip, and Sam would have easily been lost if they hadn't clung to one another.

Once they crossed the street and made it about half a block, they no longer had to dodge other fans, and Paul's pace slowed. He continued to hold Lydia's hand, of course, but Lydia let go of Sam. Tobias dropped her hand an instant later. He continued to walk next to her, though.

He still had that scowl on his face.

"Is everything okay?" Sam didn't want to hear about Emma, but she also didn't like seeing him so troubled.

Tobias sighed. He didn't look at her when he answered. "Look, Sam. It's nice that you're concerned and all, but you're not the person I want to talk to about..." He stopped and seemed to chew on his words for a moment. "There's just some stuff going on, and I don't want to talk about it, okay?"

"Okay."

It was definitely about Emma. She was sure of it.

And she felt relieved that he didn't want to talk to her about it.

SIXTEEN
𝄢

Tobias felt bad about shutting Sam down that way, but this had to stop.

He didn't even know what *this* was. He couldn't define it in his own mind. It was the way Sam sensed his moods and called him out when he was being a jerk. It was the way she gazed at him and blushed when he looked at her. It was the way his friends treated him because of Sam. It was the way his mom nudged him and wagged her eyebrows and seemed to read his thoughts, even the thoughts he didn't want to have. It was the way his stomach did a somersault when he held Sam's hand.

She was a seventh grader, for crying out loud!

It had been a mistake to find his friends at the game.

Friends. Could he even call them that anymore? It made him angry that he'd been treated so unjustly, that the people he'd thought were his friends could be so cruel.

Tobias had hoped to find Luke at halftime to tell him that he understood about Emma, that he would step back and stay out of Luke's way. But when he found him, Luke had already made his move. He and Emma were wrapped around each other, making out behind the announcer's booth.

Tobias hurried away before they saw him and found the rest of their friends — Fiona, Ceci, Colton, Hunter, Will, and Ollie — by the equipment shed near one of the end zones.

"Decide you were done playing with babies, Toby?" Fiona sneered when he approached.

The whole group chortled.

Something snapped. It was one thing for Luke to tease him, but now

57

they were all in on it, and Tobias had had enough. "Shut it, Fiona."

"Ooh, Lover Boy is mad," Colton sniped.

"Lighten up, Toby, it was a joke."

"But isn't it cute how he jumps to defend her?"

"He must have it real bad."

"Enough!" Tobias yelled. "I'm sick of you guys making a joke out of this whole thing. Sam's parents are in the hospital. Do you understand? They might never get out of the hospital. She has no other family. She's alone, completely alone. And you guys are here laughing at her and making fun of her and me and I'm sick of it. I'm sick of you. All of you."

He stormed off, cheeks and neck flushing, heart racing, thoughts black.

Maybe Luke was right. Maybe he had given Sam priority over the rest of them, but now that he'd seen his friends' true colors, he didn't regret it.

Tobias spent the rest of the game on his own, pacing the chainlink fence that marked the edge of school property. Over and over again, his outburst replayed in his mind, and he wondered if he'd overreacted.

By the time he noticed the game clock winding down, he had calmed his emotions, but he had also concluded — even though he knew it was through no fault of her own — that Sam was ruining his life.

Blessed are those who are invited to the marriage supper of the Lamb.

Revelation 19:9

SEVENTEEN

On Sunday morning, Sam went to Mass with the Howards.

Lydia had asked her the day before if she wanted to go with them and insisted she didn't have to if she didn't want to. But not going meant staying at the house alone, and Sam didn't feel quite that comfortable in the Howard home yet. Still, she figured she better find out what *going to Mass* actually meant before she committed to doing it with the family.

"What does that mean, going to Mass?" Sam inquired.

"Oh, well..." Lydia was obviously surprised by the question. "It's what Catholics call their church service."

"Oh." How had Sam never heard of it before? She had known some Catholics somewhere, hadn't she? Or at least read about them in a novel? "So... you're just asking if I want to go to church with you."

"Yes. Exactly. But like I said, only if you want to. I know your folks aren't religious, and I don't want to overstep."

Sam thought about it for a second.

"Do I have to dress up?"

"We always dress up, but that doesn't mean you have to."

"Why do you guys dress up?"

"To remind us how special the Mass is."

"But you go every week."

"Mm-hm. Just because it happens frequently doesn't mean it's not special. If you had a wedding to go to every weekend, you'd dress up for each one, wouldn't you?"

Sam thought about that and nodded after a moment.

"Well, the Mass is a wedding, too. Between Christ and his Church."

Now Sam was really confused. She must've looked it, too, because Lydia laughed.

"Have I scared you off?"

"No." Lydia's description of it as a wedding, in fact, intrigued Sam. She'd never been to a wedding, but they seemed wonderfully romantic, and she was eager to go to one. Maybe there would be dancing, too? And Tobias might ask her to dance...

"I'll go. And I'll dress up."

Sam briefly wondered how her parents would feel when they woke up from their comas and learned that she had gone to Mass with the Howards. She hoped they wouldn't be mad.

But, she thought, what harm could it do? She was only curious.

| ♩ ♪ ♩ |

Sam had never been so full of questions in her life.

She tried her darnedest to pay attention at Mass because she was genuinely curious, but the way the priest spoke seemed foreign even though it was all in English. And she kept waiting for the bride and groom to show up, but they never did. There certainly hadn't been any dancing.

Hadn't Lydia called it a wedding?

In the car after Mass, squished between the boys in the back seat (she tried her best not to think about her shoulder pressing into Tobias's arm), Sam couldn't hold her questions inside any longer.

"Lydia," Sam started.

"Yeah?" Lydia turned around in her seat to look at her.

"I thought you said it was going to be a wedding." Sam had even dragged Lydia back to her own house to help her pick out her fanciest dress.

Bear snorted a laugh, and Tobias gave her an odd look out of the corner of his eyes.

"It was," Lydia replied simply.

"Are you making a joke?" Maybe Sam was just too dense to get Lydia's humor this time.

Lydia laughed but said, "No, not at all. Let's see, how can I explain this?" She pondered it for a few moments. "See, God loves us so much that he wants to be one with us, his Church, just like a husband and a wife become one. And God accomplishes that — becoming one with us, marrying us in a sense — when we receive Communion at Mass."

Sam didn't get it.

"The Eucharist, the little wafers we went up to receive," Tobias added, sounding irritated for some reason.

"When I had to stay in my seat?" Sam asked to clarify.

"Right," Tobias said. "They're not just wafers of bread. It's really Jesus. That's what she's talking about. We receive Jesus when we receive Communion."

Sam thought about their explanations, tried to sort their words into something that made sense. "So... Jesus *is* God? They're the same?"

"Yes. God is a Trinity — three persons, one God. Jesus, the Son, is the second person," Lydia explained.

Only Sam felt like it explained nothing.

"You know when we pray, and we make the sign of the cross?" Tobias asked, still sounding annoyed. He demonstrated the motion of touching his head, his chest, and each shoulder. "And we say, *In the name of the Father, and of the Son, and of the Holy Spirit.*"

Sam nodded.

"The Father, Son, and Holy Spirit. That's the Trinity," he said, as if that made any sense.

"So... which one is God?"

"The Trinity is God. Three persons, one God," Lydia repeated.

"And Jesus is?"

"The Son. The second person of the Trinity," Lydia answered.

It still made no sense to Sam, and she still hadn't received a satisfactory answer about the missing bride and groom.

But she felt that the more they talked, the more confused she became, so she just nodded and said, "Oh. Okay."

|𝄾 ♩ ♪ ♩ |

After consulting with Lydia, Sam decided that she would go to the hospital to see her parents every Sunday evening (unless their situation changed, of course).

She didn't really want to see them, but not going made her feel too guilty.

It wasn't that she didn't care about them. She cared very much, but she didn't like dwelling on things she had no control over. Her visiting wouldn't make them come out of their comas any faster, and seeing them that way pained her. Nevertheless, she convinced herself that any good daughter would go anyway.

And she wanted — almost more than anything — to be a good daughter.

FALL

Her sandal ravished his eyes,
her beauty captivated his mind,
and the sword severed his neck.

Judith 16:9

EIGHTEEN

𝄞

Before Sam knew it, Halloween approached.

Her parents had been in the hospital for two months. Her father woke up in mid-October, but he still couldn't speak or move on his own. They had moved him to another part of the hospital, and when Sam had visited, he'd stared at her blankly, as if he didn't recognize her. That was almost worse than when he'd been in a coma.

Her mother had yet to regain consciousness.

Even though she'd fallen into a routine fairly easily, it had taken the better part of September for Sam to feel some sense of normalcy living with the Howards. For the most part, Paul and Lydia treated her no differently than they treated their own children. Lydia even scolded her sometimes.

The first time it happened, it caught Sam off guard — Lydia had been so gentle and consoling since the accident, and she constantly joked and laughed. But Sam had to admit that she'd been pushing her luck, and she had deserved Lydia's reprimand. On a day when Jason the Meathead had been particularly annoying, Lydia's cheerful greeting grated on her, and Sam responded with nothing more than an eye roll. When Lydia started needling her with questions, Sam snapped at her. Lydia snapped back, and Sam knew she'd crossed into new territory. She'd grown so comfortable with the Howards that she'd begun to let out a part of herself that she normally only showed to her parents — the part that wasn't all that compliant or helpful or respectful.

Bear treated her the way she imagined most big brothers treated little sisters. Of course, she also thought he probably landed on the nicer end of the big brother spectrum — she'd heard students in her class tell horror stories about how cruel older brothers could be. Whenever he and Tobias went out somewhere or played basketball on the driveway together, Bear invited her to join them and made sure she felt included. He taught her how to shoot a basketball and how to dribble (she was terrible at both) and bought her popcorn at the movies and won a stuffed raccoon for her at the traveling carnival that went through town. In return, Sam became his biggest fan at the football games, out-cheering everyone and waving a homemade poster with his name and jersey number on it.

Tobias acted less brotherly. Not that she wanted him to act like a brother — she had rather another sort of relationship in mind — but he wasn't even what she would classify as friendly. He wasn't mean or anything. He just seemed perpetually annoyed with her very existence. If Bear invited her to join them tossing the football in the backyard (she was also terrible at this), Tobias would roll his eyes and heave a sigh like it was the worst sort of burden to have to throw a pigskin in her direction.

When, a few days before Halloween, Lydia told him he would be taking Sam trick-or-treating, he whined about how he was *too old for that baby stuff.*

Then Sam quipped, "Really? Then why are you whining like a baby?"

Tobias scowled and blushed, and Lydia cackled.

"She's got you there, Tobias," Lydia crowed.

"Why can't Bear take her?"

"He's going to a party."

"Well, what if I have plans with my friends?" Tobias pushed.

"Do you?" Lydia asked.

"Well... no, not yet. But... I can't make any plans with them if I have to babysit," Tobias complained.

"Babysit?!" Sam protested. "I'm not a baby! I can go by myself if you're too big and important to tag along."

"Oh, no ya don't," Lydia said. "Either you go together or no one goes."

"Why can't you take her? Or Dad?" Tobias whined.

"We have concert tickets."

Sam's ears perked up. "Concert tickets? What kind of concert?"

"A boring, grown-up concert. The symphony," Lydia answered.

Sam felt the sting of sudden tears. She hadn't realized how much

70

she missed going to symphony concerts with her parents until that moment. Tobias could take Halloween and stuff it. She wanted to go to that concert with Lydia and Paul.

"Can I come?" she begged.

"Oh, honey," Lydia said, "I don't know if there are any tickets left. And if there are, I doubt it'll be near the ones we already have."

Sam was crushed.

"Do you really want to go? You'd rather do that than trick-or-treating?" Lydia asked.

Sam nodded. "My parents used to take me to concerts all the time. It was the one thing..." She swallowed, having a hard time pushing the words past the lump in her throat. "The only thing we did as a family."

"Oh, Sam." Lydia's face softened and she pulled Sam close. "Let me talk to Paul. We'll see what we can do."

"What about me?" Tobias griped.

"What about you?" Lydia turned the question back on him.

"You guys are all going to a concert, Bear is going to a party. So what? You're just going to leave me here alone?"

"I thought you had big plans to make with your friends," Lydia pointed out.

Tobias did that thing, opening his mouth and shutting it again before any words came out. "Fine." And he stormed out of the room.

After he was gone, Lydia turned back to Sam. "What's up with him?" She jerked her head in the direction Tobias had gone.

Sam shrugged. "I don't think he likes me very much."

Lydia raised an eyebrow. "I think you're wrong."

"Well, his friends don't like me very much. I *know* that's true."

Sam didn't see them often, but whenever she did see one of Tobias's friends, they made rude gestures at her and gross remarks about her and Tobias. She was young and probably naive, but she understood well enough what they were getting at. She often wondered why Tobias was friends with them at all.

Sam had also spotted his friend, Luke, and that girl, Emma, holding hands. She wondered how Tobias felt about that, but they hadn't talked — not really — since that first football game. He avoided her as much as possible, ignored her when he couldn't avoid her, and barely tolerated her when he couldn't ignore her. Arguing about trick-or-treating had been the most extensive conversation they'd had in weeks.

"Sam. Have Tobias's friends been mean to you?" Lydia asked.

They certainly hadn't been nice, but Sam didn't want Lydia to get involved. That would only make Tobias dislike her even more. She regretted having said anything.

"Sam?" Lydia expected an answer.

Sam shrugged. She didn't want to lie to Lydia. Ever. But she didn't want to tell her about the things Tobias's friends had said to her. "It's no big deal."

The way Lydia looked at her made her feel ashamed *for* Tobias's friends. She blushed.

"And Tobias?" Lydia said. "Has he been mean to you?"

Sam shook her head vehemently. "He mostly just ignores me."

Lydia's eyes narrowed. She sat in thought for a moment, gazing off at nothing. Then, suddenly, she chucked Sam gently under the chin and winked.

"I'll go talk to Paul about those tickets."

NINETEEN
𝄢:

Tobias sat in the treehouse in the backyard, bouncing a baseball against the wall like he'd seen some POW do in a movie once.

He hadn't gone to the treehouse since he was a little boy, but he didn't want to be found.

He was miserable. Worse, he felt like he had no right to be miserable. Not when he thought about everything Sam had gone through.

Tobias hadn't told anyone in his family that he didn't eat lunch with his friends anymore, that Luke and Emma hadn't talked to him in weeks, that he had exactly zero people to make plans with for Halloween.

Somehow he'd believed his friends would just *know* that he'd tried to distance himself from Sam since that night at the football game. He expected them to notice that he... That he what? Ignored her while they walked home? How would they know that? But his only other option — at least the only other option he could see to get his friends back — was to go straight up to them and convince them that Sam meant nothing to him. Which would be a lie, technically, and wholly unfair to Sam.

But wasn't he already being unfair to her?

If Tobias were honest with himself, he would have to admit that, as much as he had pushed Sam away to regain lost friendships, he had also put distance between them because the way she made him feel absolutely terrified him. It didn't matter how many times he told himself she was too young for him; the other half of his brain immediately responded that their age difference would be moot in a couple of years, maybe even a few months.

She would be thirteen in January.

But then he'd be fifteen the following August.

Then she'd be fourteen.

But then he'd be sixteen.

On and on it went. For half the year it would matter, and then it wouldn't. And then it would again. But why did it work that way?

Sam had called him a baby. Yet she was the one just barely out of elementary school. And he was practically in high school. When Tobias thought about it in those terms, he felt disgusted with himself.

But then he'd think about how her maturity surpassed that of most of his classmates, not to mention her intelligence. And he'd think about how she went to symphony concerts and had suffered such terrible tragedy with such great poise. He'd think about the sincere curiosity she expressed about his family's faith and about God and Mass — things she'd never been exposed to before living with them — and how she absorbed it all and asked the most profound questions. It was like Sam was a much older person who had taken up residence in the body of a twelve-year-old girl. Tobias had even heard his mom call her an *old soul*. When he thought about it that way, he wondered why he cared what his friends thought at all.

Tobias was still berating himself for being a jerk to Sam *and* for liking her when his mom's head suddenly popped up through the floor hatch.

"Figured I might find you up here," she said as she rested her arms on the floor and set her chin on her arms.

Tobias was half-convinced that his mom really could read his mind. There was no other explanation for how she'd found him so easily.

Tobias bounced the ball off the wall one more time. "Did you come to tell me what a baby I'm being?"

"I don't think you need me to tell you that."

Tobias frowned at her.

"No," she continued, "I came to ask if you would like to join us at the symphony concert on Halloween."

"Sam's going?"

"Yes."

Tobias leaned his head back against the wall.

His mom waited patiently for his answer.

"What makes you think I want to go to a concert with her when I didn't want to take her trick-or-treating?" Tobias knew that she had trapped him, and he knew that she knew it. If he said no, he'd spend Halloween alone. If he said yes, he was admitting that he had nowhere else to be — and thus no real reason why he had refused to take Sam trick-or-treating in the first place.

"I didn't ask if you wanted to go to the concert with Sam. I asked if you wanted to go with us. Your dad and I are going, too, ya know."

Tobias sighed. He had a feeling his mom knew more about the turmoil going on inside him than she pretended.

"Sure. I'll go."

He could tell that his mom was trying not to grin in triumph. Instead, she pursed her lips and nodded sagely. "I'll tell your dad to order the tickets."

She disappeared.

Tobias resumed bouncing the ball against the wall.

|𝄽 𝅘𝅥𝅭 𝅘𝅥𝅮 𝅘𝅥 |

That evening, Tobias's sister, Liz, wanted to video chat with all of them.

She was a senior in college, and he only saw her a few times a year. She called his mother often, but didn't do much to keep in touch with him and Bear. It was unusual for her to request to speak to the whole family at once. To make matters worse, Tobias hated video chat — the delay and goofy eye-lines made the whole thing feel uncomfortably inauthentic to him.

They all gathered around his dad's laptop in the family room. They set the computer on the coffee table, and he and Bear squeezed in on either side of their parents on the couch. Sam started to excuse herself to her music room — Tobias did a mental double-take when he realized he had begun to think of it as *her* room instead of Jake's — but Bear stopped her.

"Where are you going, Sam?" Bear asked. "Get over here. You're family."

Sam turned bright red. Tobias couldn't tell if it pleased or embarrassed or angered her that Bear had called her part of the family.

"There's no room," she protested.

"Sure there is," Bear insisted. "Tobias, get on the floor."

Tobias shot an incensed look at his brother, but he moved to the floor, making space for Sam on the couch.

Sam settled in next to his mom just before the video chat jingled.

Liz's face appeared on the screen, but she wasn't alone. A guy with a buzz cut and a serious expression sat next to her.

Tobias could hear his mom's sharp intake of breath and what sounded like, "Oh my goodness, she's getting married." But she said it so quietly and so quickly that he wasn't sure anyone else caught it.

Everyone exchanged awkward hellos. Liz even made a valiant effort to include Sam and ask about her parents.

"So," Tobias's mom said. To his ear, her voice sounded half an octave higher than normal. "Are you going to introduce us to your friend?"

Liz and Buzz Cut exchanged a lovey-dovey look that made Tobias want to fake-vomit.

"Everyone, this is Micah," Liz started, and Micah waved. "Um. We've been dating for... Well, technically, for only a couple months, but we've been good friends for..."

"Since freshman year," Micah filled in for her.

"Yeah, so... he proposed last night. And I said yes!" Liz was ecstatic.

For a moment, everyone seemed frozen. Tobias could see all their faces in the video chat, the shock they all wore, and he felt horrible knowing that's what Liz saw, too. And then:

"Congratulations!" It was Sam. "That's amazing! How did he do it?"

Before Liz and Micah could begin to tell their engagement story, the rest of the family finally came to their senses and stumbled over each other to offer their congratulations. Tobias felt immense gratitude that Sam had filled in the blank silence while his brain (and apparently, everyone else's brains) struggled to unfreeze.

"Have you set a date?" Again, it was Sam. Why did Sam have all the right questions? It hadn't even occurred to Tobias to ask. Suddenly, he was glad that Bear had insisted Sam stay for the video call — he could only imagine how awkward the conversation would have been had she gone downstairs.

"We were thinking spring. April maybe," Liz answered.

"Wow. That's pretty fast," his mom retorted.

"Well," Micah explained, "once we graduate, I'll be commissioning straight into the Army."

"He's been in ROTC, but he wants to go Active Duty," Liz added.

"And we want to be married before I leave for my first duty station," Micah finished.

"Besides, even though we haven't been dating that long, we've known each other for a long time, so it's really not that fast," Liz rationalized.

The conversation continued in fits and starts, Sam carrying it as often as anyone, until it finally fizzled. Everyone said their goodbyes, offering congratulations one more time before Liz and Micah's faces disappeared.

They were all silent for a time. Liz's announcement had been so unexpected, so startling — they didn't even know she was dating anyone, for goodness' sake!

"Welp. Looks like the family just keeps on growing," Sam joked.

It wasn't even a good joke, but it was exactly what they needed to break the tension. They all laughed the giddy laugh of release, even Sam. His mom laughed so hard she snorted, and then they all laughed harder.

After a while — Tobias didn't know how long — the silliness wore down and everyone dispersed. Bear went to his bedroom, Tobias's parents went to the kitchen for dessert, and Sam went to her music room.

Tobias continued to sit on the floor of the family room, thinking that having a growing family, perhaps, wasn't so bad.

TWENTY

$\flat$

Sam could hardly contain her excitement for the concert.

The symphony would be playing selections from the scores of spooky movies. It was a pops concert, the kind her parents would have called *cheesy*, but Sam's ears craved the sound of a live orchestra, no matter what they played.

Paul managed to secure two extra tickets, but the seats were in a different section than the ones he and Lydia already had. Sam had discussed the seating arrangement at length with Lydia. Lydia had presumed that Sam and Tobias would sit together, but Sam insisted that Tobias wouldn't be on board with that. She tried every kind of logic she could think of to persuade Lydia that pairing her with Tobias was a bad idea. But in the end, Lydia pulled the *beggars-can't-be-choosers* card, saying that Sam could either sit with Tobias or sit at home. Sam relented.

Apparently, costumes were encouraged. Sam had always dressed up in a nice dress or at least a skirt for symphony concerts, so the idea of wearing a Halloween costume to the concert hall seemed unconscionable to her. Lydia had to show her the program description on the orchestra's website to convince Sam that wearing her squirrel costume would be acceptable.

Tobias also thought wearing a costume was a stupid idea, but for a different reason. He claimed it had nothing to do with concert etiquette — he just thought costumes were childish. But when Lydia told him that she and Paul were going as Dr. Frankenstein (Lydia) and his monster (Paul), he rolled his eyes and agreed to wear Bear's old pirate costume.

Sam finished getting ready first, and she paced by the front door waiting for the Howards.

Bear had already left for his party dressed as a merman. Sam could almost see the steam coming out of Lydia's ears when he came down the stairs wearing nothing but a fishtail. It made Sam giggle, though. Bear was a big guy, and she had no doubt he was very strong, but his muscles weren't what she would call sculpted. His bare belly hung over his green, scaly waistband.

"No way are you going like that," Lydia declared, shaking her head. "Put on a shirt."

Bear just snickered and hugged his mom. "You're adorable when you're angry," he said.

As he walked away, Lydia wound up her kitchen towel and snapped him on the butt. He yelped like a little girl, and Sam howled with laughter. She could tell Lydia was genuinely upset with Bear, but she didn't push it for some reason — she let him go as he was.

Sam's bushy squirrel tail dragged on the floor as she paced. She made a mental note to take care that it didn't get caught in any doorways. Lydia had found the costume at a secondhand shop. It was a full, furry bodysuit — like footy pajamas — that zipped up in front, and the head was just a hood with little tufted ears on it. Sam carried a papier-mâché acorn the size of a basketball to make sure no one mistook her for a cat or some other fuzzy creature.

Surprisingly, Tobias — the boy who always ran late — was the next one to appear.

Sam could practically hear herself gulp when she saw him. He looked so dashing as a pirate. The costume came with a tricorn hat, but Tobias had opted to simply wear a red bandana tied around his scalp. Sam thought the pirate boots and red waist sash belt really sold it.

They stared at each other for a moment.

"Nice costume," Tobias said. "It's cute."

Cute? What did he mean? Cute, like a little kid? Or cute, like attractive?

"Thanks," Sam said. "I like yours, too." She hesitated, but decided Halloween was a good cover to make her next comment seem innocent enough: "You make a very handsome pirate."

"Thanks."

They were caught in a kind of spell then. Sam wished she could think of something more to say to keep him talking to her — Tobias wasn't often so civil lately, and she didn't want to waste the opportunity. But her big brains had evidently taken the night off. She could think of nothing. So they just stared at each other.

Tobias was the one to break the spell.

"I'm sorry I was a such a jerk about trick-or-treating," he said.

She hadn't expected an apology, and she didn't know how she should respond. She shrugged. "I didn't really want to go anyway."

"You don't like trick-or-treating?" Tobias asked.

"I've never had friends to go with." Sam's own answer surprised her. It sounded pitiful, and she didn't want Tobias's pity. To make it less pitiful, she continued, "And you know, we moved around so many times, and we didn't always live in nice neighborhoods like this one." It was getting worse, not better. "And my parents never really liked Halloween, so they never liked taking me trick-or-treating, even when we did live in nice neighborhoods." Stop talking! She wished she had a piece of duct tape to put over her own mouth.

Tobias listened. She could see the pity in his eyes. But all he said was, "Well, you didn't miss much. Trick-or-treating is totally overrated. Unless you like candy and fun, of course."

Sam couldn't help but smile. She didn't often hear Tobias make jokes — he usually left it to the more boisterous people around him. And she was grateful that he'd spared her the pity party. Seeing her smile gave him permission to smile.

Sam clung to this moment, treasured it — the two of them standing by the front door in their ridiculous costumes and grinning at each other.

She took a snapshot of it in her mind and tucked into a safe place in her brain so she could take it out later and remember that, once upon a time, a dashing pirate had called her cute and made her feel a little less pitiful.

| ‽ ♩ ♪ ♩ |

Even though Lydia had tried to paint the concert as *boring, grown-up* stuff, Sam estimated that families with kids made up nearly half the audience, most indeed wearing costumes.

Lydia and Paul walked Tobias and Sam to a box on the balcony level, Box B3, before finding their own seats on the mezzanine below. Sam could see them when she leaned over the railing. They waved at her, and she smiled and waved back.

As many times as she'd gone to concerts with her parents, Sam had never sat in a box seat. Part of her had secretly longed to because she had seen so many movies with characters sitting in box seats at the opera — it seemed such a high class thing to do — but her mom had snootily maintained that the sound and view of the stage were best in the very center of whatever section was just behind and above the orchestra level. Now that Sam sat here with Tobias, she couldn't care less about the sound or the view of the stage. There was a kind of intimacy in sharing a box with someone, and it delighted her that her someone — at least tonight — was Tobias.

Sam glanced over at Tobias and saw something like begrudging wonder in his face. It struck her that this was probably his first time at the symphony.

"Isn't it beautiful?" she remarked. "My favorite part is that big chandelier in the middle. When they dim the lights, it'll go up into the ceiling."

"Really?"

"Yup. And it'll come back down for intermission."

"Intermission?"

"Like halftime," she explained.

"I know what an intermission is," Tobias replied. He wasn't irritated, though, not like he had been lately. He said it with a laugh. "I just didn't know the concert was gonna be that long."

"Well, look at the program. Sometimes they tell you how long each piece is."

Sam reached over to grab the program from his lap. When the usher had offered them a second program, Tobias told him they would share a program, and the declaration had made the tips of Sam's ears burn.

Before Sam had an opportunity to investigate the running times of the evening's pieces, the lights dimmed. The chandelier receded into the ceiling, just as she'd claimed it would. She watched Tobias's face as he watched the chandelier.

"Now, the concertmaster — that's the first chair violinist — will come out and tune the orchestra," Sam whispered.

Tobias's gaze dropped to the stage.

Sure enough, the concertmaster came out, and the audience dutifully applauded.

"Why do we clap for her?" Tobias leaned close and asked in a whisper. She could feel his breath on her edge of her ear, and it tickled.

Sam shrugged and laughed. "I don't know actually. I've never thought about it before. It's just tradition, I guess."

As the orchestra tuned, Sam added, "The conductor will come out next, and we'll clap again."

"I'm ready." Tobias held his hands ready to clap, and Sam giggled. He kept his eyes trained on the stage, but he smiled.

The orchestra finished tuning, and moments later the conductor emerged from backstage. Tobias started clapping before anyone else. The conductor bowed with a flourish, stepped on his podium, and gave the orchestra an energetic downbeat, kicking off a gloriously cinematic overture.

It didn't take long for Sam to lose herself in the music. Everything else faded from awareness — even Tobias — until it was just her and the sound of the orchestra. The music washed over her and moved through her and swept her away.

She closed her eyes and breathed it in.

TWENTY-ONE
𝄢:

Because of the way the chairs were arranged in the box, Tobias couldn't watch the orchestra without also watching Sam. And soon, he only watched her.

She fascinated him. The rapture — that's the only word he could think of to describe it — on her face mesmerized him. The music had done something to her, and he ached to feel what she felt, to hear the music the way she heard it.

When the first piece ended and the audience began to clap, Sam opened her eyes and exhaled as if she'd been holding her breath the entire time. She turned to him with wide eyes.

"That was amazing!" she exclaimed.

"Yeah," Tobias agreed, nodding. "It was great."

The clapping died down, and the next song began. Afraid that Sam might eventually catch him staring at her, Tobias made a concerted effort to keep his attention on the stage. It was hard. Really hard. His rebellious eyes constantly flicked to her upturned face, and he found himself wondering what it would be like to kiss her on the cheek. And then he got mad at himself for thinking such things.

After every piece, Sam turned to him to say, "Wasn't that awesome?" or "Did you hear those French horns?" or "Now I *have* to see that movie."

Everything the orchestra played was supposed to be from scary movies, but they played just as many songs from action or adventure movies that happened to have a great theme for the villain.

When his mom had first asked him if he wanted to go, Tobias had honestly expected it to be dull, and he didn't think he would recognize any of the music. But he found that he had seen most of the movies and enjoyed hearing the music live.

Mostly, though, he enjoyed watching Sam enjoy the music. He had known that music was one of her interests, but he'd had no idea just how deeply that interest affected her. Seeing her in this setting somehow made her make more sense to him.

At intermission, Tobias's parents came up to the box to check on them. Sam gushed about the concert and the seats and showered his mom and dad with gratitude for bringing her.

She threw her arms around Tobias's mom and repeated, "Thank you, thank you, thank you."

Tobias's mom chuckled and hugged her back. "If only *all* my children were so grateful." She winked at Tobias, and he smiled back at her.

"Thank you, Mom and Dad," Tobias said. "This is actually really cool."

But Sam's expression had suddenly become more serious as she withdrew from Tobias's mom.

The lights flickered, signaling the end of intermission.

"We'll meet you on the mezzanine level at the end of the concert," Tobias's dad reminded them.

"Sounds good," Tobias answered.

His parents left to return to their own seats, and he and Sam sat in their chairs again. She was more subdued than before.

He nudged her. "You okay?"

She turned to him. "She said *all her children*. If only *all her children* were so grateful. Like I'm one of her children. One of you."

"I'm sorry," Tobias apologized. He thought he understood. He thought it might have been a painful reminder that she was stuck with a borrowed family while her own parents were fighting for their lives.

But Sam shook her head, even as tears formed in her eyes. "No. It was…" Her bottom lip trembled, and she took a moment to collect herself. "It was the nicest thing anyone's ever said about me."

He wanted to hug her. To tell her that she could stay with them as long as she cared to. That she would always be a part of his family. That she was wanted.

Before he could say any of that, the lights dimmed and Sam turned back toward the stage.

Tobias spent the entire second half of the concert wondering about Sam's life before the accident. He replayed in his mind the handful of things he had learned about her in the last few days — how much she loved concerts because they were the only thing the Ingrams did as a family, how Sam had rarely or maybe even never gone trick-or-treating, how being thought of as someone's child was the nicest thing she'd ever been told — and almost couldn't believe he'd never considered how much her life must have changed the night she moved in with his family.

Truthfully, he'd taken it for granted that her parents were probably a lot like his parents. But Tobias realized now how very wrong he had been. And he felt a little ashamed that he'd never even bothered to find out what her parents were like, and what her life had been like before. He felt like he'd learned more about her in the last three days than he had in the entire three years that they'd been neighbors.

When the concert ended, Tobias didn't hesitate to grab Sam's hand. He figured she'd assume he held her hand so that they wouldn't get separated as they made their way through the crowd, but in truth, he just desperately wanted the contact. Her hand fit so snugly inside his, like it was meant to be there.

Aware that he'd have to let go once they made it outside, he took his sweet time navigating the swaying crush of bodies.

Tobias looked down at Sam — the top of her head barely came to his shoulder — and thought she looked adorable with her tufted ears and her papier-mâché acorn tucked under her other arm. He asked over the noise, "Did you like it?"

Sam smiled up at him and nodded. "Did you?"

He nodded. "Way more than I thought I would."

She gave his hand a squeeze. "I'm glad you liked it. The symphony is one my favorite things in the whole wide world."

Almost without realizing it, Tobias squeezed back. "Then we should come again sometime." As the words left his mouth, his heart doubled its pace.

Had he just asked Sam out on a date? What was he thinking? What would Sam think?

TWENTY-TWO

♪

Sam was sure she was dreaming, and she would wake up any second now.

Had Tobias just asked her out on a date?

She didn't know; she'd never been asked on a date before. But then she convinced herself that Tobias was just being nice because of what she'd revealed during intermission.

"I would like that a lot," she responded. Vague enough, she decided, that it could go either way: if he was asking her on a date, her answer was yes (obviously!), but if he was just being nice, she was just being agreeable.

Tobias grinned, and Sam nearly swooned.

When they reached the stairs to go down to the mezzanine level, holding hands became awkward because there were too many other people for them to descend side-by-side. Tobias pulled her hand up to his shoulder and patted her fingers.

"Don't let go," he ordered.

They reached the bottom of the steps, and Lydia and Paul stood there waiting for them. The four of them moved to the side to let the crowd thin before they continued on to the parking garage. Sam wished they would brave it just so she would have an excuse to hold Tobias's hand again.

"Well," Lydia started, "what did you guys think of the concert?"

"It was awesome," Tobias raved.

Sam nodded in agreement. "I loved it." It was true. Shaped by what she now thought was snobbery in her parents, Sam had expected to find the program corny, but the orchestra had enthralled her as it always did.

"The box seats were okay?" Paul asked.

"They were perfect," Sam assured him. "This whole night has been perfect."

So perfect that she still expected to wake up from a dream.

And then she did.

Because she felt guilt.

Why her guilt decided to rear its ugly head at that precise moment, she would never understand. But it did. And it crushed all the evening's delights out of her.

Her parents were in the hospital — her mom still in a coma, her dad technically awake but not really in any better shape than her mom — and she was here enjoying one of their favorite pastimes. And instead of thinking about them, Sam had indulged in thoughts of holding Tobias's hand and (maybe) being asked out for the first time.

Worst of all, she had felt immense pleasure when Lydia implied that she was — in Lydia's eyes — really and truly as much a member of the Howard family as Tobias or Bear. That pleasure was a betrayal, plain and simple.

As the crowd became a trickle, Paul led them to the ground floor and the exit to the parking garage.

Tobias didn't grab her hand again — he had no reason to — but he did walk so closely to Sam that they rubbed shoulders and brushed fingers now and then. Her skin tingled each time. She ached to hold his hand. But she was plagued by the thought that it was wrong to be as happy as holding his hand would make her. And it would continue to be wrong until her parents got out of the hospital.

So she shifted her papier-mâché acorn to her other arm to put space between them.

During the car ride, Sam felt Tobias's gaze flick to her now and again. She swore she saw his fingers twitch like he was about to reach over and touch her hand. But he didn't. Sam leaned her head against the window and pretended to fall asleep so he would stop looking at her — or at least so she would stop noticing when he looked at her.

From now on, she had to keep her feelings under a tighter rein. She couldn't allow Tobias to distract her from being a good daughter.

And she couldn't allow Lydia and Paul to burrow any deeper into her heart than they already had. There wasn't room for them and her parents.

Sam was an Ingram, not a Howard, and she'd better not forget it.

TWENTY-THREE
𝄢:

Tobias had a hard time falling asleep.

Luckily, Halloween fell on a Saturday, so he could sleep a little later in the morning. Maybe his parents would even decide they were going to evening Mass instead of the one at 10:00 a.m. At this rate, Tobias wouldn't even fall asleep until it was morning anyway.

He was confused. Confused about how he felt about Sam. Confused about how she felt about him. Confused about how they should proceed if they both felt the way he thought they both felt.

Things had been so much clearer back when he liked Emma. They'd been lab partners in seventh grade science class, and Emma had utterly charmed Tobias. Luke and Fiona and a couple of the others were in that class, too, and their current configuration of friends had taken shape there.

When Tobias caught Luke and Emma making out, it was a shock. And it hurt. But the hurt had healed without Tobias really noticing. The fact that they both ignored him pained him more than the fact that they were together. Whatever he'd felt for Emma was long gone.

In any case, Tobias couldn't recall ever feeling about Emma the way he now felt about Sam. He'd been attracted to Emma, yes, but what Sam did to his insides was different. Tobias wondered why all his friends, and perhaps his mom, had been able to see her effect on him before he did. How could he have been so clueless? So blind?

But did Sam truly feel the same way?

Tobias had often guessed that she had a crush on him, but now that his heart was on the line, he felt less confident. Maybe he had misread her all this time — flattered himself that, because he was an older boy who sometimes deigned to pay attention to her, of course she would have a crush on him.

Thinking about it that way made him cringe at how poorly he had treated her. He had a lot to atone for.

Tobias heard the sound of the front door opening and closing and footsteps on the stairs. Bear must finally be home from his party. He heard the door to Bear's bedroom shut an instant later.

Tobias crept from his bed and into the hallway. He knocked softly on Bear's door. Bear opened it — he looked like an idiot in his merman fishtail — and invited Tobias inside with a jerk of his head.

"What's up, little bro?"

"How was your party?" That wasn't really what Tobias wanted to ask, but he had to ease into this conversation.

"Fan-freaking-tastic. How was your night?" He didn't sound fantastic, though, and Tobias wondered if Bear needed to talk about something, too.

"The concert was really good." Tobias paused. "You okay?"

Bear heaved a sigh and slumped onto his bed. "Can you keep a secret?"

"You know I can."

"I think I'm being called to the priesthood."

It wasn't even remotely close to what Tobias had expected Bear to say. He stared at his brother, unsure how to respond.

"I heard three different confessions tonight, and I just kept thinking, *If only I could give them absolution*," Bear mused. "Who thinks that? Who does that happen to?"

Tobias shook his head and shrugged, bewildered.

"You think I'm crazy?" Bear asked with a smirk.

"No," Tobias assured him, and he meant it. "I think you'd make a great priest, actually. You're good at making people feel comfortable and… important."

Bear cocked his head to the side as if thinking it over.

"Like Sam," Tobias continued. This was how he would introduce his own troubles, he decided. "You're so good with her. You make her feel like part of the family."

Bear shrugged. "Sam's a sweet kid."

"Yeah. She is." Tobias felt his chest tighten with nerves. Once he said it out loud, he'd never be able to take it back. But he trusted his brother. "I really like her."

"We all do," Bear agreed.

"No, Bear," Tobias said. "I mean, I really *like* her. And I don't know what to do about it."

Bear stared at him for a long moment. And then he laughed. It wasn't a mean laugh, but it embarrassed Tobias just the same. "Oh, little bro. What do you mean, you don't know what to do about it? It's obvious Sam likes you, too. What are you waiting for?"

Tobias frowned. Was it really that simple?

"You don't think it's weird? I mean, she's only in seventh grade. And she lives with us."

Bear waved a dismissive hand. "Who cares? You were in seventh grade, what, five months ago? And it's not like she's gonna live here forever."

"You don't think I should wait?"

"For what?"

"Until she moves back into her own house, I guess. Or until she's older... I don't know," Tobias hung his head, not sure what he was trying to say.

"The age thing doesn't matter as much as you think it does, Tobias," Bear insisted. "Maybe your friends think it's a big deal, but that's their problem. And as far as her living with us — I don't know. If you're really that worried about it, ask Mom what she thinks. She's the one who makes the rules."

Tobias did *not* want to talk to his mom about it.

But Bear brought up a fair point: even if Tobias worked up the courage to officially ask Sam out, they couldn't date without his parents noticing — not while they lived under the same roof. Not that he'd want to sneak around anyway. He despised kids who did things behind their parents' backs like that. No, if he and Sam were going to be together, he didn't want to hide it from his parents. But that left him with the inescapable conclusion that he needed his parents' permission. He felt absolutely certain that his mom would be all for it if Sam were living in her own house — in fact, Tobias suspected that his mom had been playing matchmaker for three years — but under the current circumstances, he doubted his mom would be quite so keen on the idea.

"Thanks, Bear," Tobias mumbled. "Goodnight."

Tobias thought that talking to Bear about the whole situation would ease his mind, that Bear would have the perfect answer. But the conversation only compounded his worries.

Back in his bed, Tobias reviewed the list of worries and tried to plan his next step. He intended to be methodical and logical about it, setting things in the proper order in his mind. He couldn't approach Sam before he talked to his mom — if his mom nixed the idea, none of it would matter anyway. But if his mom gave him the green light, then he could think about the best way to move forward with Sam.

Then the horrible thought occurred to Tobias that Sam might very well say no — for any number of reasons. And then where would they be? Stuck living in the same house for who-knew-how-long. And how awkward and painful that would probably be for both of them.

That thought decided it for Tobias. He would forget all about it. He wouldn't talk to his mom. He wouldn't ask Sam out. He would hope that Bear took what he'd told him to the grave. He would be nicer to Sam than he had been — he owed her that much, at least — but that was all.

No more finding reasons to hold her hand. No more joking with her. No more box seats at the symphony.

His mind made up, Tobias finally fell asleep.

Is any one among you suffering?
Let him pray.

James 5:13

TWENTY-FOUR

♪

Even though that first Mass had confused the daylights out of Sam, she continued to go with the Howard family every Sunday morning.

Little by little, each week, she grasped more of the general shape of the liturgy. By her third time, she recognized that there was a rhythm to it, a formula of sorts. It became a kind of game for her, a code she was determined to crack.

The day after Halloween was apparently a special holiday at the Howards' church. It was called All Saints' Day. Sam didn't notice anything all that special about the Mass, though, except that the priest wore white instead of green. Otherwise, the Mass followed the same pattern that all the other Masses had.

Almost exactly halfway through every Mass, the priest gave a homily (Sam had heard about sermons before, but the Howards called this part of the Mass the homily; she didn't know what the difference was). Today Father Bernard's homily focused on the saints, which Sam learned was a special category of super holy people throughout history. Although every saint had a different and unique story, Father Bernard pointed out, one thing they all had in common was a life of prayer.

Sam didn't think she wanted to be super holy. Being super holy, frankly, seemed kind of boring — or at least it had until Father Bernard told stories about some saints who had lived very interesting lives. Either way, she was pretty sure she had to at least be Catholic to be super holy, and she still wasn't even sure she believed in God.

Even so, something about the way Father Bernard talked about prayer made Sam want to try it.

She had sat through the prayer the Howards recited before meals dozens of times now — in fact, she'd heard it so many times that, even though they said it *very* quickly, she felt certain she had deciphered all the words and could recite the prayer herself. But she'd never actually participated. During the homily, she resolved to try it out — she would participate in the prayer at brunch after Mass.

When they sat down for brunch that morning, and Paul started the motion for the sign of the cross, Sam made the motion, too. And when they started the prayer, Sam said it in unison with them (they said it so darn fast, she stumbled over *which we are about to receive*, but she nailed the rest of it).

Lydia noticed. Tobias noticed, too, and Sam noticed him noticing her before she reminded herself that she wasn't supposed to notice such things anymore.

But neither of them mentioned it.

Sam didn't feel any different after the prayer. The food didn't taste any better. She didn't think holier thoughts as they ate. She wasn't sure what she expected to feel after praying for the first time, but she was sure she was supposed to feel *something*. Maybe it was because she had stumbled over some of the words — maybe that had somehow invalidated her prayer.

"What do you guys feel like after you pray?" Sam asked the whole table after a while.

"What do you feel like, Sam?" Lydia turned the question back on her.

"I don't feel any different."

Lydia nodded. "What were you thinking about when you prayed?"

Sam shrugged. "Saying the right words."

"Do you know what prayer is?" Lydia inquired.

Sam frowned. She felt like she was being quizzed, and it made her uncomfortable not to know the answer. She always knew the answer at school.

"Prayer is a conversation," Lydia said. "A conversation with God."

"Then why do you say the same thing every time you pray? That's not how real conversations happen," Sam rebutted.

Lydia's eyebrows went up, and she didn't answer right away.

"This isn't the only time we pray, Sam," Paul filled in when Lydia didn't answer. "When you pray privately, on your own, you can use whatever words you want to talk to God. But when we're all praying together, it's nice that we all know the same words so we can all ask for the same thing. In this case, so we can ask God to bless us and the food."

Sam pondered Paul's explanation for a moment. She was aware they also prayed the rosary together after dinner, but she hadn't realized they also prayed on their own, privately.

"What do you ask for when you pray the rosary together? What's that conversation about?" she challenged.

"You can offer a rosary for all sorts of intentions," Lydia jumped in again. "But praying the rosary is more about meditating on the events of Christ's life."

Sam absorbed Lydia's words. Like an itch in the back of her brain, she sensed she was close to uncovering some enormous Truth about the strange after-dinner ritual, but it was just out of reach. Filing Lydia's answer away where she could return to digest it more fully later, Sam moved on to the other bit Paul had explained about praying privately.

"When else do you pray?"

"Lydia and I get up early and pray before any of you kids are even awake. And I pray while I'm at work sometimes. And when I'm driving. And I pray again with Lydia before we go to bed at night," Paul explained. "The Bible tells us to *pray without ceasing*. I'm not quite that good yet, but I'm working on it."

Sam turned to Bear. "What about you, Bear? Do you pray like that, too?"

She had no intention of asking Tobias.

Bear seemed a little embarrassed, which was odd because he was never embarrassed about anything. His eyes flicked to his parents, then Tobias, and finally to her.

"I'm no saint, but yeah. I pray on my own," he confessed.

Sam very definitely did not notice the corner of Tobias's mouth lift as he watched his brother.

They ate in silence for a few moments as Sam thought over what they'd told her.

"So... if I pray on my own — have a conversation with God — then I'll feel something?" she asked.

Lydia shrugged. "God speaks to each one of us differently. I can't tell you what you'll feel."

That blew Sam's mind.

"Wait," she said, "he speaks back?"

All four of them grinned, but she didn't know what was so funny.

She had only repeated what Lydia had said.

"Not the way you're thinking," Tobias clarified. "Not usually anyway. But you never know. He could."

"I don't understand," Sam said.

"Whispers in the heart," Bear murmured, almost to himself.

Lydia and Paul both seemed surprised that he had said it.

"He mostly speaks in whispers in the heart, so you have to be very quiet and still and listen very closely," Bear continued.

Lydia actually dabbed at her eyes, as if she were starting to cry. Sam didn't know why Bear's words should make her sad, though.

"What does he say?" Sam really wanted to know. She'd never heard any of this stuff about prayer before, and it intrigued her.

"Like Mom said, he says something different to everyone. Whatever you need to hear," Tobias told her.

"You guys aren't pulling my leg, are you? Because this sounds crazy," Sam said.

They all laughed but swore they were telling her the truth.

|𝄆 ♩ ♪ ♩ 𝄇|

After the meal, Sam went up to her bedroom — she'd stopped thinking of it as her temporary quarters the day her dad failed to recognize her — and sat on her bed.

She didn't quite know how to begin, but they'd all called it a conversation, so she started with, "Hello, God. How are you doing today?"

There was no answer. But Bear had said she needed to be quiet and still and listen very closely. Maybe she just hadn't heard God's answer, so she pretended that she had.

"That's nice. I'm having a pretty good day so far. I guess. Actually, that's not true. I mean, today's not so bad, but just in general. These last couple months have really sucked. Sorry. I'm probably not supposed to say *sucked*. But you know what I mean, right?"

She waited, trying to be as quiet and still as possible. But she grew impatient to continue.

"See, God, my parents were in a really bad accident, and they've been in the hospital ever since. My dad, he woke up, but he didn't know who I was. My mom, she's still in a coma. I've been staying with the Howards, and I guess you know they're pretty great people, but... I miss my parents, God. I know I wasn't a very good daughter, and maybe they weren't great parents always, but they're my parents and I miss them."

For some reason, Sam had fallen short of admitting that to herself before now, let alone to someone else — not that she was fully convinced that God existed and he was listening. She'd clamped down on those feelings and buried them deep, as if missing her parents made her weak. And weakness scared her.

But now, with the honest admission, came tears.

Sam hadn't cried much since that first night in the hospital when she'd blubbered on Lydia's shoulder. She had successfully distracted herself with school and learning the trumpet and Bear's football games. And Tobias.

But now that she poured her troubles out to God — if he was there — the tears poured out of her, too. Sam stopped praying and just cried. For a long time, she cried.

And then she felt it. That little whisper in the heart that Bear had mentioned. Only it was more like a gentle pressure than a voice. Like someone hugging her soul.

It took her breath away.

And then it was gone.

And so were her tears.

"Thank you," she whispered.

$$| \quad \text{♩.} \; \text{♪} \; \text{♩} \; |$$

Visiting her parents at the hospital that evening felt different, more peaceful. Sam had less of an urge to crawl up the wall and out the window.

She sat for half an hour with her mom (the longest she'd sat with her yet), and she even told her a few things (she'd never had the courage to speak out loud to her unconscious body before). Mostly, she told her how much she missed her and hoped that she recovered soon. Sam also told her mother about school and band and the Halloween concert. She didn't tell her about praying and going to Mass.

It still unsettled her to visit her father. He seemed more curious this week, less blank, but he still didn't seem to recognize her. Sam told him she was his daughter and that she missed going to symphony concerts with him. She couldn't think of much else to say because there wasn't much else she and her dad had in common. It made her sad that she didn't know what to talk about, and in the deepest part of herself, she wondered if that were her fault or his. At the end of her visit, Sam squeezed her father's hand and kissed him on the forehead.

His eyes followed her every movement, but he didn't respond otherwise.

On the ride back to the Howard home, Lydia asked Sam how the visit went.

"I wish I was older," Sam answered.

"Why is that?" Lydia asked.

"Because older people always know the right thing to say. I never do."

Lydia laughed softly. "We might be better at pretending we have the right thing to say, but believe me, grown-ups say plenty of the wrong thing, too."

"What would you say to your parents if they were in the hospital like that?"

"My dad has been in the hospital like that," Lydia responded. "Well... sort of. He had a heart attack and spent several days in the ICU."

"What did you say to him?"

Lydia fell silent for a moment, apparently recalling her experience. "That I loved him very much. That I wasn't ready for him to leave yet. That my mom wasn't ready for him to leave yet." Lydia paused. "And I prayed with him."

"How?"

"I don't know," Lydia said. "I just held his hand and prayed."

"And God spoke to you?"

Lydia fell silent again, as if she hadn't considered it before. "Not in so many words. But he was there. I could feel him there with us."

"Like someone hugging your soul?"

Lydia looked over at her, curious, and then back at the road.

"I prayed today, and that's what I felt," Sam told her. She hadn't planned to tell anyone, but somehow it felt right to tell Lydia.

Lydia half-smiled, but she also looked like she might start crying. Her chin trembled.

"Sam," she whispered. "That's beautiful."

They drove in silence for a moment.

"Beautiful."

TWENTY-FIVE

⚓

Lydia debated telling Paul what Sam had told her about her prayer, but decided against it in the end. Sam had opened her heart to her, and Lydia wouldn't betray that confidence.

The girl constantly surprised Lydia. Her frank inquisitiveness produced questions that Lydia often had a hard time answering.

And her boys. Bear and Tobias made her so proud when they jumped in to answer the questions she couldn't. As a mother, she would always worry whether she had done enough to prepare her children for the moral perils that life would surely throw in their path. She'd failed Jake. But hearing her other sons talk with such conviction about faith and prayer filled her heart to brimming.

The truth was, Lydia adored Sam. She had come to love her as one of her own. And in such a short time!

The Ingrams' future was so uncertain. Lydia had hoped for Sam's sake that when John woke up, things would look more hopeful. But his apparent inability to recognize his own daughter made Lydia wonder if Sam's parents would ever again be in a condition to take care of her.

The word *adoption* came to her almost unbidden. Was it selfish to think of such a thing? Wasn't it, in a twisted sort of way, hoping that Sam's parents *didn't* recover? What kind of monster did that make Lydia?

But in reality, they had to prepare for the possibility. If Sam's parents never recovered enough to bear the responsibilities of custody, and no other family members were ever discovered... Were Lydia and Paul ready for that kind of commitment?

She asked Paul that night as they lay in bed together. "What if Sam's parents are never able to take her back?"

"She has no other family, right?"

"Right."

"Well, then. It seems obvious to me."

"What does?"

"You don't really want to put her into the foster care system, do you? Not when we could give her a good home."

Lydia smiled and snuggled against her husband. "Sometimes I forget just what a wonderful man I married."

"Shall I remind you?"

TWENTY-SIX

♪

Monday. Mrs. Gordon droned on about poetry forms, and Sam's eyes glazed over.

Jason the Meathead sat in the seat behind Sam. Twice during the first half of class, he kicked her backpack over, forcing Sam to crawl half out of her desk to retrieve its spilled contents. Before he could do it a third time, she zipped every possible opening. He kicked it over again, and Sam felt some satisfaction when nothing fell out and the Meathead grunted in disappointment.

Just as Mrs. Gordon finished explaining sonnets, Sam experienced the most troubling sensation. She felt as if she'd just peed herself, but there had been no urge to warn her. Luckily, it was only a tiny trickle. She prayed it would dry before she had to stand up.

But it was not to be.

Only a few minutes later, it happened again. Sam crossed her legs, trying not to think about what horrible medical condition might cause a twelve-year-old to pee herself and desperately hoping she hadn't gotten her chair wet. If the Meathead noticed…

Sam shuddered involuntarily.

Right before the bell rang to dismiss them from class, it happened a third time. And it was no trickle this time.

Utterly mortified, Sam did not rise from her seat when the bell rang. Jason the Meathead swung his backpack around purposely so that it would strike her in the shoulder as he passed her.

"Oops," he sneered. "Nice socks, orphan."

Sam waited for the room to empty before she risked getting out of her chair. When she did and saw a streak of bright red on the yellow plastic, she didn't know whether to be more embarrassed or less. She hadn't peed herself.

She'd gotten her first period.

|𝄇 ♩ ♪ ♩ |

Sam skipped her last class of the day and practically ran to the Howard home.

After she'd noticed the blood on her chair, she had surreptitiously checked behind her to see how much blood was visible on her jeans. Enough that she certainly couldn't make it through another class without someone pointing and snickering and ruining Sam's entire life. It made her feel like a dork slipping off her sweatshirt and tying it around her waist, but then again, people already thought she was a dork because of her fondness for crazy knee-high socks that didn't necessarily match anything else she wore.

If ever a girl needed her mother...

And as if she hadn't suffered enough calamity this year...

Tears of self-pity stung Sam's eyes.

At least Tobias had basketball practice after school, so he wouldn't notice that she'd left school early.

Sam barged through the front door of the Howard home and ran straight up to her bedroom.

On the stairs, she heard Lydia's voice calling, "Hello?"

Sam ignored Lydia and shut her bedroom door behind her. She felt that sensation again, and it made her squirm. Not being able to control it was the most uncomfortable experience she could imagine. Suddenly being a girl felt terribly unfair — why were women cursed with this horrible humiliation?

Sam looked around her bedroom.

Now what?

She had vague notions about how tampons and maxi pads worked, but she didn't have any of those things. And she didn't know where she could possibly find any.

"Sam?" Lydia called and rapped on her door lightly. "Are you okay? You're home early."

Sam had grown as comfortable with Lydia as she had ever felt around anyone. And she supposed Lydia, being a woman herself and having had four children, one of them a daughter, would appreciate exactly what Sam was going through and would know what to do about it.

Still, Sam wished it were her own mother on the other side of that door.

"Sam?" Lydia sounded even more worried since she hadn't answered.

Taking a deep breath and a moment to gather her wits, Sam opened the door. She knew she wore her discomfort on her face because Lydia gasped when she saw her.

"What happened? Are you okay?"

Sam shook her head and, unable to make herself verbalize her shame, she slowly turned around so Lydia could see it for herself. A sob shuddered through her, but she didn't release it.

"Ohhh," Lydia murmured, "I see. I'll be right back."

Lydia disappeared and returned less than thirty seconds later bearing a gift: an opened and half-empty package of maxi pads.

"That's all I have on hand at the moment, but I'll have Paul pick some up on his way home," Lydia said.

Sam's eyes bulged and she shook her head. "Don't tell Paul. Or Tobias. I'll die. Please."

Lydia laughed, not unkindly, and ran a hand over Sam's hair. "I'll tell him *I* need more," Lydia promised and winked.

Sam breathed a sigh of relief.

She felt indebted to the Howards for taking her in and caring for her while her parents couldn't, but something about this moment made her gratitude for Lydia overwhelming. Sam lunged forward and embraced Lydia in a tight hug.

"Thank you," she whispered.

Lydia returned the hug.

"Come down for a cup of tea when you get changed," Lydia whispered back and planted a kiss on the top of Sam's head.

♩ ♪ ♩

Sam feared that, when she went down for a cup of tea, Lydia might want to talk about awkward things, like periods and maxi pads.

She was right about the awkward part, but not about the subject.

"Sam, have your parents talked to you about sex?"

Sam froze with her cup of tea halfway to her mouth. She'd had a little sex ed in school, of course, but she'd tuned most of it out. The subject would surely interest her at some point down the road, but she'd never even been kissed. She figured she had plenty of time to learn about all that stuff long before any of it actually applied to her.

But yes, her mother had talked to her about sex. Once.

Sam set her cup of tea down. Lydia studied her unabashedly, as if she didn't feel awkward bringing it up, but Sam felt awkward and refused to make eye contact.

"My mom just said to let her know when I was ready so she could get me on birth control," Sam answered with a half-shrug.

Lydia's eyebrows lifted in surprise. "That's all?"

Sam knew the reaction implied some failure on her mother's part, but oddly, it made *her* feel guilty. Maybe Lydia felt obligated to buy her birth control now.

"You don't have to worry about it," Sam assured her. "I'm not ready."

Lydia shook her head, speechless for a moment. She muttered, almost to herself, "Sometimes I forget how the rest of the world thinks."

Sam hoped that was the end of it, but Lydia had more to say.

"Sam, I'm not sure what your parents believe," she started, "but in this house, we believe that no one is ready until they're married."

Sam knew that couldn't be true. She'd seen plenty of movies proving otherwise.

"That is..." Lydia took a deep breath. "A lot of people think they're ready before they're married, but when you're truly ready to do something, Sam, it means being ready for all the possible consequences of doing that thing. In this case, that means you're not truly ready for sex unless you're also ready for the natural consequences of sex."

The natural consequences? Was Lydia talking about STDs? Sam remembered the sex ed teacher spending a lot of time on that topic.

"A baby, Sam," Lydia clarified, apparently recognizing the confusion in Sam's face. "If you're not ready to have a baby, you're not ready for sex."

"I already told you I'm not ready," Sam reminded her.

"I know you did," Lydia replied.

"I'm only twelve," Sam added.

"I know you are," Lydia responded.

They sat sipping their tea in silence for a time.

"Just promise me, Sam," Lydia said, "that you'll never be afraid to ask or tell me anything. Even if you think I might be disappointed or upset, I can't help you if you're not honest with me."

Sam briefly thought of Jason the Meathead. She'd never told Lydia about the bully in her English class, but then again, she didn't think he was worth mentioning.

Another, completely unrelated question popped into her mind. Something she had begun to wonder about but had been too self-conscious to bring up before now.

Sam looked up at Lydia, and Lydia's brows rose expectantly.

"Will you show me how to shave my legs?"

You are the fairest of the sons of men;
grace is poured upon your lips;
therefore God has blessed you for ever.

Psalm 45:2

TWENTY-SEVEN
𝄢

Tobias's first basketball game of the season was on the first Tuesday of November.

Tryouts had taken place a couple weeks earlier, and Ollie and Colton had also made the team this year. Luke, who played last year, had been cut. Ollie was tall and had earned the start at center. Tobias was a starting forward. Colton, the shortest of the three of them, played at the guard position, but he wasn't a starter.

Since he had practice everyday after school, Tobias only walked to school with Sam; she had to walk home alone. The route was only six blocks through a nice neighborhood, but Tobias worried about her walking alone. A couple of times, Sam had let it slip that she had a bully in her class — Jason the Meathead, she called him — who sometimes bothered her. The one time Tobias had even come close to expressing his concern, though, Sam swore she could take care of herself.

On the day of his first game, his mom arranged to meet Sam at the gym so together they could form Tobias's cheering section. His dad wouldn't get off work early enough to come to the game, and Bear still had football practice — the playoffs started at the end of the week.

As he dressed for the game, Tobias tried not to think about his nervousness. He always felt nerves before a game, but they were worse than usual today. He attributed his jitters to the fact that it was the first game of the season — a season that actually mattered because, unlike in seventh grade, there was a state championship at the end of it. He was definitely not nervous because Sam would be in the stands.

Even though Ollie hung out with that group of friends who had ditched Tobias — or had Tobias ditched them? — he and Tobias played basketball well together. Many of the team's offensive plays revolved around their chemistry and ability to find each other in open space. Ollie didn't say much one way or the other about what had happened with their group of friends, and neither did Tobias.

Colton, on the other hand, thought that *Lover Boy* was the most ingenious insult in the history of mankind, and he continued to call Tobias by that nickname. At first, it really got under Tobias's skin, but the effect wore off as Tobias realized that Colton's smallness was not in his height but in his confidence. In hindsight, Tobias could see that Colton had always parroted everything Luke said, especially if it was mean. It was Colton's way of feeling important.

When the team ran out of the locker room for the pre-game warmup, it surprised Tobias how many people already packed the bleachers. In seventh grade, the games had never drawn much of a crowd — just the players' parents, really. But eighth grade sports drew other students as spectators, and they were a rowdy bunch.

It took Tobias several moments to spot his mom and Sam about halfway up in the parents' section. His mom waved at him, and he waved back. She nudged Sam, whose attention had been elsewhere, and pointed him out. Sam waved — reluctantly, it seemed to Tobias — and he nodded to her in return.

"Aw, that's precious. Your girlfriend came to watch, huh, Lover Boy?" Colton sneered.

Tobias clenched his jaw and focused on the warmup routine.

TWENTY-EIGHT

𝄞

Sam had mixed feelings about watching Tobias's basketball game.

On the one hand, it made it awfully hard to wrangle the emotions she needed to forget — he was just so darn handsome and athletic! — which frustrated her. But on the other hand, ever since that day Tobias had promised to show her video clips of a basketball game (he hadn't shown them to her after all, but she'd eventually looked them up on her own and been captivated), she'd wanted to watch a live game.

While the boys warmed up before the game, she saw Colton say something to Tobias. Tobias ignored him, but the look on his face told her it had been something nasty.

Tobias wasn't a boaster. In fact, he didn't talk about himself much at all. Sam, then, was entirely unprepared for just how excellent a player he was.

Within the first minutes of the game, it became clear that he carried the team on his shoulders. The big kid under the basket — Ollie, maybe? — was no slouch either, but Tobias dominated. He could shoot from anywhere, and when he didn't have the open shot, he found the teammate who did.

Soon, Sam was screaming her head off the same way she did at Bear's football games.

And she wasn't alone.

The student section was considerable, and they were obnoxiously loud to begin with. But once they realized that Tobias had taken control of the game and no one could stop him, they began to cheer his name: "To-by! To-by! To-by!"

"Paul's gonna be mad he missed this," Lydia commented during a timeout.

"None of you told me how good Tobias is," Sam accused. "He's scored sixty percent of our points. A little more actually."

Lydia gave her a strange look, and Sam realized too late that she'd hidden her big brains from Lydia, too. She didn't do it because she didn't want Lydia to know. It was just a habit at this point to let all adults believe she needed their help with math.

"We didn't tell you because we didn't know," Lydia told her.

Sam whipped around to face her.

"That's why Paul's gonna be mad," Lydia continued. "I've never seen him play like this."

TWENTY-NINE

𝄢:

It wasn't until halftime that Tobias realized the student section cheered his name.

He had been so focused on playing that he'd completely tuned out the crowd noise.

As the team jogged into the locker room, Ollie slapped him on the back. "You got fans, Howard!"

Behind them, Colton sneered, "He's showing off for his little playmate."

Ollie stopped and turned so suddenly that Colton ran right into him. "Grow up, Colton. That joke got old two months ago."

Colton shoved past both of them and entered the locker room.

"Thanks, man," Tobias said.

"I'm no hero. Shoulda said it ages ago," Ollie muttered.

When the second half started, the other team's strategy — their only hope, really — was to double-team Tobias. That's when Ollie came alive. Tobias felt just as comfortable serving as the decoy — pulling the defense outside to leave Ollie open — as he was being the scorer.

Tobias had natural athleticism and had worked hard on his fundamentals, but he loved the strategy of the game most. If his ball-handling skills had been slightly better, he would have been a formidable guard. Last season had been a disappointment for that reason: in his first year playing forward, he had taken the entire season to adjust to the expectation of being a scorer instead of a general directing his troops. With Bear's help, he had worked hard during the off-season to improve his catch-and-shoot and step-back moves. The step-back had become particularly lethal, forcing his defender backwards and giving him space to shoot from behind the arc.

But now that he faced a double-team, Tobias had a chance to show off what had once made him an effective guard despite his less-than-stellar dribbling skills. He had great vision, seeing who would be open before they even made it to their mark. The ball would leave his hands and reach the open man — usually Ollie — before the defense had even finished closing out on Tobias.

By the end of the game, Ollie took over as the high scorer. Tobias earned the first double-double of his life — 24 points and 13 assists — and they won the game by nearly 30 points.

He and Ollie clasped hands and bro-hugged in celebration.

Colton never even got in the game.

$$ |\kern-2pt\text{\raise1pt\hbox{$\flat$}}\ \ \text{\musDoubleWhole}\ \ \text{\raise2pt\hbox{$\eighthnote$}}\ \ \text{\musWhole}\ | $$

Tobias knew that Sam and his mother would be waiting to walk home with him.

He took his time showering and getting dressed, hoping that most of the students would be gone by the time he emerged from the locker room.

As much as he enjoyed the game, he didn't enjoy the spotlight. Some people thrived on being the center of attention, but not Tobias. The more eyeballs on him, the more uncomfortable he felt. That was another reason he hadn't done well last season — he had choked too many times, passing the ball away instead of shooting for fear of the attention, good or bad.

Pulling on his button-up shirt (they always dressed up on game days), Tobias wondered why today had been different — why the crowd hadn't bothered him and why he hadn't been scared to take the shot. Truthfully, he'd been so focused that he hadn't noticed the crowd much at all.

And then it hit him, the moment that his focus had become like a laser: the moment Colton had made that snide remark about Sam during warmups. Tobias had chosen to shut out Colton's words, along with everything else, and concentrate on every moment of the game. Colton's teasing could have become a distraction from the game, but Tobias had flipped the script — he had used the game as a distraction to keep from thinking about what Colton had said.

The realization made him wonder how the next game would go, and the one after that, and the one after that.

When Tobias finally came out of the locker room, his mom and Sam stood there in the middle of the gym. He couldn't hear her, but he could read his mom's lips when she tapped Sam on the shoulder and said, "There he is!"

Sam turned toward him, beaming.

Darn it all, he couldn't stop himself from grinning like an idiot.

THIRTY

𝄞

Sam felt a thrill go through her when Tobias smiled like that, and it made her already wide smile stretch even wider.

"Tobias, that was amazing!" she exclaimed. "You're so good!"

Lydia hugged him and said, "That was quite a game, mister. Bet you can't wait to tell your dad all about it."

Tobias shrugged, but Sam could tell he was tickled to have made his mom so proud. He turned bright red, and the grin didn't leave his face.

"What got into you anyway?" Lydia chided. "I've never seen you play with so much confidence."

Tobias shrugged again. "Just felt good, I guess. Like I couldn't miss."

His eyes flicked to Sam when he said that last part, and her heart skipped a beat. Boy, was he making it hard to keep her emotions under control.

Lydia threw an arm around each of their shoulders and guided them toward the exit. Tobias was just as tall as Lydia, and Sam felt small walking next to them.

Halfway down the hall between the gym and the doors leading outside, Sam stopped dead in her tracks.

"My trumpet!" She'd forgotten to retrieve it from her band locker before the game. "Can I go get it?"

"Of course," Lydia said. "We'll wait."

"You can go on home, Mom," Tobias suggested. "I'll wait."

Lydia gave them both that look she sometimes had — like she knew something but wasn't gonna say that she knew it. Part of Sam wanted Lydia to wait, too, but part of her — the rebellious part — felt overjoyed that Tobias wanted to be alone with her.

Or maybe he was just being nice. Yeah, that was probably it.

"All right, see you soon," Lydia said and left.

It was already dark outside and quite cold, and Sam didn't envy her walking alone.

Sam started toward the band room, and Tobias fell into step beside her.

"You don't have to come. You can wait by the doors," she offered.

"It's no problem. Unless you don't want me to come with you?"

"Um." Sam wasn't often speechless — sometimes she chose not to speak, but it was rare that she actually couldn't think of anything to say. Now, with her emotions in such a jumbled mess, she was good and truly speechless. She just sort of shook her head and half shrugged.

Tobias took it as an invitation and continued on toward the band room with her.

"Did you really like watching the game?" he asked.

What was this? Tobias starting the conversation? Wasn't Sam the one always trying to get *him* to talk?

"Yeah," she replied. "It's different than the football games. More exciting. Faster."

"Don't let Bear hear you say that," Tobias warned with a smile. "He'll think I've stolen your loyalty."

Sam giggled a giddy, ridiculous giggle. It was mortifying.

They reached the band room. Locked.

"Darn," Sam muttered. She really needed to practice tonight. Her first concert was tomorrow night, and she still struggled to hit that G.

"Bummer," Tobias said. "How bad did you need it?"

Sam shrugged. "Doesn't matter."

Tobias tapped her shoulder with the back of his hand. "Come on, let's go."

Just outside the building, they passed Tobias's friends, Colton and Luke. But oddly, Tobias didn't say anything to them, and they didn't say anything to him. Luke did whistle, though.

No, not whistle. It was a catcall.

Half a block later, Sam's curiosity got the better of her. "Weren't those your friends back there?"

"Used to be," Tobias replied. "Not sure what they are now."

"What happened?" Sam asked, then immediately backtracked. "You don't have to tell me, it's none of my business."

"Naw, it's okay," Tobias said. "They just turned out to be jerks, that's all."

"Because Luke stole the girl you like? Emma?" Sam almost kicked herself for her boldness. She didn't even want to know. But she had to know. She'd been wondering about it for weeks, ever since she saw Luke and Emma holding hands.

Sam saw Tobias's cheeks flush slightly as they passed under a streetlight. He swallowed. "No," he answered. He gave her that sidelong look that she adored. "Because he made fun of the girl I like. Not Emma."

Sam's heart smashed into a billion tiny pieces. There was *another* girl that she didn't even know about.

Good. It was better that way. Now her heart had no excuse to yank her in multiple directions. She could concentrate on feeling sad and sorry for her parents instead of feeling happy and hopeful about Tobias.

"That must have been hard for you." Sam made an extraordinary effort to sound sympathetic rather than pathetic.

Tobias shrugged. "Luke had his reasons. Well... for being mad at me, anyway. And that's really the only reason he made fun of..." Tobias glanced at her.

"The girl you like," Sam finished for him.

"Yeah."

They continued in silence for a moment as Sam's emotions battled each other for prominence.

"That's immature," Sam blurted, letting anger win for the moment.

Tobias gave her a look of surprise.

"Making fun of someone because you're mad at someone else? If you ask me, you're better off without that kind of friend," Sam declared.

Tobias remained quiet for a long time, and Sam thought maybe she'd overstepped. At least she'd spoken something true, though. Luke hadn't exactly been nice to her either, and she believed Tobias deserved a better friend.

Snowflakes started to fall when they had a block yet to go. They both halted and gazed up into the night sky. Sam stuck out her tongue, trying to catch a snowflake, and Tobias chuckled at her.

"Shut up," she said, scrunching her nose and giving his arm a light shove. "We can't all be as talented as Tobias Howard the basketball star."

Tobias stuck out his tongue then and chased a snowflake. It floated away from him, and they both giggled as he lunged for it and missed.

They spent the final block of their walk chasing snowflakes and laughing.

THIRTY-ONE
𝄢

Ollie invited Tobias to eat lunch with him the next day.

They sat with several other basketball players, whom Tobias had never hung out with outside of practice and games. He'd assumed he wasn't *cool* enough to fit in with them — they were part of the popular crowd that mysteriously forms at every school — but when Ollie led him to their table, they made room for him as if he'd been expected.

Most of their conversation didn't interest Tobias, and he had little to contribute. At least the basketball boys didn't spend half their lunch tearing other people down, as Tobias's old group of friends often did. Tobias regretted ever having belonged to that old group and berated himself for having allowed their charm to blind him to their cruelty and immaturity. It seemed that Ollie had taken his blindfold off, too.

Still, Tobias wondered whether the basketball boys would all react the same way his old friends had if they knew about Sam.

But what was there to know, really? Tobias had made up his mind that he wouldn't pursue anything with her — it was a risk he couldn't take while they lived under the same roof. So the only thing his teammates could possibly find out was that his family had taken in the neighbor girl until her parents got out of the hospital. But had his old friends really known more than that? Luke had acted like there was more, but there hadn't been until recently.

"So what do you think, Tobias? You in?" someone asked.

Tobias had stopped listening several minutes ago and didn't know how to respond. "What?"

"Tonight. You in?" It was Patrick, one of the starting guards.

Not knowing what Patrick referred to, Tobias answered, "Um, no,

I'm busy. Sorry."

"Too busy to study for Jackson's test tomorrow?" Ollie challenged. "What are you doing instead?"

A study group. They had invited him to join a study group. And he badly needed to study for that science test.

Funny. He'd always thought of the basketball jocks as partiers. It never occurred to him they might care about their schoolwork. His old friends had never taken studying seriously. He had misjudged these boys, and he didn't want to miss the opportunity to form new, better friendships — not to mention cram for a class he struggled in.

"No, you're right," Tobias agreed. "It's not as important as studying. Count me in."

"Cool," Patrick said. "What's your number? I'll text you my address."

They hammered out the details.

By the end of lunch, Tobias felt proud to hang out with his teammates. He texted Bear to ask if his brother would drive him to the study group.

The response was a gut punch.

You're not going to Sam's concert?

Tobias had forgotten all about the concert. He didn't want to miss it, but he couldn't back out on the study group, not without a lot of questions and awkward answers. Feeling rotten, but afraid to renege on his commitment to his new friends, Tobias texted back:

I really need to study for this test tomorrow.

It was a lame excuse, but Tobias couldn't think of anything better to say. It was true, but it wasn't the whole truth. He couldn't start off these new friendships by ditching them for Sam.

That's what had gotten him into trouble with the last group of friends, and he didn't intend to make that mistake again.

THIRTY-TWO

𝄞

Sam would never let on, but it devastated her when she found out Tobias would not be coming to her band concert.

He claimed it was because he had a study group with his basketball teammates, but Sam secretly wondered if that other girl — the one he liked — would be there, too.

Sam tried to tell herself she had no reason to be upset, that Tobias had zero obligation to attend her concert and that it was absurd to think he would ever choose hearing her play over hanging out with his friends. But it didn't matter what she told herself.

The plain, stupid truth was that his choice made her angry. Really angry.

All the people that mattered most to her would miss her very first band concert. Maybe that wasn't fair — Lydia and Paul and Bear were important to her, too, and they would all be there.

But she had looked forward to the chance for Tobias to see her in a different light, to see her in her own element. The symphony concert had given him a glimpse of her passion for music, but she wanted him to see that she had talent in her own right, too.

She was foolish to have thought such a thing, she knew. It wouldn't matter how many different lights he saw her in, he would never see her as anything more than the annoying neighbor girl who moved in when her parents got hurt.

Her parents. They made her angry, too. Sure, they couldn't help missing her concert, but why had they driven together that night anyway? They never went on dates, never went anywhere together except to take her to symphony concerts. What had they been doing?

Whatever it was, she hoped it had been worth missing their only daughter's first band concert.

Sam knew her anger was petty, but she couldn't help it. She was sick and tired of holding it together, of feeling guilty about not being a good enough daughter when the truth was that *she* needed *them*. And they simply weren't there.

The entire Howard family had been inconvenienced — no, burdened — with taking care of a girl who, by all rights, was not their responsibility.

How was that fair?

| ♩ ♪ ♩ |

Lydia and Paul showered Sam with praise after the concert, but it didn't make her feel any better.

She had missed that G after all, which made her mad and glad at the same time — mad that she had failed and glad that Tobias hadn't been there to hear it.

Most of all, it made her miss her piano. As much as she enjoyed learning the trumpet and playing with the band, she missed playing the instrument she was best at. She didn't fancy herself a prodigy or anything like that, but playing the piano came easily to her. Her hands hadn't grown enough to play the full chords in some pieces, but she found ways to modify the composition to make it sound like she played all the notes. Running her fingers over the keys relaxed her in a way that playing the trumpet just didn't.

As they walked back from the concert (Bear had left to pick up Tobias from his study group, so it was only Paul and Lydia), Sam decided to mention it: "I miss playing my piano."

"Would you like to start lessons again?" Lydia asked.

That's not what Sam had meant or expected. She didn't particularly like her piano teacher.

"No," Sam responded. "I just think I would like to go over to my house sometimes to play."

"Well, it's your house, Sam," Lydia told her. "You can go over there any time you want. You don't need to ask permission."

She had only gone back to her own house to pack more stuff, and Lydia had accompanied her every time. Thinking of going to that empty house alone, just to play the piano, gave her a creepy feeling.

"I meant..." Sam shook her head. "Never mind. It's not that big a deal."

"Would it be easier if we moved your piano into your music room?" Paul suggested.

That was an idea, and one she liked. The thought of having a piano in that room excited Sam. A little niggling in her chest tried to tell her she should feel guilty about taking things from her parents' house and making herself so at home in someone else's. But it was *her* piano — her parents had gifted it to her when she turned five. Why shouldn't she pack it up and move it just like she'd moved the rest of her life into the Howard home?

Sam nodded. "I'd like that."

♩ ♪ ♩

Moving the piano didn't turn out to be quite that simple.

That Saturday, Paul, Bear, and Tobias managed to load the upright piano onto a furniture dolly, but it took them a long time to figure out how to get it through the door. Finally, Sam suggested they take it through the sliding glass door that opened to the backyard. A path of smooth paving stones led around the house, through a side gate, and to the concrete driveway.

They rolled the piano across the street and up the Howards' driveway, but then they ran into the same problem — how to get it through the door. Lydia was no help at all. She laughed the whole time and kept saying, "This is the most ridiculous thing I've ever seen. The neighbors probably think we're nuts."

"Will it fit if you take the door off the hinges?" Sam offered.

Paul took out his measuring tape and nodded. "Just barely. We'll be careful, Sam, I promise."

Bear and Paul set to work removing the front door, but that still left the problem of getting the piano up the two steps to the front door. It had taken enormous effort from all three of the guys just to get the thing on the dolly.

With his hands on his hips and sweat rolling down the side of his face, Tobias declared, "Mom, I think you and Sam are gonna have to help us get it up the steps."

Lydia cackled her head off, but Sam felt up to the challenge. Sure, she might be smaller than all of them by a long shot, but she'd lend every ounce of strength she had to get that piano inside. The clouds threatened snow again, and there was no way she would leave her piano in the elements.

Once the door came off, Lydia and Sam and Tobias stood at the back to push while Paul and Bear lifted and pulled the front. They heaved and groaned.

One step. Stop. Pant.

Again. Second step. Stop.

Paul ran around to help from the bottom now that they bore most of the weight. Bear positioned the dolly at the top of the stairs, and somehow between the five of them, they managed to get it back on the dolly and through the door, Lydia snickering the whole time.

Now that they had the piano inside, it became obvious that the piano would never make it to Sam's music room in the basement. They would have to find a spot for it on the main floor. Paul tapped Bear and Tobias, already tired and sweaty from lifting the piano, to rearrange the furniture in the family room so that the piano could sit against the room's inside wall.

When all was said and done, Sam giddily sat down on the piano bench, which she and Lydia had carried over while the boys had argued about how to get the piano on the dolly in the first place. She played the first thing that popped into her head, a simple but pretty piece by Mozart that she'd mastered long ago. The piano was out of tune, but she didn't care. It felt good just to play again.

At the piece's conclusion, Sam turned to see all four Howards staring at her. Lydia and Paul beamed, but Tobias and Bear just looked shocked.

"Damn, Sam," Bear murmured.

Lydia punched him in the shoulder, hard. "Language, mister."

"Oh, come on," Bear chuckled. "You know you were thinking the same thing."

"What I was thinking was how beautiful that was," Lydia retorted with a frown she didn't really mean. She turned to Sam. "Truly, Sam. You play *very* well."

Sam grinned and curtsied. "Thank you."

"What other songs do you know?" Tobias asked.

"Lots," Sam replied. She didn't mean to be boastful. Just honest. Pianists were expected to memorize the pieces they performed, and Sam had a gift for memorization. Every note of every piece she'd ever played had a permanent place in her big brains.

"Anything I would know?" Tobias flashed a self-deprecating smile that made Sam's insides buzz.

She sat back down on the bench and played something she suspected Tobias had heard, even if he didn't know the name of it or who composed it: the first movement of Beethoven's Piano Sonata No. 14 in C♯ minor, more popularly known as the *Moonlight* Sonata.

When she finished, everyone clapped as if it were a real performance.

"Sam, you're incredible," Tobias breathed as he plunked down on the bench next to her. "You just have all that in your head?"

Sam only half-noticed that the other three left to get on with their own activities.

"Yes," she answered, suddenly self-conscious about her unnatural talent for memorization. What if he thought she was a freak?

Tobias looked at her temple as if he could see inside her skull. "You must have a huge brain."

"So?" Sam didn't know if he meant to insult her, but she felt that way, and it made her a little defensive.

But Tobias just smiled at her. "So nothing. I always knew you were super smart, but this — memorizing all that — that's crazy skill."

Sam tilted her head and raised one eyebrow.

"Is crazy a good thing?"

That spell happened again, the one where they just stared at each other for a precious, frozen moment.

"Yeah," Tobias finally whispered. "A very good thing."

THE HOLIDAYS

The Harness

Admonish the idle, encourage the fainthearted,
help the weak, be patient with them all.
See that none of you repays evil for evil,
but always seek to do good to one another and to all.

1 Thessalonians 5:14-15

THIRTY-THREE

♪

November zoomed by even faster than September and October had.

Between Bear's football playoffs and Tobias's basketball games, Sam had something to do most nights of the week.

Bear's team reached the semifinals before they were eliminated. The night they lost, Bear shrugged and quipped, "Still got next year."

Tobias continued to shine on the basketball court, but that first game of the season remained his personal, statistical best.

His teammates somehow learned Sam's name and waved at her in the hallways. At first, she thought she might be the butt of some joke, but eventually she realized they simply appreciated her enthusiastic cheering at the games. She felt pleased but also terrified of the attention it drew. Jason the Meathead became more bothersome all the time, and being a sort of pet to the eighth grade basketball team made her a target in a big way.

Sam's mother came out of her coma the week before Thanksgiving and, happily, recognized her daughter. It was an emotional reunion for both of them. Even though her mom's cognitive skills seemed well on the road to recovery, her motor and verbal skills had apparently taken the worst of the accident. She had a hard time forming words and would need to relearn even simple things like dressing herself and going to the bathroom. They moved her to an inpatient rehabilitation center, where Sam understood she would stay for several months.

Sam's father, on the other hand, had just begun to breathe and eat without the help of machines. He still looked at her blankly and said nothing at all when Sam visited him. When he had first awoken from his coma, Sam had assumed that the intubation was all that prevented him from talking. But now, no longer intubated, he still didn't speak to her. She didn't know whether he couldn't or wouldn't.

Although she revealed it to no one, not even Lydia, Sam continued to pray alone in her room. Even when she didn't sense that little soul hug or hear a whisper in her heart, praying made her feel better. Sam likened it to writing in a diary, except it had the added bonus that no one could ever go back and read it again. She could get her thoughts and feelings out in the open, out of her own head, without worrying about someone else's reaction or judgment. Each time she prayed, she ended with a humble request that God would heal her parents. It was what any good daughter would do. But always in the back of her mind lingered the secret and selfish desire that, when her parents did get better, they might show her the same love and affection Lydia and Paul did.

In truth, Sam still hadn't quite made up her mind whether God was real or not — what she experienced as soul hugs and heart whispers might only be in her imagination, merely things she felt and heard because she *wanted* to feel and hear them — but she continued to ask the Howards whatever questions came to mind regarding their faith. They never took offense at her questions, and they discussed the answers patiently and candidly. Sometimes none of the Howards knew the answer, and then Lydia would bring Sam a book a few days later with the answer bookmarked. It was smart and maybe a little sneaky on Lydia's part. Sam craved knowledge and always read the entire book, not just the bookmarked page. She had a feeling Lydia knew that would happen.

On the day before Thanksgiving, Sam left the school eager to continue the book Lydia had lent her most recently — one on the meaning behind all the quirky little things Catholics did. Already Sam had read about the sign of the cross, the rosary, the pope, holy water, incense, and medals and icons. She was fascinated by the tangibleness of Catholic practices, and much of the artwork around the Howard home began to make more sense to her. Tonight's chapters promised to delve into the meaning of the structure and symbols of the Mass and other Sacraments (she wasn't quite clear on what *Sacraments* were exactly, but she'd caught on that they were *very* important, and she was keen to understand why).

Lost in her reflections, Sam failed to notice Jason the Meathead following her until she'd reached the alley about halfway to the Howard home. The barking dog tipped her off. That same dog, which could be heard but not seen behind a cedar fence, had barked at her and Tobias the first few weeks they'd walked that route. But it grew used to them, apparently, because it finally gave up barking at them sometime in September.

Today, it barked moments after Sam passed it. She turned at the sudden noise and saw Jason not ten steps behind her.

Her eyes widened, and she froze.

THIRTY-FOUR

𝄢

Tobias expected to find Sam waiting for him when he came out of the school, but she was nowhere in sight.

She must have forgotten that he had no practice today because of the holiday weekend. He figured if he ran, he might catch up with her before she reached home.

Tobias jogged across the street, down the first block, and across another street. When he turned left at the corner, he skidded on a patch of ice that hadn't fully melted after the last storm. A block and a half later, he turned right into the alley.

What he saw when he rounded the corner stunned him. It took a moment for his brain to register what it meant, a moment that couldn't be wasted.

That bully, Jason the Meathead, had backed Sam up to a dumpster, his grubby fingers digging into her upper arms. He towered over her. She tried to push him away. It was like watching a mouse try to move a mountain. Jason shoved Sam against the dumpster, and the impact made a hollow metallic *boom*.

Tobias couldn't breathe, couldn't think, couldn't make his feet move.

Jason leaned close to whisper something in Sam's ear. Her whimper jolted Tobias into action.

He ran full speed. The Meathead never heard him coming.

Tobias grabbed a handful of coat and backpack and ripped Jason away from Sam. The Meathead probably outweighed him by twenty pounds, but adrenaline and the element of surprise gave Tobias the advantage. He hurled Jason across the alley, where he crashed into the fence opposite. The Meathead bounced off the cedar planks and fell to his hands and knees on the concrete.

Sam's whimper still rang in Tobias's ears, and he had no control over the rage it had unleashed.

He hauled Jason to his feet and punched the Meathead's face. A second punch shattered Jason's nose, and blood erupted from it. He threw a third punch that caught the Meathead in the mouth and split his lip. Tobias would've thrown more, but someone caught his arm from behind mid-swing.

"Tobias!" It was Sam, and her voice had a note of hysteria in it.

She pulled on his arm, and he released his grip on Jason.

The Meathead collapsed in a heap, holding his bloodied face and gurgling in pain as Tobias and Sam backed away.

"Don't you ever touch her again!" Tobias roared. His voice had finally stopped cracking, and he sounded like a man delivering his warning. But hearing the fury and menace in his own thundering voice brought the reality of what he'd done crashing into him. He panicked.

They had to leave. Now.

"Come on."

Tobias gripped Sam's arm and dragged her away down the alley. She resisted, and it made him panic even more.

"Wait, Tobias. My trumpet," she wailed.

Sam freed herself from Tobias's grip and ran back toward Jason and her discarded trumpet case.

Tobias's eyes darted all over. Had anyone seen what he'd done? Couldn't she just leave the stupid trumpet? Didn't she know they had to get out of there?

"Would you hurry up," he urged, feeling more panicked every second.

Tobias watched Sam pick up her trumpet, but its weight slowed her down. When Jason started to get to his feet, Tobias rushed to take the trumpet from Sam and hustle her out of the alley.

They ran another block and stopped when Sam put a hand on Tobias's arm. He snatched his arm away from her.

"What is it?" he snarled.

A hurt look flickered across Sam's face. But the image of blood exploding from Jason's nose clouded Tobias's vision. The sound, too — the cracking of bone and that sickening, fleshy sound would haunt him.

"Tobias, your hand."

She was right. The knuckles of his right hand had already begun to bruise and swell, and one of them had split — probably from connecting with Jason's teeth. Most of the blood on his hand was Jason's, though.

Tobias uttered a swear word, an awful one he'd never used before. His heart hammered in his chest, and blood rushed through his ears. He couldn't believe what he'd done. What she'd made him do.

He cast a fearful look back the way they came even though he didn't think Jason would be in any kind of shape to follow them. If anyone else had witnessed his brutality, though…

"Sam," Tobias said gruffly, "you have to promise you'll *never* tell my parents what just happened. They can never know. Never."

Sam looked at him with eyes like saucers. "I promise," she whispered.

He had acted like a monster, a brute, a madman. Was she scared of him?

He probably should have asked her if she was hurt instead of making her promise not to tell his parents. But the rage that still pumped through his veins rattled his brain. Or maybe the shock of what he'd done. He couldn't think past the need to get away from there and hide.

Without another word, Tobias started walking again at a hurried pace.

"I've never seen you that angry before," Sam murmured, practically jogging to keep up with him.

"Well, what did you expect me to do? Stand there and watch?" Tobias snapped. "What were you thinking anyway?"

"What was *I* thinking?"

"Didn't you notice he was following you?"

"No. Not until—"

"Damnit, I told you it wasn't safe walking alone, didn't I tell you that. I told you that, and you wouldn't listen," Tobias accused. "You told me you could take care of yourself. Well, it sure looked like you were doing a helluva job."

Tobias was scared. Scared of what he'd done, of what might've happened if he hadn't arrived when he did. And his fear made him angry. Some part of him, a voice in the back of his brain, told him he shouldn't be taking it out on Sam. But the adrenaline and too many powerful emotions muted that little voice.

Sam didn't respond to him, but Tobias heard her sniffle.

Great. She was crying. He'd made her cry. For some absurd reason, it made him even angrier. And now that the adrenaline from the fight began to wear off, his hand started to hurt. Badly.

If she expected an apology after what he'd just done for her, she would be waiting for a long, long time.

THIRTY-FIVE

𝄞

Why was Tobias being so mean to her?

Sam felt herself shaking all over, and as much as she tried to stop them, the tears came anyway. Jason the Meathead had terrified her — truly terrified her. She would never repeat to a living soul what he whispered in her ear. And then Tobias had shown up out of nowhere to rescue her. Watching him pummel her nemesis had been equal parts thrilling and horrifying. The look on Tobias's face when he broke Jason's nose — she was a hundred percent sure she'd heard it snap — was a look she never wanted to see again.

But then Tobias turned his fury on *her*. And she didn't understand why. What had she done to become the target of his anger? It wasn't *her* fault Jason had followed her and cornered her. Was it because she'd gone back for the trumpet? Or because Tobias had injured his hand saving her? Or did he think she wouldn't live up to her promise never to tell his parents?

Sam's misery grew the closer they got to the house. And as her misery increased, so did her tears. A block from the house, she couldn't keep up with Tobias any longer. She cried uncontrollably, and she knew she had to get hold of herself before Lydia saw her. Sam stopped and bent over, hands on her knees, to give herself a moment to rein it all in.

Tobias didn't notice she'd stopped until he was ten paces in front of her. He turned around and scowled at her.

"What are you doing?" he demanded.

Sam shook her head, unable to answer.

With a sigh of frustration, Tobias marched back to her and set her trumpet in front of her. "Pull yourself together. And remember. Not a word."

He left her there.

Sam didn't have any tissues, so she pulled one arm out of her coat and used the sleeve of her sweatshirt to wipe her nose. It was disgusting, but she couldn't walk into the house with snot and tears all over her face. There'd be no hiding what happened if Lydia saw that she'd been crying.

Her heart felt like a squashed bug.

Yes, Tobias had rescued her like some chivalric knight out of a fairytale, but he also made it clear that he still didn't like her one bit. Somehow, Sam had let herself believe that she and Tobias were friends. She knew he liked some other girl — he'd told her so — but ever since the Halloween concert, they'd gotten along so well. It was obvious now that he hated her. They would never be friends, let alone anything more.

The realization crushed her.

$$|\!\!\!\!\!\; \; \downarrow \; \flat \; \downarrow \;|$$

Over the past three months, Tobias had purposely avoided or ignored Sam plenty of times.

It had been annoying, awkward, even hurtful at times. But tonight Sam's pain cut especially deep.

Tobias had immediately disappeared into his bedroom, and Lydia hadn't even seen him, so she didn't know about his hand. True to her promise, Sam didn't give him away.

Lydia could tell that something was going on — Sam had never been good at hiding her emotions, and the wild events of the day, and perhaps the evidence of tears, must have been plastered all over her face — and she asked if everything was okay. Sam had promised herself that she would never lie to Lydia. She respected her too much. So she tried to think of an answer that was both vague and honest.

"It was kind of a weird day, but I don't really feel like talking about it," Sam said.

Lydia let it go at that, but Sam had a feeling it would come up again sooner or later.

Bear evidently tried to get Tobias to come out of his room to play video games with no luck. He asked Sam if she would like to play, and she agreed, reasoning that it would help her focus on something *not* her feelings. She couldn't even name all her feelings, and she instinctively knew it would take her longer to sort through them than the time they had before dinner — and it was a process she definitely didn't want to be in the middle of when they all sat down to eat.

At dinner, Tobias wouldn't even look in Sam's direction.

Not that she looked in his either.

At one point, their hands collided when they both reached for the asparagus at the same time. Tobias recoiled and turned red all the way up to the tips of his ears. Sam thought she might be turning red, too, but she was determined to play it cool.

With an effort, she made her voice sound as casual and relaxed as possible. "Sorry. Go ahead."

Tobias shook his head but didn't look up from his lap. "Ladies first."

That was just like him to be all gentlemanly when all she wanted was to be mad at him. She wasn't even sure why she wanted to be mad except that it would be easier than feeling whatever it was she felt now.

Tobias used his left hand for everything so he could keep his right hand — the bruised, swollen one — under the table. No one else noticed — at least they didn't say anything — but since Sam sat right next to him, she could see his injured hand in his lap. It looked awfully painful, and it made her feel guilty.

He'd hurt his hand to save *her*, and he didn't even like her!

After dinner, Sam went to her bedroom and left the door ajar. Half an hour later, after the Howards finished praying their family rosary, Sam heard Tobias pass her room and slam the door to his own.

While everyone else was occupied, Sam snuck into the kitchen and nabbed an icepack from the freezer. She tiptoed up the stairs and down the hallway to Tobias's room. She knocked softly.

"Who is it?" came Tobias's muffled voice.

"It's Sam."

Her heart pounded waiting for him to come to the door. Or maybe he would tell her to go away? She could actually see her shirt front pulsing with her heart when she looked down. Under normal circumstances, she would never dare knock on his door. It seemed particularly foolish now.

The door opened.

You have ravished my heart, my sister, my bride,
you have ravished my heart with a glance of your eyes.

Song of Solomon 4:9

THIRTY-SIX

𝄢

Sam stood there outside his door, looking worried and beautiful.

She held up an icepack before Tobias even had a chance to ask what she was doing there.

"For your hand," she said.

Why? Why would she be so nice to him when he'd been such a raging jerk?

He took the icepack from her, and their fingers brushed in the exchange.

"Thanks."

Having had time to calm down and review what had happened in the alley, Tobias knew he'd been way out of line snarling and snapping at Sam. He knew he should apologize, but the words stuck in his throat.

Sam lingered.

Tobias willed her to go away. If she didn't, he was sure he would lean forward and kiss her any second now.

"I felt bad, you know, since it's kinda my fault you hurt your hand," she murmured.

"It's really not that bad," Tobias responded. It was a lie. His hand hurt like hell.

Still, she didn't leave. She just stared at him.

Here she was, apologizing to him, when *he* was the one who owed *her* an apology. He had to set things right.

"Sam, I'm really sorry," Tobias started. "Seeing him grab you like that — it just… Something snapped, and I had to do something. And then I couldn't stop. And then… I shouldn't have yelled at you like that. I should've asked if you were okay instead of blaming you for what stupid Jason the Meathead did to you. But I was just so scared of what I did and thinking about how much worse it could've gotten if I didn't show up when I did..."

He was babbling, and he felt like an idiot. Sam continued to stare at him, her eyes going wider and wider. Before Tobias could even think about it, he continued, "I'm so sorry for yelling at you, Sam. I like you, and I hate the idea of someone hurting you. Even more, I hate the idea that *I* hurt you."

Sam's mouth fell open.

"Um. Will you forgive me?" Tobias asked in a small voice.

"You *like* me?" Sam asked in an even smaller voice.

For an instant, Tobias thought about taking it back. He could play it off as the kind of *like* someone feels for a friend. But lying to her now, after everything they'd gone through today, felt especially wrong.

Tobias nodded. "A lot."

"When you said Luke made fun of the girl you like. You were talking about *me*?" she asked.

Tobias had almost forgotten that conversation and thought it both odd and endearing that Sam recalled it at this particular moment. He nodded. "I kinda thought you knew."

Sam shook her head and almost laughed. "No." She paused. "I like you, too, Tobias. A lot."

Even though he'd had some inkling of her feelings, hearing her say it out loud did something whacky to Tobias's brain, and all he could think to say was, "Really? Why?"

"Why? You're asking me why I like you?"

"Well, yeah. I haven't always been very nice to you."

Sam huffed. "I can't believe this is happening."

"Me either."

Tobias looked down at his feet, suddenly embarrassed.

"So now what?" Sam asked.

Tobias shrugged.

Sam looked disappointed, and Tobias guessed that she had expected more than a shrug. He should have said something. But what?

And then he knew exactly what he *had* to say. It tortured him, but they had to be practical about this.

"Sam, I really, *really* like you," Tobias stressed. "But we can't... While you're living with us... I don't think we should... you know...?"

THIRTY-SEVEN

♪

Sam didn't know.

What was Tobias trying to say?

"Don't think we should what?"

Tobias sighed and looked away from her. "I don't think we should act like boyfriend and girlfriend. Or anything."

Sam's emotions couldn't keep pace with the day's events. She had gone from abject terror to utter heartbreak that afternoon. At dinner, she'd been visited by her old enemy, guilt. Then Tobias admitted that he liked her, and her heart spasmed with joy.

Now... Well, now the rapid rollercoaster of emotions must have made her brain fuzzy: she couldn't comprehend what Tobias could possibly mean.

She said so. "I don't understand."

"I know. It's not the way I want it to be, either, but I think it's for the best," Tobias said.

"No," Sam returned, "I mean I actually don't understand. What are you saying when you say we shouldn't act like boyfriend and girlfriend?"

Tobias sighed again. "I don't know how else to say it."

"So..." Sam closed her eyes, hoping that if she blocked out Tobias's handsome face, she might be able to get her thoughts in order. "You just told me that you *really* like me, and I told you that I like you back. But you don't want me to be your girlfriend?"

Now that she'd spit it out, she felt disappointment. And anger. Why would he tell her that he liked her just to take it back?

Tobias looked sad. "I do want you to be my girlfriend. But not yet."

147

"That makes no sense," Sam declared.

"It does," Tobias countered.

He opened his mouth to continue, but Sam cut him off.

"Is it because I'm only in seventh grade? Because your friends will make fun of you? Like Luke did?"

"No, definitely not," Tobias asserted. "It's because we live together, Sam. We can't be boyfriend and girlfriend until you move back in with your parents."

Sam's heart squeezed painfully. What if that never happened? Her parents' progress so far had been slow and not very encouraging. It could take them years before they were ready to take care of a child again. Who knew if she'd even *be* a child by the time they recovered?

More to the point, Tobias might meet someone else and lose interest in her long before her parents improved enough for her to move home.

"Why does that matter?" she challenged.

"It just does."

"Is it your parents? You think they wouldn't like us being together?"

"I wouldn't if I were them."

"Why? Because I'm younger than you?"

"No, it's not about your age. It's about..." Tobias stopped, frustrated. Whatever the big deal was, he didn't want to say it. Tobias took a moment, and Sam patiently waited for him to figure out how to explain it to her. He sighed again. "It wouldn't be appropriate for us to be together like that while we live in the same house because it would be"—Tobias searched for a word—"scandalous."

Wow. Sam hadn't been thinking along those lines at all. She was only twelve, for goodness' sake! What did he think would happen? That she might start sneaking into his room at night? How absurd.

Well, considering she stood outside his room right now, maybe it wasn't so absurd.

Besides, Sam had to acknowledge that he was probably right about his parents. And maybe even other people. Hadn't Tobias's old friends already made insinuations about that kind of thing? How much worse would it be if she and Tobias actually *were* dating?

Did that really matter, though? Why should they care what other people thought? It was none of their business.

Except his parents, she supposed.

In all fairness, Sam had to admit it *was* their business — because Tobias was their son, and she was in their care, and it was their house they lived in. Not to mention, Lydia had taken pains to have that horribly awkward sex conversation with her — and now it crossed Sam's mind that perhaps Lydia suspected something already.

The conclusion was inescapable. Sam had come to love and respect Paul and Lydia, and she couldn't bear the thought of their disapproval.

Sam slumped, defeated.

THIRTY-EIGHT

𝄢

Tobias hated the look of disappointment on Sam's face, and he hated even more that he had caused it. But it didn't change his certainty that it would be foolish to date while they lived together.

"I'm sorry, Sam," Tobias whispered. "About... About everything."

Sam shook her head and looked away. "Don't be." She paused, took a breath like she was going to say something, paused again. Finally, Sam looked up at Tobias again, her eyes full of intensity. "Do you think you'll still like me when my parents get better?"

Tobias's heart lodged in his throat, and he couldn't answer for a long moment. It hadn't occurred to him that it was even possible to *stop* liking her. In the three months she'd lived with his family, they'd both seen the best and worst of each other. She'd certainly seen the worst of him, anyway. What could possibly happen to change what he'd come to feel for her?

"I know I will," Tobias promised.

Sam almost smiled. She nodded to herself. "Don't forget to use a towel with that." Sam nodded at the icepack in his hand.

Tobias smiled a little. "Yes, ma'am."

"And Tobias?"

"Yeah?"

"Thank you. For what you did today." Sam bit her lip. It seemed like she had more to say, but she didn't continue.

"You'll let me know if he ever bothers you again, right?" Tobias asked. He meant it. If he ever saw that Meathead even look at Sam sideways, he was ready to do it all over again.

"I don't think he will," Sam said. When Tobias gave her a look, she quickly added, "But I promise, I'll tell you if he ever does."

They stood a moment longer, saying nothing but reluctant to part.

"Well," Sam finally said, "goodnight, Tobias."

"Goodnight, Sam."

Let them thank the LORD for his steadfast love,
for his wonderful works to the sons of men!
For he satisfies him who is thirsty,
and the hungry he fills with good things.

Psalm 107:8-9

THIRTY-NINE

𝄞

Thanksgiving with the Howards was a day Sam would never forget.

They went to Mass that morning. Sam thought it was weird because it wasn't Sunday, but Lydia insisted that Mass was "the *real* Thanksgiving." Every time Lydia said it, she winked, and it started to annoy Sam — as if Lydia were telling a joke she didn't get.

Even weirder, Tobias and Bear drove to Mass separately. When Sam asked Lydia about it, she merely shrugged and told her that Tobias wanted to get there early for some reason. Tobias never got anywhere early, and the whole thing made Sam suspicious.

On the car ride to Mass, when Lydia made another joke about the *real* Thanksgiving, Sam asked in exasperation, "Why do you keep calling it the *real* Thanksgiving? What does that mean?"

Lydia grinned as she turned around in her seat. "It's because the word *eucharist* is Greek for *thanksgiving*."

Sam frowned. She didn't believe her. Lydia's name might be Greek, but Sam felt certain that she didn't know the Greek language.

Lydia laughed at the look on her face.

"What?" Sam complained. "What's so funny?"

Paul glanced at her in the rearview mirror with a smile of his own.

"I'm not teasing you, I promise," Lydia claimed. "*Eucharist* really does mean *thanksgiving* in Greek."

"You know Greek? For real?" Sam still didn't believe her.

Lydia laughed again. "No, not at all," she said. "But I wouldn't let any of my children receive their first Communion until they knew *that* Greek word."

Sam didn't get it.

She thought she'd had the whole Eucharist thing figured out — supposedly the Body and Blood of Jesus, it was how God achieved union with his people — but now Lydia had thrown another wrinkle into the definition. Perhaps *wrinkle* was the wrong way to think about it; perhaps it was more like another *layer*.

Whatever it was, Sam knew she would be thinking about it all through Mass.

‖ ♩. ♪ ♩ ‖

After Mass, they left Bear's car at the church and rode all together to the rehabilitation center so Sam could spend a little time with her mom.

The rehab center occupied half of a building in the same complex as the hospital where her dad was still being cared for. They would go there next before they made the two-hour drive to Paul's parents' house.

The Howards lounged in the waiting room while Sam visited her mother.

Sam's mom had never been overly affectionate with Sam, so it struck her deeply when they hugged that day and her mom, weak as she was, clung to her for almost a full minute. Sam told her that she would miss spending the day with her and that she loved her very much and that she was very, very thankful for her. Her mother groaned and slurred words that Sam couldn't decipher, but she felt sure her mom had said something lovely and comforting.

When Sam came out to the waiting room, she decided that she didn't want to see her dad that day. If he even knew what day it was, it wouldn't mean anything to him that she, still a stranger to him, had come to visit. And it would ruin her mood for the rest of the day. Sam pulled Lydia aside to tell her what she'd decided, and Lydia understood, as always.

They left, and Sam felt grateful that no one mentioned what a bad daughter she was.

‖ ♩. ♪ ♩ ‖

Paul was one of eight children — a fact that absolutely blew Sam's mind — and six of the eight would be at the Thanksgiving gathering.

As if that many people weren't overwhelming enough, all of Paul's siblings had multiple children of their own. The eldest even had grandchildren. All told, more than forty people would gather for the

Howards' Thanksgiving dinner. Sam couldn't wrap her mind around a family that size until she saw it with her own eyes.

The noise when they entered the door almost made her turn and run.

As if sensing her instinct to flee, Tobias put a gentle hand on her back and whispered in her ear, "Don't worry, none of them bite."

Tobias moved in front of her to partake of the hugs and exuberant greetings from aunts and uncles and cousins. Her skin tingled where his hand had touched her.

"And this must be Sam," cooed an elderly woman not much taller than Sam as she wove through the crush of bodies. The woman reached out and took both of Sam's hands in her own. "You can just call me Grandma Jo."

"Grandma Jo?"

"Short for Josephine," the woman explained.

"That's my middle name," Sam told her. "Samantha Josephine Ingram."

Grandma Jo smiled brightly. "Well, isn't that something? I'm awfully glad to meet you, Samantha Josephine Ingram."

Sam couldn't help but smile back. "I'm glad to meet you, Grandma Jo."

She'd never called anyone *Grandma* before, and saying it warmed her insides, like drinking hot tea. Sam felt as if she'd found something she hadn't realized was lost. Until that moment, she'd never known that she desperately wanted a grandmother.

Sam bookmarked the thought in her brain, knowing she would have to return later to ponder her parents' parents — why her mom and dad never spoke of them and why she knew nothing about them. In fact, meeting so many members of Paul's family made her wonder a great deal about where her own parents had come from and how they'd grown up. She searched her memory — and she had a very good memory — and could find no recollections of her mom or dad talking about places they'd lived or family members they'd loved and hated or even childhood friends they'd known. It was as if their lives were a complete blank before they married and had Sam.

Grandma Jo drew Sam forward and introduced her one by one to each and every family member. Most smiled and offered a friendly hand to shake before returning to whatever conversation Sam and Grandma Jo had interrupted. A few of the women were more enthusiastic and wrapped Sam in a hug before she knew what was happening. It wasn't unpleasant, just unexpected.

All of Paul's family members apparently knew something of Sam's story. At least, she assumed they must because none of them asked who she was or what she was doing there or why she lived with Paul and Lydia.

Suddenly, Sam realized she'd been separated from *her* Howards. She found herself in the kitchen, surrounded by people she didn't know, and Tobias and his immediate family were nowhere in sight. Grandma Jo had disappeared, too. It made her a little panicky.

"Sam!"

She turned at the sound of her name and saw Liz and Micah making their way toward her. Liz hugged her.

Sam had only met Liz in person a handful of times, but a kind of bond had cemented between them the night Liz announced her engagement. The rest of the family had been shocked, but Sam felt genuinely excited for Liz and Micah. Since that night, Liz always asked after Sam whenever she called, and Sam always asked after Liz.

"You look a little overwhelmed," Liz noted.

"I am," Sam admitted. "This is my first Thanksgiving with more than three people."

"I know how you feel, Sam," Micah commented. "My family's not nearly this big. It'll take some getting used to, huh?"

Sam nodded but wondered if she'd truly have the chance to get used to it. Micah, presumably, would be around for Howard Thanksgivings for years to come.

Would she?

FORTY

𝄢:

Somehow, Tobias had lost track of Sam.

He and Bear had been catching up with three of their cousins close to their age — Jessica, fifteen; Lorraine, seventeen; and Bryce, thirteen. When Tobias turned to introduce Sam to the group, she wasn't there.

He spotted her disappearing into the next room with Grandma Jo. A few minutes later, Tobias managed to slip away to search for her. He went all through the house but couldn't find her.

Tobias told himself he was just looking out for her. They had agreed, after all, that they were not going to be a couple yet. So he definitely didn't look for her because he just wanted to be near her or anything like that.

Tobias found his mom talking to his Aunt Miranda near the hors d'oeuvres table.

"Looking for something, Tobias?" his mom asked. "You look a little lost."

"Um. I just was gonna introduce Sam to Jessica and Lorraine, but I can't find her," Tobias replied.

"I think I saw her in the garage with Liz and Micah," Aunt Miranda told him.

"Thanks."

Tobias's grandparents always had a ping-pong table set up in the garage for family gatherings. There was usually loud music and plenty of alcohol out there, too.

Bear and Tobias didn't drink (at least, Tobias didn't think Bear drank), but some of their cousins did even though they were still minors. Tobias worried what Sam would think of his family if they got too out of hand.

When he reached the garage, he found Sam playing ping-pong with a fierce look of determination on her sweet face. She played against Bryce, and she was way overmatched. Bryce didn't take it easy on her at all, whacking the ball in her direction with ferocious speed, and Sam flailed hopelessly after it.

Liz and Buzz Cut (once Tobias had nicknamed Micah in his mind, it stuck, and he knew he would have to take care not to say it out loud) sat in camping chairs that had been set up in a loose circle away from the ping-pong table. Two of Tobias's uncles sat with them, and they all nursed beers.

Sam and Bryce focused so intently on their ping-pong match that neither had noticed Tobias yet. He picked up a spare paddle from the workbench and approached from the periphery. Bryce slammed the ball over the net, and Tobias reached in from the side and smacked it back. It shot off the lip of the table, and Bryce swung right over top of it.

"Point for Sam!" Tobias called.

He surprised her, but it looked like a good surprise. She beamed at him.

"Get Jessica out here," Tobias ordered Bryce. "We'll play doubles."

Bryce seemed perturbed that Tobias had interrupted their game, but he left to find Jessica.

"I don't know if you want me on your team," Sam said with a grin. "I'm not very good."

"You think I'm gonna let Bryce have you?" Tobias teased.

Sam tilted her head and raised one eyebrow. He'd seen her make that face before, and it drove him crazy. "Are we still talking about ping-pong?"

So much for not being a couple. Tobias couldn't think of a clever response before Bryce returned with Jessica.

Sam smirked at him.

He wondered where she'd learned to tease like that. It was maddening.

FORTY-ONE

𝄞

The ping-pong game quickly climbed the charts of *The Most Fun Sam's Ever Had*.

Tobias and Bryce both took the game much more seriously than Sam and Jessica, who were more often giggling than hitting the ball. Just like all other sports she'd tried, Sam was terrible at ping-pong; and just like all other sports she'd seen him play, Tobias was exceptional at it. Bryce managed to keep the game close, but Tobias was obviously the better player.

Sam noticed that the swelling on the knuckles of Tobias's right hand had gone down considerably, and he used that hand — his dominant hand — with no apparent trouble. Still, an ugly purple bruise covered three of his knuckles and spread almost halfway to his wrist. If either of his parents had noticed, they hadn't said anything about it in front of her.

When Sam and Tobias were up 19 to 17, Bryce served a spinning shot across the net. Tobias extended into Sam's half to return it, but his thigh caught on the corner of the table.

There was a loud *r-r-rip!*

Tobias looked down aghast. His jeans had torn just below the front left pocket. The rip was easily four inches long.

Sam and Jessica and Bryce howled with laughter.

"It's not funny," Tobias said, but he had trouble keeping a straight face himself.

He picked up the ball from where it had bounced to a stop on the floor and flicked it toward Bryce. Bryce caught it and readied to serve again.

"Eighteen serving nineteen," Bryce announced before slapping the ball across the net.

This time Tobias returned it without ripping his pants, and it whizzed past Jessica off the bounce.

"Game point," Tobias proclaimed.

Bryce readied to serve again. "Game point. Eighteen serving twenty."

The ball came flying at Sam. Tobias lunged to bat it back, but it sailed too far to her side of the table. Sam threw her paddle up in front of her more in self-defense than any actual intent to return the ball, but — miraculously — it worked. The ball struck her paddle at just the right angle. It cleared the net by a hair and squibbed off the edge of the table before Bryce could reach it.

Tobias whooped triumphantly, tossing his paddle on the table and throwing his arms up in victory. Before it completely sank in that she'd scored the winning shot, Tobias wrapped his arms around Sam's waist and lifted her off her feet. Sam squealed in surprise, and Tobias twirled her around.

He set her back on her feet and turned to his cousins to gloat. "Did you see that shot? Did you see it?"

Even though they'd only twirled around once, Sam's head spun. She didn't know whether the thrill of victory caused it — or having Tobias's arms around her or something else altogether — but she felt like a feather floating on a breeze of pure happiness.

Tobias grabbed Sam's hand and raised it as if he were declaring the champion of a boxing bout.

"Ladies and gentlemen, the luckiest ping-pong player in the whole wide world, Samantha Ingram!"

| ♩ ♪ ♩ |

When the meal started, Sam and Tobias sat at the kids' table with several of his cousins, including Bryce, Jessica, and five others younger than Sam. Bear and Lorraine sat with the adults in another room.

Tobias constantly snuck sidelong glances at Sam that made her cheeks flush and her heart skip a beat.

She finally understood why most people looked forward to Thanksgiving dinner: the food was divine. Although her parents celebrated Thanksgiving, most of the meal they picked up from a restaurant the day before and reheated. Today, Sam had her first taste of a real, honest-to-goodness Thanksgiving meal. She overstuffed herself, but she couldn't bring herself to regret it.

As Sam shoveled pecan pie into her mouth long after most of the kids had finished and left the table, she wondered if anything about her life before her parents' accident had actually been *normal*.

This was normal — great, sprawling families eating a hearty, home-cooked feast together, toasting to the things that made them thankful, playing games and watching football and snickering at Grandpa snoozing in the recliner. As much as she missed her parents and wanted them to get well, the world into which the Howards had welcomed her filled her up in a way nothing else ever had.

Tobias nudged her elbow.

She looked at him.

"You okay?" he asked.

Sam nodded. She didn't think she could put her thoughts into words without getting all sappy, though, so she took the opportunity to ask Tobias something that had been on her mind all day. "Why did you and Bear go to Mass early this morning?"

Tobias raised his eyebrows in surprise. "Is that really what you were thinking about?"

Sam grinned. "No. But that's what I want to know. If you tell me, I'll tell you what I was thinking about."

Tobias considered her offer. Then, with a look of resignation, he said, "Deal. I wanted to go to Confession before Mass so I could receive Communion."

Sam cocked her head at him, hoping he would say more. Still knowing so little about Catholicism, she struggled to grasp the context of his statement.

"You're not supposed to receive Communion if you have a mortal sin on your soul," Tobias explained. "Not until you've gone to Confession for that sin."

"Because you beat up Jason," Sam said, comprehension setting in. Then she frowned. "But you were defending me. That can't be a sin."

Tobias shrugged. "Defending someone isn't a sin, but I didn't have to do what I did to defend you. I didn't have to hurt him like that. And I did hurt him, Sam. Really bad."

"He deserved it."

"Fighting wrong with more wrong doesn't make anything right," Tobias insisted gently. He paused. "Either way, that's not the only thing I had to confess. I was pretty mean to *you* yesterday, too. And you most definitely *didn't* deserve it."

Tobias smiled, and Sam returned the smile. Her insides hummed with pleasure.

"Your turn," Tobias said, nudging her elbow again. "What were you thinking about?"

"I was thinking about what I'm most thankful for."

"Yeah? What is it?"

"You," Sam answered frankly and paused for just the barest moment. "And your family. You guys didn't have to take me in, but you did. And you made me feel like I belong."

"You do," Tobias replied simply.

"What are you most thankful for, Tobias?"

Tobias swallowed, and for a moment, Sam thought he might kiss her. But he didn't.

"I'm thankful for a lot of things. Like... that I got to go the symphony with you. And that I get to listen to you play the piano. And walk to school with you." He grinned. "And win ping-pong games with you."

Sam grinned, too.

They were caught in that magical spell again, gazing at each other and saying nothing. Sam had always liked Tobias — even when he didn't like her back or, more recently, when he pretended not to. She'd even gone so far as to admit to herself that she was in love with him.

Now, when Tobias was being so sweet and charming, Sam thought her heart might explode with the intensity of her feelings.

FORTY-TWO
𝄢

Tobias knew he played a dangerous game.

They had agreed. He had convinced her, hurt her feelings telling her how they couldn't be together yet. But here he was, pouring his heart out to her again and allowing her to burrow deeper into his. How could they possibly keep up this charade for... however long it would take for her parents to recover?

After what Tobias told her last night and just now, he no longer had the option to pretend that he *wasn't* falling for Sam. No, not *falling*. *Fallen*. It was a done deal.

But neither could they show their real affection for each other. Not while they lived together. Whether they crossed any lines or not in reality, everyone would assume they had simply because they lived under the same roof. And if they weren't careful, even conversations like this one would get people talking. Sam didn't deserve to have those kinds of nasty rumors told about her.

Even when they could openly date sometime in the future, even when they were a few years older, Tobias had no intention of going too far with a physical relationship. Despite knowing that the world thought it old-fashioned, he firmly believed what his parents had taught him about the sanctity of marriage, and he fully intended to wait for marriage to indulge certain desires. That was a conversation for a much later time, of course — he and Sam were both way too young to even think about it.

But that was just the point: the rumor mill wouldn't care how young and innocent they were, and Tobias resolved to protect Sam from that for as long as possible.

And that's why Tobias used every ounce of willpower he possessed *not* to lean in and kiss her.

Instead, he made himself turn away from her adorable face and leave the table.

FORTY-THREE

𝄞

They left Grandma Jo and Grandpa El's shortly before 9:00 p.m.

After Tobias left Sam at the kids' dinner table, they didn't cross paths again. Sam had a feeling he was trying to avoid her again. It irritated her that he acted so warm and almost flirtatious one moment and so standoffish the next.

She had conceded to his logic that it would raise too many eyebrows if they acted on their true feelings. As far as she was concerned, she'd kept up her end of the bargain. Well, except for when she'd brought the icepack to his bedroom last night. But that was justifiable in her mind — she had simply wanted to make amends for getting him injured in the first place.

Tobias, on the other hand, had been the one to follow *her* into the garage. He had been the one who insisted on playing doubles at ping-pong and who teased her about not letting someone else have her and who celebrated their victory with a twirling hug and who claimed the seat next to her at dinner and who basically confessed his feelings all over again when she asked what he was most thankful for.

And now he avoided her again.

As they made the rounds saying goodbye, Sam received a hug from every single member of Paul's family. She couldn't recall ever having received so many hugs in one day, and each hug filled in a bit more of the hole in her heart that she was just now coming to recognize. She added physical affection to the growing list of things she never knew she had always longed for.

At the door, Lydia finally got a decent look at Tobias.

"Tobias Howard, what in the world did you do to your pants?"

Lydia demanded. Sam could tell she tried to keep a straight face and act mad, but by the end of the question, Lydia had cracked. She couldn't help herself, Sam decided — Lydia saw humor everywhere.

Tobias looked down at the rip that exposed the fabric of his pocket and blushed. Bear guffawed, but Paul seemed less amused.

"And your hand?" Lydia pointed to his right hand and the bruise that colored his knuckles. "What have you been doing today?"

"Playing ping-pong," Tobias answered with a shrug.

"Oh, brother." Lydia rolled her eyes and shook her head.

They waved their final farewells and got into the car. Sam settled into the middle seat between Tobias and Bear and made a conscious effort not to act any differently than she normally would. If Tobias wanted to act like nothing had happened between them, that's how she would act, too.

Lydia turned in her seat as Paul pulled out of the driveway.

"All right, mister," she started. "The truth now. There's no way you got those bruised knuckles playing ping-pong." She raised her eyebrows. "Unless you play ping-pong by punching people."

Tobias's eyes went wide, and his mouth dropped open. Sam felt him tense.

She froze, too. She willed herself not to look at Lydia, to pretend that she wasn't even hearing this conversation.

"You punched somebody, Tobias?" Bear asked. The surprise and the amusement in his voice were both real. It had occurred to Sam that Tobias might have told Bear about all that transpired yesterday, but his reaction indicated otherwise.

"It's not funny, Bear," Lydia said quietly.

Bear wisely kept his mouth shut. Lydia's good humor had disappeared, and that was never a good sign.

"Who did you hit, Tobias?" Lydia asked.

When Tobias didn't answer right away, Sam spoke up. "Maybe he smashed his hand in his locker or something." It wasn't a lie exactly. It was a suggestion — Lydia could choose to take it or not.

Lydia turned her hard gaze on Sam, and she feared that, with those few words, she had damaged Lydia's trust. Still, she wasn't about to let Tobias take the heat alone, not when it was her fault that he had beaten some kid to a pulp.

Lydia's eyes flicked back to Tobias. "She's not helping your case, Tobias. You hit someone *and* you asked Sam to lie for you."

Tobias licked his lips and swallowed. He cleared his throat. "You're right. I punched a guy yesterday because he was…"

"Yes?"

Sam's stomach clenched. She didn't want Paul and Lydia to know that she had been bullied.

"I saw him hurting Sam."

Lydia's gaze shot back to Sam, only there was concern in her eyes now, too. "Sam?"

Sam nodded. Much as she didn't want to cry, her lip started to tremble and tears formed in her eyes. "It's true. His name is Jason. He followed me after school yesterday and caught me in the alley." She barely finished the sentence before she started to blubber. It was embarrassing.

"What?!" Bear exclaimed.

"Oh, Sam," Lydia murmured. It sounded like she had tears in her voice, too, but Sam's own crying was too intense for her to look up.

She felt Tobias's fingers curl around hers and squeeze. Lydia reached back and touched her knee.

"*I* want to beat that kid up!" Bear declared. "Did he really hurt you, Sam? Are you okay?"

Sam could only nod.

Lydia pulled a couple of tissues from her purse and handed them to Sam. It mortified Sam to blow her nose in front of Tobias, but she couldn't breathe.

"I don't think he had a chance to do much more than grab her before I got there," Tobias told them hoarsely. "But he looked like he was getting ready to do something a lot worse."

Sam could only nod again. It certainly hadn't felt good when Jason shoved her against the dumpster, but she had escaped without any real injury. Unlike Jason and Tobias.

"I'm sorry I didn't tell you, Mom," Tobias said.

Sam calmed down some, but tears still rolled down her cheeks and she still hiccup-sniffled.

"We'll talk about this more tomorrow. Both of you," Lydia said. She didn't sound as angry anymore, but Sam thought she detected disappointment.

Tobias didn't let go of her hand. She didn't want him to. In fact, as the motion of the car lulled her to drowsiness, Sam allowed her head to rest on Tobias's shoulder.

She slept.

FORTY-FOUR

⚓

Lydia managed to make it to the safety of her and Paul's bedroom before bawling her eyes out that night.

In the car, she gave the kids the impression that she would wait until tomorrow to continue the conversation out of concern for their feelings. But in truth, she would not have made it through any more of that conversation without completely losing it herself.

Paul sat on the edge of the bed with her and held her while she cried into his shoulder. He rubbed her back but said nothing. He had learned after 23 years of marriage that the best thing to do was just to let her get it out of her system.

Lydia was a failure.

She had spent months mentally patting herself on the back for her selflessness: she had taken in the poor neighbor child whose parents were tragically incapacitated, had given up countless hours of her life to work with case managers and lawyers and judges and doctors and nurses to ensure that all three of them received the best possible care. Without meaning to and without realizing it, she had built herself up as some kind of hero, a saint, a martyr.

Worse, Lydia had fooled herself into believing that she was, in fact, a better mother than Renee Ingram. That the Howards were a better family for a girl like Sam to grow up in. They were wicked thoughts, and she was disgusted with herself for having thought them.

She felt all the more sickened having realized that she had failed Sam so spectacularly. A bully had terrorized the poor girl — who knew how long it had gone on — and Lydia hadn't had a clue. She had failed at a parent's most important job: she had failed to protect a child in her care. And because of her failure, her fourteen-year-old son had felt the need to step in, violently.

When Lydia verbalized all these things to Paul, he smiled and gently shook his head.

"Tobias didn't do what he did because you failed," he commented. "Tobias did what he did because he's in love, and his beloved was being threatened by a villain."

Lydia blinked. In her heart of hearts, she'd always thought it would be cute and perfect if Tobias and Sam ended up together, but in her mind, it would happen years from now.

"What makes you so sure?" she asked.

Paul gave her a look that said, *Are you serious?*

"Okay, okay," Lydia conceded. "Say you're right. Still. When we took Sam in, we took responsibility for her safety. Doesn't it bother you that we didn't even know she was being bullied?"

Paul shrugged. "Of course it bothers me. But there could be a million reasons we didn't know, none of them *your* fault. I think, going forward, we just need to reinforce with Sam that she should come to us if there's something like that going on."

Lydia nodded. Paul made it sound so simple.

"What about Tobias?" Lydia pressed.

"What about him?"

"Do you think we should be worried about him?"

"I think we should be proud of him."

"What?"

"I know, we don't want him thinking that problems can be solved with his fists, but"—Paul shrugged again—"all I'm saying is, a lot of guys his age wouldn't have had the courage to step up and defend a young lady in distress."

Lydia raised her eyebrows skeptically.

Paul smiled. "If someone were hurting you, I'd beat his brains out. How can I expect less from my son?"

"Oh, honestly." Lydia rolled her eyes and shoved him.

"I suppose we should talk to this boy, Jason's, parents, though," Paul reflected.

"And the school."

"Mm," Paul agreed.

Lydia sighed. "Do you think we should be worried about Tobias's feelings for Sam?"

"Why would we be worried about that?"

"Do you remember being a teenager?"

"Sure."

"And would it have been tempting to you if you lived in the same house with a cute girl that you really liked?"

"Ah." Paul nodded, finally catching her drift. But then he shrugged again. "No, I don't think we should be worried."

"No?"

"No."

"Why not?"

"Because it wouldn't change anything. It's not like we're going to send Sam into foster care just to help Tobias avoid temptation. That would be cruel. And you're not going to convince Tobias to *not* like Sam. You could tell him that hanky-panky is off limits as long as he lives under our roof — whether Sam lives here or across the street — but I'm pretty sure he already knows that. So worrying about it? Waste of energy."

Lydia tried in vain to find the hole in his argument. He was right, of course. Worrying never changed anything.

But she was a mom, and that's what moms do — they worry.

FORTY-FIVE

𝄞

The morning after Thanksgiving, the Howards began to decorate the house for Christmas.

Sam knew most other kids loved Christmas, and she supposed the Howard family probably loved it, too. It was normal to love it. But her family, she realized now, was not normal.

To her, Christmas was like Valentine's Day — a day that the world made a huge deal about, but one that was just kind of annoying and depressing if you didn't have anyone to celebrate with. Her parents didn't celebrate Christmas. They didn't decorate. They didn't listen to Christmas music. The only Christmas gifts she ever received came from teachers. And so it was a holiday Sam actively ignored.

It made her anxious thinking about the act she would have to put on for the Howards. She would have to pretend that, like all the other kids, she loved Christmas and couldn't wait for Christmas morning (she'd seen enough movies and commercials to know that opening presents on Christmas morning was ultimately why everyone made such a big deal about the holiday). Otherwise, they would feel sorry for her that she'd been that poor kid whose parents never cared enough to get her Christmas presents. But her parents did care about *her*; they just didn't care about a silly holiday whose only purpose was to make people break the bank buying gifts nobody really needed.

Decorating at the Howard home was a family affair, apparently, and Sam was invited to help. She didn't really want to, but she also didn't want to be the only one *not* decorating. Lydia put Sam and Tobias in charge of setting up a miniature Christmas village on the bay window seat in the family room while Bear and Paul hung the outside lights.

Sam unwrapped each piece of the village and handed it to Tobias to put in its proper place on the window seat. She had fallen asleep on his shoulder and they'd held hands the entire car ride last night, but this morning, Tobias barely said two words to her.

Sam looked around to make sure they were alone and that Lydia was out of earshot.

"So—"

"I'm sorry about yesterday," Tobias interrupted, but he didn't take his eyes off the Christmas village.

"Why?" Sam suspected she knew why, and a knot of fear settled in her stomach. She didn't want him to be sorry for making her feel cherished.

"I shouldn't have…" Tobias stopped moving pieces around, but still wouldn't look at her. "We agreed not to be boyfriend and girlfriend yet, but then the ping-pong game and last night in the car…"

He trailed off, perhaps hoping Sam would know exactly what he was getting at, but she honestly thought that statement could go either way. Did he regret their original agreement? Or did he regret the ping-pong game and holding hands in the car?

When Tobias didn't go on, Sam hissed in frustration, "Which part are you apologizing for, Tobias?"

He hung his head. The fact that he still refused to make eye contact with her confirmed her fears, but she wanted to hear him say it. She didn't want to let him off that easy.

"I think we need to be more careful about… not flirting and stuff," Tobias muttered. "Otherwise it's kind of like cheating — saying we're not together but still kind of acting like we are. We can't do that anymore."

Sam glared at him, but Tobias still wouldn't look at her. His ears turned red, though, and that gave her some satisfaction.

"It's like…" Tobias chewed his lip. "I know you don't know this, but when you go to Confession, you have to say the Act of Contrition at the end. And part of it is promising to avoid the near occasion of sin."

"You think we sinned yesterday?" Sam scoffed, offended.

"Not exactly, no," Tobias was quick to say. "But it's the same idea. When we flirt with each other, that just makes it harder to do the right thing. It's… It's too much of a temptation."

Sam thought perhaps in some other context, being considered *tempting* might be a compliment. But right now, it just felt like an insult. It made her feel dirty somehow. And that made her angry. She stuffed her hands into the box of village parts and pulled the rest of them out in one big pile. She dumped it in Tobias's lap and stood to leave.

"Where are you going?" Tobias asked.

"Removing the temptation," she spat. "Isn't that what you wanted?"

"Sam…" Tobias sputtered.

Sam stomped out of the room.

|𝄾 𝅗 𝅘𝅥𝅮 𝅘𝅥 |

When Lydia gave the promised talk to Sam later that day, all Lydia really told her was that the next time someone bullied her, she needed to tell an adult.

Apparently, while Lydia talked to Sam, Paul talked to Tobias. Sam was glad Lydia and Paul had separated them. It would have been unbearable to witness each other's humiliation, and she was still mad at Tobias.

"Am I in trouble?" Sam asked.

Lydia sighed. "No. But remember that chat we had a few weeks ago? And I said I can't help you if you're not honest with me. You remember that?"

"Yes." Sam looked away, tears of shame pricking her eyes despite Lydia's assurance that she wasn't in trouble. "I'm sorry I disappointed you."

Lydia drew her into a close hug.

"Oh, Sam. I *am* disappointed that you didn't feel comfortable enough to tell me you were being bullied, and I *am* disappointed that you tried to hide what Tobias did," Lydia said. "But I'm mostly disappointed in myself, Sam. I should have recognized that something was going on."

Sam thought that was ridiculous — of all the people in her life, Lydia knew more of what was going on in Sam's life than anyone else. Other than the bullying, the only thing she didn't know about — although it was entirely possible she did — was Sam's dilemma with Tobias.

When it was over, Sam sought refuge in her music room, not particularly interested in being seen by anyone for a while. Instead of playing her trumpet, though, she spent an hour or more writing music. She settled into one of the huge bean bag chairs and tipped her music stand into her lap to convert it into a hard writing surface. She had no staff paper, so she used the edge of her band folder to draw straight lines to make staves on printer paper. She hadn't composed in several months, and she regretted that the piano never made it down to her music room — writing was easier when she could check what she'd written against the way it was supposed to sound. The process of jotting down notes and rests, clefs and time signatures, sharps and flats, nonetheless soothed and refreshed Sam's soul.

Almost without realizing that she did it, Sam prayed while she composed. It was nothing more than a running conversation with God in her head. He didn't always respond — in fact, he mostly didn't — but she thought maybe he was just quiet the way Paul and Tobias were quiet. She told God about everything that had happened since Tuesday, when they'd last spoken. There was quite a lot to tell. Then she told God how confused Tobias made her and asked if God had any advice for her. She waited for an answer (she didn't often ask him direct questions and figured it was worth giving him a little time to think about an answer), but grew impatient after a minute or so.

Eager to try out her composition on the piano, Sam headed upstairs. She still wasn't in the mood to talk to anyone, but she felt relatively confident that she could carry on a civilized conversation without devolving into tears should she run into any Howard on the way.

At the piano, Sam propped her piece of printer paper on the music rack and settled onto the bench. She exhaled slowly as she placed her fingers lightly on the keys.

She played.

FORTY-SIX
𝄢

Tobias had just come in from the garage where he'd talked with his father when the music started.

Sam played the piano, but it was a strange piece. Strange and beautiful. Tobias had never heard it before, and it had a different style than most of the other songs she played.

He stopped just outside the family room to listen, not wanting to disturb her.

The talk with his dad had not gone at all the way he'd expected. Tobias thought he'd be in big trouble for fighting, hiding it, and making Sam lie for him. But as his dad wandered all over the garage cleaning and rearranging and organizing — a lifelong project Tobias didn't think he'd ever finish — they didn't even talk about the fight. Much. Sure, his dad had given the cursory *can't-solve-problems-with-your-fists* platitude, but then he mostly talked about goals and planning and managing expectations.

Tobias was frankly baffled. He had no idea how any of what his dad said connected to what had happened that week. And he tried, he honestly tried. But he just couldn't follow the thread of his dad's dissertation.

At the end, his dad had looked up from his work and said, "Patience, Tobias. That's the key. Just be patient, and let the Lord do his work. Things will turn out the way they're supposed to — not always the way you expect, but the way they're supposed to."

Tobias nodded and said, "Yes, sir."

And then they came back in the house. Tobias's dad didn't seem to notice Sam's piano playing, but it drew Tobias like a mosquito to a bug zapper.

That's how he felt, too. Like an insect buzzing helplessly toward his doom. Only two days had passed, and already Tobias was discovering how hard it was to keep away from Sam. No, not hard. Impossible. She was irresistible, and he was weak.

Perhaps he should have taken the opportunity to ask his father's advice.

There was a pause in Sam's playing, and Tobias started forward, but then she started again from the beginning. He didn't have a great ear, but he thought what she played this time differed slightly from what she'd just finished playing.

"I think she wrote it," his mom whispered at his shoulder.

Tobias nearly jumped out of his skin. He hadn't heard her approach, and he flushed with embarrassment that she'd caught him listening.

But his mom listened just as intently. They stood there together, mother and son, letting Sam's mysterious music seep into their souls.

The song ended, and there was silence. And then Sam started over again, and again it was a subtle variation from the last time.

"Amazing," his mom breathed.

Tobias nodded in agreement. He thought of all the times he'd heard Sam humming to herself, and he pictured her breathing music like air.

When Sam finished that time, they heard her get up and leave the room the other way, toward the stairs to the basement.

Tobias's mom locked eyes with him. She spoke very quietly. "She's a special girl, Tobias. Very special. But she's been through a lot. More than we know, I think. Just... be careful."

Tobias stared, dumbfounded.

What did she mean? What did she think had happened to Sam that they didn't know about? And what was he supposed to be careful with? Did his mom know how he felt about Sam?

Before Tobias could form the words for any of his questions, his mom patted him on the arm and left him standing there.

Praise the LORD!
Praise God in his sanctuary;
praise him in his mighty firmament!
Praise him for his mighty deeds;
praise him according to his exceeding greatness!
Praise him with trumpet sound;
praise him with lute and harp!
Praise him with timbrel and dance;
praise him with strings and pipe!
Praise him with sounding cymbals;
praise him with loud clashing cymbals!
Let everything that breathes praise the LORD!
Praise the LORD!

Psalm 150

FORTY-SEVEN

𝄞

At Mass that Sunday, Sam noticed the priest wore white again as he had on All Saints' Day.

Lydia explained that a new liturgical season was starting, the season of Advent, which was supposed to prepare them for Christmas.

Ugh. Christmas again.

Sam detested Christmas, and she wasn't too keen on having a whole liturgical season — whatever that meant — to prepare for it.

But Sam noticed one other thing at Mass that Sunday. The parts of the Mass that stayed the same week to week, which Sam had memorized after her second Mass, suddenly changed. Or rather, they were the same words, but in a different language: Latin.

Feeling like a complete dolt, Sam realized she knew these Latin words — not because she'd ever heard them at Mass before, but because she'd heard them set to music in several pieces by Mozart and Verdi and Bach and Beethoven and many others. Sam had never heard those pieces performed outside a concert hall, and the melodies the choir sang that morning were unfamiliar to her. But the words were the same. The words of the Catholic Mass.

Sam was stunned. She couldn't believe it had taken her this long to make the connection. It had been right there in the names of those pieces: Beethoven's Missa Solemnis in D Major and Bach's Mass in B Minor and Mozart's Great Mass in C Minor. The Masses written by the greats were *Mass settings*, music for the liturgy. All the famous Requiems, too, for they had the same words. She'd known they were religious pieces — she *must* have — but the knowledge was like a string of lights with one bad bulb, and it took hearing the Latin in its

181

rightful context to replace the bulb and illuminate the entire string.

Suddenly, the liturgy of the Mass seemed more beautiful to her, and the Requiems and Mass settings seemed to have far more depth. It was a new thing to ponder — the intersection of religion and art, how beauty could help people worship — and she couldn't wait to retreat to her music room and listen to her favorite Requiem, the one by Dvořák (she had a weakness for the late Romantics).

Her epiphany excited her so much, Sam shared it with everyone in the car after Mass.

"You guys are gonna think I'm dumb, but I just realized today that Requiems are Mass settings," Sam announced.

All of them gave her the strangest look, as if she'd lost her mind. Even Paul glanced at her in the rearview mirror with a furrowed brow. Wow. They really did think she was dumb for not making the connection earlier.

"Can you say that again in English?" Bear quipped.

"Ha ha, very funny." Sam rolled her eyes, assuming he was trying to be witty about the Mass parts being in Latin instead of English.

"No, seriously," Bear said. "What did you just say?"

Sam gave him an annoyed look. She couldn't tell whether he made fun of her or really didn't understand. "The parts of the Mass they did in Latin today. I've heard them before. And it made me think, of course, because Requiems are Mass settings. But it took me until today to…"

Did she slur her words or something? They all still had that look like she was crazy.

"Give me your phone." She held out her hand for Bear's phone.

"What for?"

"You guys are looking at me like I'm crazy, so I'm gonna show you what I'm talking about," Sam ranted, letting her frustration bubble over a bit.

Before Bear could get his phone out of his pocket, Tobias had his out and handed it to Sam.

Lydia had turned to face forward again, but before she did, Sam saw her grinning.

Sam hit the home button, but Tobias's phone was locked. With a half smirk, he held up his index finger. Sam had to concentrate in the bouncing car to press the home button to his finger so that it would read his fingerprint.

The phone unlocked, and she navigated to his music app. Sam

searched *mozarts requiem*, thinking they were most likely to recognize that one (she'd learned by now that none of the Howards were well versed in classical music). When she found it in the search results, she hit play on the *Sanctus* movement.

The music started, the chorus singing out, "*Sanctus, Sanctus, Sanctus Dominus Deus Sabaoth.*" Sam mouthed along with it so the listeners could decipher the words more easily. She hit pause after the first minute or so.

"See, this is Mozart's Requiem, that he wrote right before he died. He didn't even finish it before he died, actually, but anyway, the point is — the Requiem, it's music for a Mass. They're singing the same words we sang today," Sam explained.

"Wow. That's cool, Sam," Bear said, but he didn't sound like it was cool. He sounded like he was trying to humor her.

Sam turned to Tobias for support. He shrugged apologetically and took back his phone.

None of them understood. And she didn't know how to make them understand.

After that book on Catholic practices Lydia gave her, Sam had come to appreciate the rich *concreteness* of the Howards' faith. But this — magnificent, glorious music written by the most brilliant composers the world had ever known — drew her into the *transcendence* of what they believed. It was like a veil being drawn aside, granting her a glimpse into this Heaven that they were all trying to get to.

Sam had often thought that symphony concerts had an almost supernatural ability to connect her across time and space to the composers who had dreamed up that music. The experience of listening to live orchestral music was, for her, a kind of spiritual ecstasy, a brush with the sublime. She wondered now if perhaps, instead of whispers in the heart, God spoke to her through music. Perhaps he spoke to everyone that way, but few people ever learned to hear his voice there.

It gave Sam goosebumps to think what it might be like to hear Mozart's Requiem — or any Mass composed by one of the greats for that matter — at an actual Mass.

She might even become Catholic herself just to hear such a thing.

Mend your ways, heed my appeal,
agree with one another, live in peace,
and the God of love and peace will be with you.
Greet one another with a holy kiss.

1 Corinthians 13:11-12

FORTY-EIGHT

𝄞

It was decided that, to keep Sam from having to walk alone after school and risk being cornered again, she would go to the gym after school and do her homework during the boys' basketball practice. Then Tobias could walk with her as usual.

Tobias suggested that Lydia come to the school to walk with Sam so she wouldn't have to wait around for him, but Sam vehemently objected. It was one thing to wait for a schoolmate so they could walk together and another thing entirely to be escorted by a parent like a baby.

Sam was secretly convinced Jason would never come near her again after the beating Tobias gave him, but the Howards wanted to be cautious. In fact, Sam opined that they were being far *too* cautious. Paul wheedled Sam into giving him Jason's last name so he could contact the Meathead's parents, and Lydia informed her that she would be talking to all of Sam's teachers and administrators. She appreciated their concern. Truly. But the whole thing made her feel incapable, and she hated that feeling.

On Monday, Sam's guess about Jason proved correct.

In English class — where he'd previously made a habit of sitting in the seat directly behind her so that he could pull her hair and flick her ears and poke her with his pencil and mutter epithets like *freak* and *orphan* and *Adèle* so only she could hear — Jason sat as far away from her as possible. The bridge of his nose was still a little puffy, and bruises colored the skin under his left eye and the corner of his mouth a sickly purplish-yellow.

Seeing his face like that, Sam realized just how much trouble Tobias could be in if Jason or his parents wanted to press the issue. If anyone divulged the details of the incident to school officials, Tobias could very well be suspended from school, expelled even. Could they arrest a fourteen-year-old for assault?

But when Mrs. Gordon asked Jason what happened to his face, he blamed the bruises on a game of Thanksgiving football that had gotten too rough.

It made Sam wonder if perhaps he hadn't seen Tobias's face clearly and therefore couldn't identify him. Or maybe he had seen his face and simply didn't know who he was — Tobias wasn't in their grade, after all. Or maybe Jason regretted what he'd done to Sam and felt he deserved the beating Tobias had given him. Or maybe Paul had already contacted Jason's parents, and they'd come to some agreement.

Whatever Jason's reason for not revealing Tobias's part in his broken face, Sam breathed a prayer of thanksgiving to God.

After school, even though she had been right about Jason, Sam went to the gym and set herself up in the bleachers. She had plenty of homework to do — her teachers had moved on from feeling sorry for her and, despite her best efforts to keep them hidden, discovered that she had really big brains, so of course that meant extra work *to keep her from getting bored* — but she had a hard time focusing on her assignments. Her eyes constantly drifted to the court to watch Tobias play. She had to remind herself not to stare at least a dozen times.

Truthfully, Sam was still annoyed with Tobias. They had successfully avoided each other or at least remained somewhat aloof for most of the weekend after Tobias had accused her of presenting too much of a temptation for him. Even though she had originally agreed to that course of action, she quickly came to regret it. Stupidly, after only a few days of pretending they wanted nothing to do with each other, she began to doubt that he'd ever told her he liked her at all. Like maybe she had dreamed it. Or maybe he was getting over her already. It made her apprehensive and insecure in a way that irritated her to no end.

It shocked Sam, then, when Tobias shyly reached for her hand a block away from the school. She snatched it away.

"What are you doing?" she demanded.

Tobias had clearly expected a different response. He did that thing, opening and closing his mouth with no words coming out. Sometimes she thought it was cute, but not today.

"You're the one who said we couldn't act like boyfriend and

girlfriend, remember?" Sam reminded him. "And I definitely don't need someone to hold my hand to make sure I don't get lost."

She stomped away from him, not sure *why* she was so angry, but absolutely certain that she had every right to be.

"I'm sorry," Tobias said when he caught up to her. "I just thought — I don't know what I thought."

They walked in silence for a couple blocks.

"I think my mom knows," Tobias blurted.

Sam stopped, and Tobias stopped with her. She looked right at him. "And Bear." She stated it. She didn't ask it.

Tobias looked away and nodded almost imperceptibly. "I told him a long time ago that I liked you."

"And your dad?"

Tobias shrugged.

"So… if everyone knows…?" Sam flipped her hand to finish the question.

Tobias held her gaze for a long time before shaking his head. "I don't know what to do, Sam. I don't like pretending, but I'm…" He sighed and looked away again. "It's not just my family. I don't want people thinking we're doing things we shouldn't be doing."

Sam frowned. "Luke and those guys already think that," she retorted. "Other people probably do, too. But so what? Why do you care what other people think?"

His gaze shot to her in surprise. "I didn't think you knew."

"About Luke and Colton and the rest of those jerks?"

Tobias nodded.

"They've only been making gross gestures and comments to me every chance they get since the day I moved in with your family."

"Sam, I had no idea," Tobias said. He was genuinely distraught.

"It doesn't matter," Sam snapped. She wasn't particularly proud of the disdain that had slipped into her voice. "I don't care what they think about me, and you shouldn't either. They're not your friends anymore. If you ask me, they were bad friends to begin with."

Tobias shook his head. "If I had known—"

"You would've what?" Sam waited, but just as she suspected, he didn't have a response. "Whatever."

Sam started walking again.

Tobias followed, and they walked the rest of the way in silence.

FORTY-NINE
𝄢:

Tobias did not attempt to hold Sam's hand again.

Her reaction had been unexpected and hurtful. It made him wonder if she didn't like him anymore, if he'd blown his one and only chance with her. It also made him recall what his mom had said about how much Sam had been through and her warning to him to be careful.

Maybe his mom was more insightful than he gave her credit for.

Already by Tuesday, Tobias regretted the decision they had made about Sam doing homework in the gym during practice. He dearly wished she hadn't been so stubborn and prideful about his suggestion that his mom walk her home. Having her sit there in the bleachers made it hard to concentrate on basketball.

At least his teammates had been cool about it (other than Colton, of course, but Tobias knew his loyalties would never change). Trying not to reveal too many details about what had happened, he told Ollie that his mom didn't want Sam walking home alone anymore, and Ollie told the others. Since Sam had become something of a mascot — being the loudest and most enthusiastic fan at every game so far this season — the boys were quick to support that decision. In fact, a couple of them offered to walk Sam home themselves if Tobias didn't want to — a ridiculous suggestion considering the fact that he and Sam had the same destination. Tobias politely declined, of course, but their offers secretly made his insides burn with jealousy. He tried to rationalize that they were just being brotherly, but deep down he feared that he wasn't the only who had fallen for the team's number one fan.

His worst fears were realized on Thursday when, on the bus ride to their away game, Patrick came and sat next to him.

"So, Tobias," Patrick started. "You know Sam pretty well, right? I mean, since she's staying with your family and all."

Tobias glanced at Patrick. "Sure. I guess I know her as well as anybody."

"Is she, like, dating anyone?" Patrick inquired.

Tobias glared at Patrick and wondered if he were imagining Patrick's smarminess — he'd never noticed it before. "She's a seventh grader."

"Yeah. And?"

"You don't think she's too young?"

"Do you? I mean, is she, like, super immature?"

Tobias leaned his head back against the seat. "No, just the opposite, actually. She's super smart. My mom calls her an old soul."

"So she's not dating anyone?"

Technically, no. Because *he* had told her they couldn't until she moved out. Tobias couldn't make himself say it, though, so he just shook his head.

"Do you think it would be okay if I asked her out?" Patrick pressed. "I mean, would your parents have a problem with that, do you think?"

"I don't think I'm the one you should be asking," Tobias replied. He didn't say why, though.

"Do you think she'd say yes?"

Tobias clenched his jaw. He sure hoped she wouldn't. "Like I said, I'm not the one you should be asking. If you want to ask her, ask her. She knows her own mind."

It wasn't until Patrick moved to a different seat that the irony of the situation struck Tobias.

He had been so concerned that people would think his romantic feelings for Sam inappropriate, had pushed her away because of it. And here was Patrick, so oblivious to his true feelings that he thought Tobias saw Sam as nothing more than a kind of adopted sister. If Tobias had had the courage to date her himself, to hold her hand in public long before now, even to flirt with her, Patrick and everyone else would know that she was off limits. But just like with Emma, he waited too long to make his move.

And now it might be too late.

FIFTY

𝄞

Sam had never been so astonished in her life, and she knew her face showed it.

It was Friday afternoon, and she had just finished setting up her little workstation in the bleachers. One of Tobias's teammates, Patrick, came out of the locker room early and headed toward her. He made a little small talk, and then the question: "Would you like to go out with me sometime?"

Patrick seemed like a nice enough guy, and he wasn't bad looking, by any means. But Sam had never even thought about liking someone who wasn't Tobias. She certainly had never expected anyone else to like her.

"You can think about it if you want," Patrick said smoothly. "Unless"—he chuckled to himself—"I guess maybe I should've asked first if you're even allowed to date yet."

"I don't know," Sam answered honestly.

Funny that it had never occurred to her all the time she'd been pining after Tobias. Who could even tell her whether she could date or not? Lydia and Paul? They were responsible for her, but was it really their place to make decisions about her dating life?

"You don't know if you're allowed? Or you don't know if you want to?" Patrick quipped.

"Both, I guess," Sam responded.

Patrick smiled crookedly. "Well, let me know when you find out, huh?"

"Sure."

He made his way back down the bleachers to the court, and that's when Sam noticed that Tobias had been watching them. She felt her cheeks burning and knew she turned bright red.

Well. Served him right. If Tobias wasn't willing to step up and date her, why shouldn't she date someone else? Or at least make Tobias think she might. If he thought she would wait around forever for him... Well, he was probably right, but he didn't have to know that he was right. Might do him a little good to think he had competition.

And so, when practice ended, Sam called Patrick over and told him she would indeed be honored to go out with him. She didn't have her own cell phone yet — her parents had never given her one, and the Howards didn't seem eager to overrule that decision — so she told him to catch her on Monday to arrange the details.

"No problem. I have Tobias's number. I'm sure he won't mind if I call him to get hold of you," Patrick said affably. Before Sam could object, he started away toward the locker room and called back over his shoulder, "Talk to you soon!"

Sam facepalmed. Her idea to make Tobias jealous suddenly seemed petty and mean. If Patrick called her on Tobias's phone...

But how could she fix it? She couldn't very well follow Patrick into the locker room. And she didn't want to wait for him — Tobias might be with her at that point, and she wasn't about to take back her yes in front of *him*.

Tobias did, in fact, come out before Patrick. And boy, did he look steaming mad. He grabbed Sam's trumpet as he passed her, but didn't even pause to wait for her. She slung her backpack over her shoulder and ran to catch up.

He walked so fast, and his legs were too darn long. Sam had to trot to keep up with him.

Suddenly, after they'd gone almost two blocks, Tobias stopped and turned to face her.

"Do you really like him?" he grilled her. "Patrick?"

Sam swallowed.

Tobias's eyes were so intense, they seemed to drill holes through her. But then she remembered how Tobias had yanked her around like a puppet on a string — liking her one moment and telling her they couldn't be together the next, flirting with her and trying to hold her hand one day and avoiding her on another — and her anger gave her courage the boost it needed.

"Maybe," she spat. "What's it to you?"

"You know what it is to me," Tobias retorted. "Remember last week, when you were all"—he pitched his voice higher to imitate her—"*Oh, Tobias, do you think you'll still like me by the time my parents get better?*" His voice returned to its normal range. "Guess I should've been the one asking that question, huh?"

"Well, maybe if you could make up your mind for more than two seconds," Sam countered. Now it was her turn. "*Sam, I don't think we should date, it wouldn't be appropriate. Just kidding, Sam, I really want to hold your hand. But I changed my mind, Sam, holding your hand is too much of a temptation. But don't you dare date anyone else, Sam.*"

"If you want to date someone else, go ahead," Tobias growled back. "Just do it because you actually like them and not because you're mad at me."

"Well, I am mad at you, Tobias," Sam shouted. "But that doesn't mean I *don't* like Patrick."

"So you do like him."

"Enough," Sam sniped with a sassy shrug.

"What does that mean?"

"It means we're gonna go out. He's gonna call me. On *your* phone."

The hurt on Tobias's face made Sam immediately regret her words. She shouldn't have said it like that, but he just made her so mad!

"Fine, then."

Tobias continued toward the Howard home, Sam struggling to keep up the whole way.

𝄆 𝅗𝅥 ♪ 𝅗𝅥 𝄇

Sam was practicing her trumpet in her music room on Saturday when Patrick called.

She knew that's what it was when she heard the knock on the door. No one ever bothered her when she hid away in her music room, and she couldn't imagine any other reason someone would knock now.

Sure enough, when she opened the door, Tobias stood there stone-faced and held up his phone.

She took it from him and shut the door so she could have some privacy — she absolutely did *not* want Tobias listening to her conversation with Patrick.

"Hello?"

"Hey, Sam, it's Patrick."

"Oh, hey."

"So I talked to my mom, and she said she could drive us to the movie theater tomorrow afternoon. Are you free?"

"No, I'm not, actually," Sam sighed, somewhat relieved. Maybe he would give up, and she would never have to tell him that she didn't want to date him at all. "I go to the hospital to see my parents on Sundays."

"Oh." A beat. "Okay." Another beat. "Maybe we could do something next weekend?"

Darn.

"Um, sure."

"Hey, maybe we could go see the Christmas lights at the zoo or something. Would you like that?"

No.

"Sure."

"Great!" She heard him muffle the speaker and ask his mom if she would take them to see the zoo lights the following Saturday evening. He unmuffled the speaker. "She says yes. We can pick you up at six and eat dinner at the zoo."

"Sounds good."

"Don't you have to ask Mrs. Howard?"

"I'm pretty sure she'll say yes. If she doesn't, I'll call you back."

"Cool. Well, I'll see you Monday at practice, right?"

"Right."

"All right. Bye."

"Bye."

Sam ended the call. Why couldn't she have just said she didn't want to go? What was wrong with her?

She looked down at the phone in her hand and her heart squeezed.

The photo on Tobias's lock screen was a picture of her that she didn't even know he'd taken. It was from Halloween, and she wore her squirrel costume in their box seats at the concert hall. He'd apparently snapped it when she leaned over the railing to wave at his parents in the mezzanine below. She looked happy.

Sam flung the door open.

"Tobias!" she called. "Tobias, I need you to open your phone!"

They nearly bumped into each other at the bottom of the stairs.

"Open your phone." She held it out to him.

"Why?"

"So I can call Patrick back."

"No."

"Tobias, I need to call him back."

"Too bad."

She punched him in the shoulder. "I need to call him back so I can tell him I don't want to go out with him, you big doofus!" Sam exclaimed.

"Why didn't you tell him that when he called?" Tobias sneered, rubbing his shoulder where she'd hit him.

"Because I'm a dummy, okay? Now, will you open your phone?"

Tobias snatched the phone out of her hand and stuffed it in his pocket. "We all have to live with the consequences of our choices, don't we?"

Tobias turned around and marched back up the stairs.

Sam stared after him, her mouth hanging open. For a brief moment, she debated going after him, tackling him to the ground, and stealing his phone back. But she thought better of it. The last thing they needed was a wrestling match. The mental picture of Lydia walking in on them wrestling almost made her laugh, but she was too mad.

Tobias wanted to teach her a lesson. How patronizing. Just because he was older than her didn't mean she was the one at fault here. *He* was the one who insisted they couldn't be together. Patrick would never have asked her out at all if Tobias hadn't been such a weenie about what other people thought and said. If this situation was anyone's fault, it was his.

Sam returned to her music room, comforted by her own indignation.

FIFTY-ONE
𝄢:

If practice the week before had been difficult, this week was hell.

Tobias had to stomach Patrick wiggling his dumb fingers at Sam as she sat in the bleachers. At least she never looked fully committed whenever she returned his wave. But it still made Tobias's blood burn.

A little voice in the back of his mind tried to tell him he could have put an end to all of this nonsense if he had just let Sam call Patrick back. But Tobias wanted to hurt her the way she'd hurt him. Or at least he wanted her to regret hurting him.

That little voice told him he was stupid for letting her go on a date with Patrick — Tobias had overheard Sam tell his mom that they were going to see the zoo lights — but he couldn't back down now. Maybe he could get Bear to take him to the zoo lights the same night so he could keep an eye on her...

Tobias nearly slapped himself. He had to get control of himself. What kind of weird, possessive person thinks about spying on someone else's date?

The little voice argued that he just wanted to make sure she didn't get hurt the way Jason tried to hurt her, but Tobias shook it off. Patrick was not Jason. Patrick was a nice guy. Smarmy, maybe, but an okay guy. The kind of guy lots of girls would fall for.

Tobias wanted to throw up.

FIFTY-TWO

𝄞

Sam was a mess of nerves waiting for Patrick and his mom to pick her up on Saturday evening.

She and Tobias had hardly spoken to each other all week. Their walks to and from school had become painfully awkward.

To her immense relief, Patrick never called her on Tobias's phone again. If he had anything to say to her, he told her when they saw each other at practice.

Lydia expressed surprise, to say the least, when Sam asked if she could see the zoo lights with Patrick. Tobias had told her he thought his mom knew about them, and Lydia's reaction confirmed that suspicion for Sam. It shamed her, in fact. It made her feel like agreeing to go on a date with Patrick not only hurt Tobias, but also somehow let Lydia down. Something about her response made Sam think Lydia didn't just know about her and Tobias, but had actually been rooting for them to get together. And now Sam was ruining it.

No. Tobias had ruined it. Sam had to remind herself of that a lot during the week.

Still, she had to admit that she had no real desire to date Patrick, and it wasn't fair to make him think she did.

So tonight would be it.

She would let him down gently and be done with it.

FIFTY-THREE
𝄢:

Tobias was a mess after Sam left with Patrick.

He worried about her. What if Patrick's nice-guy demeanor was just an act? What if he tried to take advantage of Sam? He was an eighth grade stud, the starting guard on the basketball team, and Sam was just a scrawny, innocent seventh grader. Or what if Patrick really was a nice guy and Sam had such a good time that she never wanted to see Tobias's face again?

Tobias's mom could tell something bothered him. All through dinner, she kept shooting him this look of pity that made him want to hide in his room until *next* Christmas. It was humiliating.

Not wanting his mother to ask him what was wrong — and knowing she definitely would if he hung around long enough — Tobias made a beeline for his bedroom the moment they finished the rosary. He thought it best to distract himself.

Settling on his bed with his laptop, Tobias opened up a video streaming service his family subscribed to but hardly used and searched for a movie. The first title in the list of recently watched movies caught his eye — not because he wanted to watch it, but because it sparked a memory. It was one of the movies from the Halloween symphony concert. Oddly enough, so were the next three movies listed. He remembered Sam turning to him between pieces at that concert and saying, *Now I have to see that movie.*

Tobias slammed his laptop shut in frustration and despair, his grand plans for distraction thwarted.

Someone knocked on his door.

"Who is it?"

"Mom. Open up."

"It's not locked."

His mom poked her head inside. "We need to have a chat."

Tobias rolled his eyes, but his mom made her way inside anyway. She sat on the edge of his bed.

"You can roll your eyes all you want," she said. "It won't change what I have to say."

Tobias looked at her, refusing to prompt her — if she had something to say, he wasn't going to help her say it.

"You like Sam, don't you?"

Tobias felt himself blushing, and it annoyed him that no matter what he said, his red cheeks and ears would give him away. Still, he hedged. "Of course. We all do."

"Nuh-uh. You know that's not what I mean. Come on, now," his mom prodded.

"I don't know what you want me to say, Mom." Tobias did know, he just didn't want to say it.

"Okay, look, let's forget I asked that question." She waved her hands, wiping the metaphorical slate clean. "I've been watching the two of you for a while now, and I think you both think you can hide a lot more from me than you can."

Tobias swallowed. "I'm not hiding anything. If Sam is, you should be talking to her."

His mom narrowed her eyes. A warning. He was giving her sass, and she didn't appreciate it.

"When was the last time you hung out with your friends, Tobias?" she asked.

The change of subject caught him off guard. He tried to think back to the last time he'd done anything besides basketball and family stuff. Perhaps that study group in early November? More than a month ago.

His mom raised her eyebrows, waiting for his answer.

"A while ago." He hoped the vagueness of his reply would make it sound less bad.

"A while ago," she repeated. "I seem to remember last year, you and Luke were basically inseparable. You were either sleeping over there or he was sleeping here almost every weekend. Over the summer, too. But now, I can't even recall the last time I heard you mention his name. Or any of the others you two hung out with."

Tobias shrugged. "People grow apart."

"True, true," his mom agreed. "But I'm worried about you, Tobias.

You've always been quiet, but that never stopped you from having a lot of friends. What happened? Is it because of Sam?"

"What? No." In a way, it *was* because of Sam, but the way she said it made him defensive — he couldn't let Sam take the blame for his friends turning out to be rotten people.

"Really? Because it seems like an awfully big coincidence that you stopped hanging out with them at the same time you started hanging out with her," his mom argued.

"Hanging out with her?" Tobias scoffed. "I don't hang out with her."

His mom smiled knowingly.

"We walk to school together, and she happens to be living with us, but that does *not* mean I hang out with her." Tobias felt his anger rising. Where was she going with all this? What was she trying to get at? If she knew so much, why couldn't she see that all he wanted was to suffer in solitude tonight?

"The point is, Tobias, that neither of you has much of a social life," his mom said calmly. "You have practice and games, but when was the last time you did something just for fun with your friends?"

Tobias didn't answer.

"I get the sense that Sam has always struggled to make friends, but you haven't. Maybe you've left some old friendships behind, but the basketball boys seem like good kids." She paused. "Even Patrick."

Tobias glared at her. Boy, did she know how to push buttons.

She sighed. "So here's what I've been thinking." She clasped her hands in front of her, almost like praying. "I think it would be really nice if you started hanging out with friends again *and* if you invited Sam along."

It wasn't even close to what Tobias had expected her to say.

He thought she would tell him he needed to spend *less* time with Sam, that they had grown too close and it was obvious to everyone and they risked the entire family's reputation by making googly eyes at each other one moment and bickering like an old married couple the next (not that his mom had ever seen them properly bicker — that mostly happened in the six blocks between home and school). He expected her to tell him again to be careful, not just because of what Sam had been through but because he'd reached an age when his hormones might lead him astray without consulting him first.

Never in a million years did he expect her to tell him to spend *more* time with Sam.

"You want me to get together with my teammates and bring Sam along." Tobias repeated it just to make sure he had understood correctly.

"There must be some girls that hang out with them, too, right?" she said. "I mean, they're all probably very nice boys, but it might be more comfortable for Sam if she weren't the only girl."

There had been some girls there at the study group. And he knew a few of the guys had girlfriends.

Tobias nodded. "I'll try," he promised. "They're not really my crowd, though."

"Well." She took a deep breath and exhaled quickly. "Maybe things will be different after tonight?"

Patrick. Why did she have to remind him? Sam was on a date with Patrick. Of course things would be different after tonight. It would be just Tobias's luck that Sam would start hanging out with that crowd because of Patrick, and *she* would be the one inviting *him* along, like doing him a favor.

But what if the opposite happened? What if their date was awful, and Sam never wanted to see Patrick again (Tobias couldn't convince himself that anyone would ever not want to see Sam again)?

Tobias's mom put a hand on his knee. "Just promise me you'll try. I think having other friends would be good for both of you."

It was smart. A good solution to his problem, really. If other people always surrounded them, temptation wouldn't have any opportunities. Maybe they'd even stop liking each other because they'd both meet someone else. Well, maybe Sam had moved on already. Maybe Tobias should do the same.

He had to admit, his mom's request had merit. It *would* do him good to start hanging out with other people again. In fact, Tobias felt a little ashamed that he'd become so isolated without even realizing it.

"I promise."

FIFTY-FOUR

♭

Sam was having just as rotten a time as she thought she would.

Sure, the zoo lights were pretty, but it was bitterly cold, and she started shivering within minutes. Patrick tried to put an arm around her — whether to keep her warm or because he was making a move was irrelevant — and Sam shrugged him off.

"No, thanks," she said. It was a stupid thing to say, but she couldn't think of anything else.

Later, when they'd walked a good ways ahead of Patrick's mom, he tried to hold her hand, and again she pulled away. She did her best to make it seem as if she were distracted by something and didn't realize he grabbed for her hand, but she had a feeling she didn't sell it that well.

The cherry on top was when Patrick tried to kiss her in the monkey house. He came at her, and she panicked.

She turned her face away and blurted out, "I'm in love with Tobias."

Patrick pulled back, confused. "What?"

Sam felt her eyes bulging out of her head. She couldn't believe she'd said it out loud. And to Patrick. So much for letting him down gently.

"Did you say you're in love with Tobias?"

"I did say that. Yes," Sam confirmed, still reeling from shock at her own bold admission.

Patrick laughed. For a long time. Sam couldn't tell whether she should feel insulted or not. "Oh, Sam," he wheezed as he recovered from his fit of giggles. "I'm sorry. I'm not laughing at you. It's just — oh, man — I can't believe I didn't see it before."

"See what?"

"Well, I mean, Tobias may be kind of bland, but come on," he said, "he's the best player on the team. Tall. Good looking. Quiet — why girls like that, I'll never understand."

"Bland?" she repeated in disbelief. "Tobias isn't bland. He's... He's..." What was wrong with her? Her big brains held hundreds of words she'd used to describe Tobias to herself thousands of times. "He's deep. And thoughtful. And sensitive and kind and brave and caring and hard-working and talented. And annoyingly honorable."

"Okay, okay." Patrick put up his hands in a sign of surrender and smiled. His eyebrows had gone higher and higher as the barrage of words let loose. "I get it. He's a great guy."

They sat in awkward silence for a moment.

"I'm sorry I came," Sam muttered. "I shouldn't have said yes when you asked me out. It wasn't fair to you."

Patrick shrugged. "It *is* a blow to my pride. Being jilted by a seventh grader. But I think I'll recover." He smiled as he said it, which made Sam feel a little less horrible.

Miraculously, things felt more relaxed between them for the rest of the evening. Patrick told a lot of jokes and did impressions that had Sam giggling much of the time.

Just before they met up with his mom to leave the zoo, Patrick said, "There's a group of us getting together on Friday night. You and Tobias should come."

Sam smiled and shook her head. "I told you I like him. I didn't say we were together."

"Who knows? Maybe if you bring him along, that could change." Patrick wagged his eyebrows and nudged her with his elbow.

Patrick meant well, but he didn't know. So Sam simply nodded, hoping to end the conversation there.

When he and his mom dropped her off at the Howard home, Patrick walked Sam to the door.

"Since this will be my one and only chance... may I kiss you goodnight?" he asked, then quickly added, "On the cheek, of course."

Sam hesitated. She didn't want him to kiss her, even on the cheek, but he'd been so nice about the whole thing. She nodded.

Patrick kissed her on the cheek — it was neither brief nor lingering, just a simple kiss. He waved as he walked back to the waiting car.

Sam stepped inside, and there was Tobias, looking like he'd been kicked in the gut.

FIFTY-FIVE
𝄢:

Tobias hadn't meant to spy on them.

He'd just been passing the front room when he saw it happen — when he saw Patrick kiss Sam — and he hadn't been able to move before Sam came inside.

When they locked eyes, Tobias knew it was written all over his face.

"How was your date?" he managed to croak.

Sam marched up to Tobias, grabbed his face with both hands, and pulled his head down until their lips met. It happened so fast. And then she let go and hurried away before he could react.

Tobias's heart hammered wildly in his chest.

His mom came from the family room. "Was that Sam? Is she home?"

Tobias nodded numbly, unable to make his mouth work.

What just happened?

FIFTY-SIX

♭

What just happened? What possessed her to do such a thing?

Sam shut the door to her bedroom and leaned back against it, trying to regain control of her breathing.

It was Patrick's fault. If he hadn't kissed her on the cheek... If Tobias hadn't looked so sad and hurt and pitiful...

It was an impulse. In her wildest dreams, Sam imagined sharing her first kiss with Tobias in some romantic setting, and he was supposed to be the one to initiate. She knew it might be old-fashioned, but some deep part of her longed to be on the receiving end, the responding end. She didn't want to be the first one to lay all her cards on the table. It made her feel too vulnerable.

And she didn't even wait around to see how Tobias felt about it. Like a coward, she practically ran out of the room.

Someone knocked on the door, and Sam's heart stopped.

"Who's there?" she squeaked.

"It's Lydia. You okay?"

"Yeah, I'm fine."

"You sure?"

"Yeah. I'm just... tired."

"Your date went okay?"

"Um." Sam didn't want to have this conversation through the door, but she didn't want to let Lydia in either. Ridiculously, she had a vision of the kiss — both kisses, actually — being visible on her face, like those lipstick kisses in the movies. "It was fine. But I'm not going on any more dates with him."

A beat.

"You'll let me know if you want to talk about it, right?"
"Yeah."
Another beat.
"Goodnight, Sam."

Entreat me not to leave you
or to return from following you;
for where you go I will go,
and where you lodge I will lodge;
and your people shall be my people,
and your God my God.

Ruth 1:16

FIFTY-SEVEN

𝄞

As if by mutual agreement, Sam and Tobias did not make eye contact with one another the next day.

At Mass, they sat with all three of the other Howards between them.

In the car, Sam was acutely aware of their shoulders touching, but Tobias seemed especially careful to keep their knees from doing the same.

During breakfast, where Tobias always sat on her left, Sam made every effort to engage Lydia, who sat on her right, in conversation. Lydia was only too eager to oblige.

"I was thinking we could maybe get in a little Christmas shopping before we go to the hospital today. What do you think?" Lydia asked her.

"Oh, um." Well, this was nearly as awkward as making eye contact with the boy she brazenly kissed last night. "I don't know."

"Are you worried about paying? Because we don't mind covering it. We cover all the kids' Christmas gifts until they're old enough to earn their own money," Lydia assured her.

"It's not that." She hadn't thought of that, actually. In fact, she didn't have any money, but more importantly: "It's my family. We don't celebrate Christmas."

Sam had been prepared to act excited about receiving presents, but she'd neglected to think about how she'd also be expected to *give* presents.

Lydia seemed baffled, as if she'd never heard of such a thing. "Um. Okay," she said. "So you don't want to participate in exchanging gifts at all?"

Sam shook her head, annoyed with herself for feeling a bit disappointed. Why should she be disappointed? She didn't need anything and didn't want gifts she didn't need. Maybe refusing to participate made her feel a little less like part of the family.

"Well, that's too bad," Tobias suddenly remarked.

Sam whipped around to look at him before she remembered that she was supposed to avoid eye contact with him.

"Because I already bought you a gift." He was stone-faced, and she couldn't tell whether he was angry or joking.

"So did I," Bear added from across the table. "And I ain't takin' it back."

Shame washed over Sam. These people — these kind, good people who had taken her in when she most needed to know she wasn't alone in the world — wanted to give her even more than they already had, and here she spurned their generosity. Her rudeness was unpardonable.

Infuriatingly, and embarrassingly, Sam started to cry. She put her elbows on the table and covered her face with her hands.

"Bear. Tobias," Lydia hissed. "What is wrong with you?"

"Sorry," Bear muttered.

Tobias did not apologize. But she felt his knee nudge hers, which was better — and worse — than any apology.

"You don't have to get us anything, Sam. That's not what I meant," Bear mumbled.

"Sam," Lydia said quietly, gently, coaxingly.

Sam wiped her eyes and took a deep, shuddering breath to get herself under control. She looked at Lydia.

"You don't have to participate if you don't want to. We're still going to celebrate the way we always have," Lydia said, "whether you choose to join us or not, and I think you might feel a little left out on Christmas morning. But none of us"—she gave a hard look at each of the boys—"will judge you either way."

|♪ ♩. ♪ ♩ |

Sam went shopping with Lydia.

She reasoned that nothing else she had done in the last several months had been done the way her own family did it, so why make an exception for Christmas? For the time being, she was basically a member of the Howard family, so she would celebrate Christmas the way the Howard family did.

Lydia gave her a spending limit of $25 per person.

"How am I supposed to get you a gift when you're the one shopping with me?" Sam asked her as they browsed the sports aisle.

Lydia laughed. "Do you want to get me a gift?"

"I can't get gifts for everybody else and not you," Sam pointed out as if it should be obvious.

"I guess you'll have to ask Paul or Bear to take you shopping then," Lydia replied.

She ran a hand over Sam's head and stroked her hair as if it were the most natural thing in the world. Lydia did that often, and it never failed to give Sam a soft, warm feeling, like being cuddled.

"Can I ask you a question, Sam?"

Sam swallowed, and her stomach fluttered nervously. Did she know about the kiss? Did she want to have another sex talk?

"Sure."

"Both of your parents are making progress, but — correct me if I'm wrong — there's a chance they may never fully recover?" Lydia had a gift for saying the hardest things in the gentlest way. It was a trick Sam wanted to learn.

Sam nodded. Because of her age, the doctors never disclosed much to her. But she understood enough to know that, even if she did get her parents back someday, they wouldn't be the same.

"If — and it's a big if, Sam — but if your parents can't take care of you until you're old enough that you don't need anyone taking care of you anymore..." Lydia sighed. "What I'm trying to ask, Sam, is if you like living with us? And if you want to keep living with us?"

Sam didn't know what to say. Of course, she liked living with the Howards. She loved living with the Howards. But what Lydia asked sounded almost like adoption. She didn't want to be adopted when her parents still lived.

And — silly as it might seem for a twelve-almost-thirteen-year-old to think of such a thing — Sam didn't want to be Lydia's *daughter* when there was a possibility, however far in the future, that she might one day be her *daughter-in-law*. She would never, ever express such a foolish notion out loud, but in the deepest place of her heart, it was something Sam simply felt had to be considered.

Lydia seemed a little disappointed when Sam didn't answer right away, and she almost hid it well. There was just enough for Sam to notice, though, and it warmed her heart.

Sam hugged Lydia around the waist.

"I do want to live with you and Paul until my parents get better or until I'm old enough to be on my own, whichever comes first," Sam stated. She pulled back just enough to look up into Lydia's face. "But I don't want you to adopt me."

Lydia laughed and cupped Sam's cheeks with her hands. "You are a gift, Samantha Ingram. I hope you know how very much Paul and I love you."

Sam felt tears in her eyes. Had her own parents ever said as much? Maybe they had and she just couldn't remember.

Over the months, Sam had certainly felt loved by the Howards, but to hear Lydia say it with such conviction shattered her.

|₹ ♩ ♪ ♩ |

At first, Sam tried to find gifts she thought her temporary family would most like to have, but the task proved much more difficult than she anticipated.

She knew the kinds of things they all liked to do, but she had a hard time finding anything within budget that felt quite right. At Lydia's suggestion, Sam switched tactics. She began to look for things that would remind them of her or something they had done together.

For Paul, Sam bought a gift to commemorate the first high school football game she'd gone to with them, when he took her to the booth to meet his friend Randy and told her about the pranks they played together. Sam bought — or rather, Lydia bought on her behalf — a miniature Chevy Camaro that fit in the palm of her hand. She doubted it was a 1985 model, and it wasn't yellow, but Lydia also bought a paint set from the arts and crafts aisle so Sam could paint it.

For Bear, she bought a Blu-ray of the first movie he took her to see in the movie theater. It was a comedy. Tobias had been particularly grouchy that day — it was back when Sam's mere presence annoyed him — and he hardly laughed at the movie at all. But it tickled Sam and Bear's funny bones, and they had quoted it and joked about it together for weeks afterward, which annoyed Tobias even more.

Oddly, Sam found Tobias the most difficult to buy for. She felt she knew him better than she knew the others, and she was absolutely certain that, no matter what happened in the future, her memories of this time in her life would be mostly of Tobias. How could she possibly express all that she felt and all their memories together in a single gift? Sam tried to narrow it down, as she'd done with the others, to a specific memory, one that jumped out more than the rest.

Unfortunately, the two memories that burned brightest in her mind were of kissing Tobias and of watching him beat Jason to a bloody mess. Neither memory seemed particularly worthy of commemorating with a gift.

Finally, Sam settled on something to remind Tobias of the Halloween concert (he did have a picture of her from that night on his phone, after all). He held her hand that night, and he held it as if he wanted to, as if he never wanted to let go. Sam hadn't thought of it that way at the time, but later, after Tobias confessed his feelings, she replayed that night in her mind and saw it in a new light.

When Sam picked out a CD (a medium that had gone out of style, perhaps, but Sam hoped Tobias would appreciate the quaintness of it) of the original score for a film featured at that concert, Lydia winked at her. If she knew about Sam and Tobias — the feelings they'd confessed, the kiss they'd shared, the fights they'd had — Lydia didn't say anything.

But Sam didn't want to lie to her. Ever. Not even by omission.

"Lydia," Sam said as she stared at the CD in her hands.

"Yes?"

"You know that… that I'm in love with your son, don't you?" Sam looked up at her.

Lydia smiled gently and nodded. Her eyes twinkled. "You've got good taste."

"You're not angry?"

"No, I'm not angry, Sam," Lydia said. "I'm very proud."

Relief flooded through Sam, and she couldn't stop herself from grinning.

"But," Lydia added, holding up a finger and raising her eyebrows, "that doesn't mean anything goes. There are rules in our house. Rules about what is and isn't appropriate."

"Of course." Sam nodded, assuming what she hoped was a mature demeanor. "I would never do anything that I thought would disappoint you and Paul. Never." She meant it.

"You know. I have a hunch Tobias feels the same way about you."

Sam almost laughed. "No kidding."

"Excuse me?"

Sam did giggle then. She couldn't help it. Lydia just looked so shocked.

"You know he likes you? He told you?"

Sam nodded, but then she grew more serious. "But we decided —

er, Tobias decided — well, he thought we shouldn't do anything about our feelings until I move back in with my own parents."

Sam felt it was important, now that Lydia knew how they felt, that she understand the whole picture.

Lydia stared at her.

"He didn't think it would be appropriate. Or something," Sam added lamely.

Truthfully, Tobias's reasons for not wanting to date yet confused her. Was it because it was *actually* inappropriate? Or only because other people would *think* it was inappropriate?

"Really." Lydia was deadpan. "Tobias said that."

Sam nodded slowly. Was Lydia mad at Tobias? Had Sam told her something that would get him in trouble?

"Are you gonna tell him that I told you?" Sam asked.

Lydia considered for a moment. Sam could tell that several thoughts passed through her mind quickly by the way her eyebrows moved with each one. Lydia had very expressive eyebrows.

"No," Lydia finally said. "If any part of this conversation gets back to Tobias, it'll be because *you* choose to tell him. My lips are sealed."

Sam realized in that moment that she trusted Lydia more than anyone else in the world. More than Paul and Bear. More than Tobias. Even more than her own parents. She couldn't imagine having a conversation like this with her mother. Definitely not with her father.

In fact, the longer Sam stayed with the Howards, the more she realized how broken her relationship with her parents really was. Only she didn't know how or when it had broken. It just always was. It made her sad and angry.

And guilty.

Sam's guilt never truly left her alone, but it had receded to a dark corner of her mind for a time. Now, it was like an ancient enemy come to remind her that she didn't deserve to love and be loved by the Howards.

They were not her real family, and Sam had no right to them.

FIFTY-EIGHT
𝄢

Tobias had promised his mom that he would try to hang out with friends more and invite Sam along.

When his mom left to take Sam shopping and to see her parents, he told himself he would text one of the guys on the team, put out the feelers for anything going on in the next week.

Ollie felt like the safest bet — their friendship existed outside of basketball, and Ollie had become a sort of advocate for Tobias with their teammates. But when Tobias opened a message to Ollie, he couldn't think what to write. It felt awkward somehow. Forced.

There was no way he could text Patrick. Tobias still didn't know what had happened on Sam and Patrick's date last night. He only knew that Patrick had kissed Sam, and then Sam had kissed Tobias. The memory of Sam's lips touching his, even for so brief a time, made Tobias's ears turn pink, and he was glad Bear wasn't around to notice.

It had been his first kiss. Ever. And it made Tobias burn inside to know it definitely hadn't been Sam's first kiss. He didn't know if Patrick's kiss had been Sam's first, but it didn't matter. All that mattered was that there had been at least one before him.

Thinking about all that kissing made Tobias realize how impossible it would be to keep his promise to his mom. Whichever teammate he reached out to, it was a sure thing Patrick would be invited to any get-together — even though he wasn't the best player on the team, he was certainly the most popular. And who would be the one bringing Sam to the party? Patrick or Tobias? It would be awkward either way.

Tobias gave up, shoved his phone back in his pocket, and settled in for an afternoon of video games.

| ♩ ♪ ♩ |

"I played that level with Bear a few weeks ago. It's hard."

Tobias had lost track of time until he heard Sam's voice behind him. He paused the video game and turned in his swivel chair to see her standing at the bottom of the stairs and watching him. He had no idea how long she'd been there.

"Hey," he said. "How'd the shopping go?"

Sam shrugged. "Guess you'll find out on Christmas."

They stared at each other in silence for a moment.

Tobias cleared his throat. "You never told me how your date went last night."

Sam's eyebrows lifted. "No, I guess I didn't."

Another beat of silence.

"So...?" Tobias prompted, bracing his heart for the worst.

Sam ambled over and took a seat in the other swivel chair. "I owe you an apology, Tobias."

Here it comes.

"I shouldn't have gone out with Patrick," Sam started, and Tobias's heart did a joyful flip. She continued, "I did it because I was mad at you. I'm sorry."

Tobias started to smile, but then he remembered Patrick kissing her. "But... then why did you kiss him?"

Sam frowned. "I didn't. I kissed you."

"But before — when you were outside—"

"Patrick kissed me on the *cheek*. I didn't want him to, but I told him he could because I felt so bad about going on a date with him just to get back at you."

Tobias stared at her, not sure what to make of this new information. From where he'd stood in the front room, he realized, he'd only been able to see Patrick lean forward and block Sam's face from view. He'd assumed it was a real kiss. Now that he knew differently...

"Actually, he was really nice about it," Sam continued. "He even asked if you and I — both of us — wanted to hang out on Friday night. A bunch of people are getting together, I guess. He didn't say who."

"Wait, back up." Tobias put a hand up. "He was nice about it? And asked both of us to hang out?"

Sam nodded.

"Nice about what exactly? What did you tell him?"

Sam's cheeks colored a little, and Tobias thought it made her even prettier. "I told him..." Sam paused, swallowed, took a deep breath. "I told him that I'm in love with you."

Tobias nearly fell out of his chair. *The L-word.*

"But I told him we weren't together," she rushed onward. "I didn't tell him anything about how you feel or how we decided not to date each other until I move out or any of that. All I told him was how *I* feel about *you*. That's all he knows, I promise."

Tobias didn't deserve her, and he knew it.

"But," Sam said, then hesitated to continue. She bit her lip.

Tobias raised his eyebrows and leaned forward.

"He's not the only one I told."

"What?"

"I told your mom. Today."

Tobias was stunned. His chest squeezed, and his stomach clenched with anxiety. He'd suspected that his mom knew, but suspicions were not the same as certainties.

"What did she say?"

Sam grinned. "That I had good taste."

"Ha!" It came out several octaves higher than Tobias's normal voice, but it was the only sound he could make.

"Anyway, I was supposed to come down here to tell you dinner would be ready in ten minutes, and that was, like, five minutes ago, and I'm supposed to be helping your mom cut up the apples, so..."

Sam got up to leave, but Tobias grabbed her hand, not wanting her to go.

She looked at him expectantly, but he couldn't think of anything to say. Tobias wanted to kiss her, properly, but he still didn't know where they stood. Not really. More and more people were finding out that he and Sam liked each other, but he still felt afraid for some reason. Something about it still felt too risky.

"Five minutes," Sam said and gently pulled her hand away.

Tobias nodded.

"Five minutes."

For I know that nothing good dwells within me,
that is, in my flesh.
I can will what is right, but I cannot do it.
For I do not do the good I want,
but the evil I do not want is what I do.

Romans 7:18-19

FIFTY-NINE

♪

The week, the last one before winter break, went by quickly.

Sam had final exams for the first time. She wasn't worried. She didn't even bother to study. If she heard it in class or read it in the textbook, it was locked safely in her brain.

Tobias, on the other hand, shut himself in his room every night that week so he could study without distraction. All the studying made him grumpy. On Wednesday evening, Tobias stomped down the stairs and told Sam to stop playing the piano because he couldn't concentrate with all the noise she made.

Sam resented that he called her beautiful music *noise*, but it was one of her own compositions, which admittedly contained more dissonance than most of what she played.

Despite Tobias's grumpiness at the house, things generally changed for the better between the two of them. Their walks to and from school were more relaxed and fun than they had been in a long time — maybe ever. They still didn't hold hands, and they hadn't kissed again, but a new comfortableness marked their interactions.

Although Sam and Tobias both accepted Patrick's invitation to Friday's get-together, Sam felt nervous about it. From the way Patrick described it, a lot of people would be there — far more than just the basketball team — and making friends wasn't exactly Sam's strong suit. Plus, she didn't know how she should act around Tobias in that context.

There was little question in Sam's mind that, for all intents and purposes, she and Tobias were basically a couple. At least, she had no intention of being anyone else's girlfriend, and she felt certain Tobias didn't intend to be anyone else's boyfriend.

But what did that mean when they attended a party together?

If they didn't *act* like boyfriend and girlfriend, how would anyone know they were both off limits?

|𝄽 𝅗𝅥 ♪ 𝅘𝅥 |

The party was at Patrick's house.

Bear kindly volunteered to drive Tobias and Sam, and he entertained them the entire way by singing every Christmas song on the radio in a ridiculous falsetto.

When Bear dropped them off, more than a dozen other people were already there. Patrick greeted them at the door and showed them inside. Several kids lounged in the living room (Sam felt her cheeks grow warm when she realized the couple in the recliner were making out, and she quickly averted her gaze), and a few kids hovered around snack bowls in the kitchen.

"Make yourselves comfortable. Only place that's off limits is my sister's bedroom," Patrick told them. He lowered his voice conspiratorially and smirked. "She's in there with her boyfriend."

"Your parents don't mind?" Sam couldn't keep the shock from her voice, and she knew it made her sound like a naive child.

Patrick winked. "Ski trip. Won't be back 'til Sunday."

The doorbell rang, and Patrick left to answer it before Tobias or Sam could respond. They exchanged a look.

"We shouldn't be here," Sam whispered.

"Maybe it's not what we think," Tobias whispered back.

Sam gave him a *yeah right* look, and he shrugged.

For some reason, Tobias had been (in Sam's mind) suspiciously excited to come to the party. He built it up all week as a *chance for both of us to get out and have some fun for once.* Tobias had always had lots of friends, and Sam never had any. Perhaps that's why she felt almost the exact opposite — she would much rather have stayed in and played card games with the family.

Tobias took two plastic cups from a stack and began pouring soda into them.

"I don't believe it."

Sam hadn't heard that voice in several weeks, and it made her and Tobias both stiffen. Tobias remained stubbornly focused on the drinks, but Sam couldn't help herself. She turned around.

Luke.

He had an arm draped around Emma's neck and a gross smirk on his face.

"You must be tighter with the jocks than I thought if they let you bring a seventh grader, Toby," Luke sneered.

"Actually," Tobias said as he turned around and handed one of the drinks to her, "Sam's the popular one. I wouldn't be here at all except Patrick invited *her* and let *her* bring *me*."

Sam suddenly felt Tobias's arm snake around her waist, and it surprised her. She glanced up at him, but he was locked in a stare-down with Luke.

Luke huffed. "I always knew you'd end up boinking the freak."

Tobias's grip on Sam's waist tightened. Her face and ears felt like they were on fire. Oh, how she wished they hadn't come here tonight.

"You were right, Sam," Tobias announced. Sam looked up at him again. Even though he addressed his words to her, his hard stare remained on Luke. "They were bad friends to begin with."

With that, Tobias steered her away to another part of the house. He held her so close that Sam could feel the tension in his body, his rapid heartbeat.

Sam wanted Tobias's arm around her, wanted him to hold her close, but not like this. Not to prove something to some jerk. So she shrugged him off as soon as they reached a room Sam could only describe as a library.

A handful of other kids were in the room, gawking at a particular shelf of books and shoving and jostling and laughing.

Sam headed for the window seat across the room, and Tobias followed her.

"How long do we have to stay?" Sam asked.

"We just got here," Tobias replied.

"I'm telling you, it's one of these blue ones," said one of the boys at the bookshelf.

The boy tugged on the tops of the books, tilting one at a time. There was a *snick*, and the bookshelf — actually, a wall — rotated on a kind of giant Lazy Susan until a full bar settled in its place. Sam had seen such a thing in the movies before, and it amazed her that it existed in real life *and* that Patrick's friends knew how to access it.

When the boys grabbed a bottle of some dark amber alcohol, Sam turned to Tobias and declared, "We need to leave."

"Relax, will you?" Tobias said, although he didn't sound so sure himself. "Just because they're drinking doesn't mean we have to."

"Tobias," Sam muttered through her teeth. "I don't. Want. To be here."

"We just need to find where they're playing games or something," Tobias insisted. He stood and grabbed her hand to pull her up off the window seat. "Come on. We'll at least take one look around the house. If we can't find anyone doing anything fun, I'll call Bear."

Tobias intertwined his fingers with Sam's and rubbed this thumb back and forth across hers. The sensation had a hypnotic effect on her.

Suddenly, staying didn't sound so bad.

SIXTY
𝄢:

Several considerations warred inside of Tobias's head.

This party made him supremely uncomfortable — he'd never been at a party without parents (or at least someone as responsible as Bear) to supervise. Some of his teenage cousins drank at family holidays, but always with their parents' knowledge and consent. He felt certain the couple he saw making out in the living room wouldn't be the only couple making out that night, not to mention whatever transpired in Patrick's sister's bedroom.

On the one hand, Tobias had promised his mom he would try to expand his and Sam's social circle. But on the other hand, he realized his initial assessment of the basketball boys — as partiers — had been correct, and he didn't particularly want to join that social circle.

On the one hand, Tobias wanted Sam to see how cool he was and how none of the shenanigans bothered him. But on the other hand, he was concerned that she might be too young for such shenanigans, and witnessing them might scar her for life.

On the one hand, Tobias finally felt free to show the world how he felt about Sam (whether because he didn't think anyone would really notice them among all the other craziness at the party or because he'd turned a corner in his own interior struggle with the appropriateness of their relationship, he had yet to sort out). But on the other hand, he worried that seeing all the other couples making out would make one or both of them feel pressured (or emboldened?) to do the same.

As Tobias and Sam wandered through the house hand-in-hand, he began to lose hope that they'd find anything worth doing or anyone worth talking to. He would have to call Bear as he'd promised, but he didn't want to give up that easily. By the time they reached the game room in the basement, the party had grown to several dozen kids.

One group played shuffleboard.

Another set played foosball.

Yet another group played some kind of beer pong (at least, Tobias assumed it was beer pong, having only ever heard about it and never seen it played in real life). He briefly wondered if the cups actually contained beer or some non-alcoholic substitute.

An air hockey table sat unoccupied.

Tobias weighed the options. The group playing shuffleboard included Luke and Emma, so that was out. There was no room for them to join the foosball game. They could play air hockey, but it would be just the two of them, which meant he wouldn't *really* be fulfilling his promise to his mom to meet and hang out with new people.

Desperately hoping it was something non-alcoholic in those cups, Tobias led Sam to the ping-pong table.

"Mind if we join?"

SIXTY-ONE

𝄞

Before they even reached the ping-pong table, Sam knew it was a mistake.

Tobias likely didn't realize what he was getting them into. He was a fine athlete, after all. But Sam... No matter how many sports Bear tried to teach her, she did not possess the skill necessary to participate successfully in a drinking game that involved throwing little balls into cups.

They lost their first game by four cups.

At first, Tobias offered to drink for both of them — perhaps hoping to spare his twelve-almost-thirteen-year-old girlfriend (she relished the term *girlfriend* even as she realized just how big a mistake they made coming to this party) from getting in over her head — but the other team objected and demanded they take turns drinking. The other kids swore it was only lite beer, but never having consumed any alcohol before, Sam felt dizzy after drinking five cups filled halfway.

After another game and five more cups, she was completely sloshed.

Tobias seemed to fare better, but it was honestly difficult for Sam to tell — he seemed to be tilting, but she had a sneaking suspicion that it was just her brains doing a cartwheel inside her skull. Closing her eyes didn't alleviate the sensation at all.

The next team up jostled Sam out of the way, and someone ripped the paddle out of her hand. She stumbled and fell to her hands and knees.

Strong hands gripped her under her arms and pulled her back to her feet. Someone ushered her toward the stairs — she sure hoped it was Tobias and not someone else, but moving her head to look made her want to puke. She tripped on the first step up, and whoever escorted her held her upright.

"I just need to sit down," she mumbled. At least, that's what she tried to say, but the words sounded funny.

Sam started to sit on the stairs, but her usher wouldn't let her. He looped one of her arms around his neck.

"This'll be fun," she remarked, but it came out jumbled again.

With one arm around her back and the other behind her knees, her escort lifted Sam and carried her all the way up the stairs and out the front door. The cold December air hit her like a vicious slap, and she became alert enough to recognize Tobias's handsome face so close to hers.

Tobias set Sam down, and they both sat on the porch steps. She leaned into him and rested her head on his shoulder. He was so steady, and she loved him for it.

"This was a bad idea," Sam murmured.

"Hey, can you come get us?"

Sam glanced up, confused. Tobias talked into his phone. She didn't remember him getting it out.

"Yeah, I know. I know. Bear. Just, please, come." Tobias sounded panicked.

Sam shivered.

"Our coats," Tobias breathed. "Stay here. Don't move."

He got up and went back in the house. It felt like ages — freezing, agonizing ages — before Tobias came back out. He helped Sam put her coat on.

"This was a bad idea," she repeated.

"I know. I'm sorry, Sam," Tobias moaned, wrapping an arm around her. "I should've called Bear when you asked me to."

Bear pulled into the driveway. He got out of the car, but left the motor running.

"Can you walk?" Tobias asked Sam as Bear approached.

"I can't feel my feet," she answered.

"What's wrong with her?" Bear demanded. She must've really looked bad for him to sound like that.

"Help me get her into the car," Tobias said.

Bear didn't just help. He hoisted her in his arms as if she weighed nothing and carried her to the car. He even buckled her in like he would with a toddler.

"Don't you dare puke in my car," Bear warned as the car started moving. "Either of you. Damnit, Tobias."

"I didn't know it was going to be that kind of party, okay?"

"So what? Just because it was *that kind of party* doesn't mean *you* had to drink. Or that Sam had to. What were you thinking?"

"Shut up, will you? I already have two parents, and you're not one of them. Geez."

That was the last thing Sam heard before she passed out.

|♮ ♩ ♪ ♩ |

Sam woke up sometime in the middle of the night.

Someone, probably Lydia, had changed her into pajamas and put her in her bed. When Sam opened her eyes, she was dismayed to find that her brains still did cartwheels. Her mouth felt like she'd eaten cotton balls. It tasted horrible.

On wobbly legs, Sam made it to the bathroom and turned on the faucet. Using her hand as a scoop, she slurped up some water. She did this a few times before giving up and simply sticking her mouth under the running water.

Her tummy gurgled.

Uh-oh.

Lucky she was already in the bathroom and the toilet was only a step away.

|♮ ♩ ♪ ♩ |

The next morning, Sam did not want to get out of bed.

She felt infinitely better than she had in the middle of the night — she had thrown up a total of three times, and each time she felt better — but she did not want to face Tobias's parents. Or Bear. Or Tobias. Shame and embarrassment consumed her, and Sam wished she could hide under the covers and disappear until the sun exploded and obliterated the entire planet.

It was noon before someone came looking for her. Lydia didn't even bother to knock. Her lips were set in a straight line, and Sam could feel the tears coming before Lydia even opened her mouth to reprimand her.

Humiliated, mortified, disgraced, wretched, Sam threw the covers over her head and sobbed.

She felt the edge of the bed sink as Lydia took a seat.

"Sam," she said quietly.

Sam wasn't trying to ignore her, but she couldn't control her sobs.

Lydia waited until Sam had expended enough energy to bring the volume down to a quivering sniffle.

"Sam," Lydia repeated, and Sam felt her tug on the covers.

"I don't want you to look at me."

Lydia sighed. "Sam, I'm not going to yell at you. Will you come out and talk to me, please?"

"No," Sam answered, miserable.

"Why not?"

"Because I let you down," Sam whimpered.

Lydia sighed again. "Did you?"

Sam nodded her head but didn't know if Lydia could see it through the heavy duvet.

"Do you want to tell me what happened?"

"Tobias didn't tell you?" Sam squeaked.

"Tobias said it was all his fault," Lydia told her. "Is that how you see it?"

Sam shook her head, again not sure whether Lydia could see it.

"Then why don't you tell me what happened from your perspective," Lydia coaxed.

Sam sniffed and wiped her nose. It was gross, but she didn't want to emerge for a tissue. It was easier to talk when she couldn't see the disappointment on Lydia's face.

But how could Sam spin this to take the heat off of Tobias?

Joining the beer pong game *had* been his idea, and Sam *had* asked him to call Bear long before that. Nevertheless, Sam could have refused to drink at any point, to heck with the rules of the game. Or she could have refused to play altogether. She was old enough to take responsibility for her own choices.

"We played a drinking game," Sam confessed. "Twice. And we lost both times. I... I drank a lot of beer."

"Did anyone pressure you to play?"

"No."

"Really?"

"I chose to play, and I chose to drink. No one forced me to," Sam insisted.

"Okay." Lydia remained quiet for a moment. "Have your parents ever talked to you about alcohol, Sam?"

They hadn't. Not explicitly. But that didn't excuse Sam's behavior. She knew what she'd done was wrong. She didn't need parents to tell her she shouldn't drink a beverage legally reserved for adults.

"Sam?"

"No."

"Okay."

"But I knew it was wrong," Sam added.

"Will you promise me that you'll never do it again?"

"I promise."

"Good," Lydia said and sighed again. Boy, she must be mad to sigh so much. "I have to confess, Sam, I'm in a little bit of a pickle. If you were my own daughter, I would ground you for all of Christmas break. But you're somebody else's daughter." She paused. "So, tell me. What do you think *your* mother would do?"

Sam had no idea. She'd never done anything remotely like this before. Even if she had gotten into trouble this big, grounding her would hardly have worked — she never went out with friends anyway. The only punishment that seemed suitable...

"You have to ground me from Tobias," Sam mumbled.

"What was that?" Lydia asked, but Sam thought she could hear the tiniest bit of amusement in her voice.

"Ground me from Tobias," Sam repeated.

She didn't know how that would work since they lived in the same house, but Lydia could figure out the logistics. No other punishment seemed severe enough to purge her of the shame she felt.

"Ground you from Tobias," Lydia echoed. "There's an idea." She paused, then patted Sam on the leg. "Come eat something when you find your way out of those covers. It'll make you feel better."

Lydia left.

SIXTY-TWO
𝄢:

"Grounded from Sam?" Tobias repeated, incredulous.

What kind of punishment was that? How would that even work?

His dad shrugged. "You don't like it? Good. That's the way it's supposed to be."

They meandered around the garage again, his dad organizing and reorganizing as he delivered Tobias's sentence.

Both of his parents sat him down the night before to pry the whole story out of him as soon as his mom had finished putting Sam to bed. He felt pretty sure that, as drunk as he was, he managed to shield Sam from most of the blame. But the details of the conversation seemed a little fuzzy now.

Apparently, his mom had talked to Sam, gotten her side of the story, and suddenly Tobias found himself in the garage with his father announcing that he would be grounded from Sam for the next two weeks. What had Sam told his mom? What did being grounded from each other even mean?

"What does that mean, Dad?" Tobias asked. "Being grounded from Sam. Does that mean we're supposed to sneak around the house so we don't accidentally run into each other?"

"Don't give me attitude," his father warned.

Tobias threw up his hands. "I'm not trying to. I'm trying to understand what you want me to do for the next two weeks if I'm grounded from the girl who sleeps down the hall from me and sits next to me at the dinner table."

His dad looked up from sorting screws. "You're going to stay with your grandparents."

Tobias's jaw dropped. His parents were *actually* sending him away. Granted, staying with his grandparents wasn't much of a punishment in and of itself — Tobias wouldn't have a lot to do there, but they always spoiled him as all grandparents spoil their grandchildren — but it stung to be kicked out of his own home. And it *would* be hard not seeing Sam all that time. Not to mention Christmas...

"What about Christmas?"

"Mm, yes. Nobody should be punished on Christmas Day. We'll bring you home for Midnight Mass and Christmas Day," his dad explained, focusing again on sorting screws, "and then we'll send you back until New Year's."

| ♩ ♪ ♩ |

Poor Bear.

As if he hadn't put up with enough because of Tobias's poor choices, now Bear had been tagged to make the drive — two hours each way — to drop Tobias off at their grandparents' house. And boy, was he sore about it.

At least Bear agreed to take Tobias to Saturday afternoon Confession on the way out of town. Tobias wanted to get the sins of last night off his soul ASAP. Because she wasn't Catholic, Sam didn't have recourse to the Sacrament of Reconciliation. It made Tobias feel sorry for her, even if she didn't understand or care about the grace she missed out on.

Tobias packed his duffle with his door shut. If at all possible, he and Sam were to avoid each other until he and Bear departed.

He heard the sound of something sliding under his door. It was a folded piece of lined notebook paper, blank on the outside.

Tobias opened it.

Sam had exquisite handwriting, precise and small:

> *Dear Tobias,*
>
> *I don't know what they told you, but it's my fault you have to leave. I told your mom to ground me from you. I didn't know they would make you leave. I'm sorry. I think maybe you tried to take the blame for last night. Thanks for that, but I need to take responsibility for my choices too. I hope you understand.*
>
> *I just want you to know how much I will miss you while you're gone. I was really excited to hang out during the break, and I'm sad*

I ruined it. I hope you forgive me.

Please don't forget about me. I love you very much. I wish I had told you a long time ago. Nothing makes me happier than knowing you like me back.

See you Christmas Eve.

Love,

Sam

Tobias didn't quite know how to feel after he read it.

Sam had used the *L-word* twice now — three times if he counted each mention in her note separately. Tobias searched his heart, trying to understand how deep his own attachment ran. It hadn't really been that long ago that Tobias even realized that he *liked* Sam. He wanted to write her back, but could he honestly tell her that he *loved* her?

Maybe this separation was just what Tobias needed to figure it out.

SIXTY-THREE

⚓

In some ways, sending Tobias to spend the break with Paul's parents was an impulsive decision.

The time between Sam suggesting they ground her from Tobias and Paul breaking the news to their youngest son clocked in around two hours. In the span of that two hours, Lydia and Paul changed their minds at least seventeen times.

At first, they brainstormed ways to ground Tobias and Sam from each other without sending either of them away and could find no satisfactory solutions. Every suggestion either one made was ultimately deemed impractical and unworkable.

At one point, Paul pushed to find a different punishment altogether, but even as they argued about how to make it work, the conviction that separating Sam and Tobias was necessary crystallized in Lydia's mind. She felt absolutely certain that neither Tobias nor Sam would have drunk alcohol had they not gone to the party together. Neither would have had anything to prove. But together...

As if granted some supernatural insight into their souls, Lydia somehow understood that, in Tobias's calculations, playing a stupid drinking game had been a necessary risk in order to fulfill his promise to help Sam make friends; and that, in Sam's desperation to please Tobias and win his approval, she had been willing to go along with anything. Neither of the kids articulated their motivations in those terms, but Lydia felt the truth of her insight in her bones.

And so, the way Lydia saw it, separating the two of them was indeed the *only* suitable punishment for both. And since they had nowhere to send Sam — having agreed that she didn't know Paul's parents well enough — the solution seemed clear to Lydia. Tobias, beloved son though he was, must live in exile for a couple of weeks.

Perhaps they'd look back one day and see that they'd treated their son unfairly and they'd suffer insufferable guilt as all parents eventually do, but it was the only workable idea they could come up with in the moment.

It pained Lydia to watch Tobias leave so morose and defeated. She'd already lost one son to wild parties and worldly pleasures — they hadn't seen Jake in nearly three years, since he'd stormed out of the house in a drug-induced rage.

She was determined not to lose another.

I thank thee, Father, Lord of heaven and earth,
that thou hast hidden these things
from the wise and understanding
and revealed them to babes;
yea, Father, for such was thy gracious will.
All things have been delivered to me by my Father;
and no one knows the Son except the Father,
and no one knows the Father except the Son
and any one to whom the Son chooses to reveal him.
Come to me, all who labor and are heavy laden,
and I will give you rest.
Take my yoke upon you, and learn from me;
for I am gentle and lowly in heart,
and you will find rest for your souls.
For my yoke is easy, and my burden is light.

Matthew 11:25-30

SIXTY-FOUR

$\oint$

If someone had told Sam in August that she'd feel lonely eating dinner with three other people, she would have scoffed.

It amazed her how much her life had changed — how much *she* had changed — since her parents' accident. She had a boyfriend (sort of). She prayed. She'd gone on a date and faithfully attended Catholic Mass every Sunday. She had gone Christmas shopping and gotten drunk at a party — both firsts — in the same week. And now, she felt lonely despite being surrounded by people who cared about her.

Perhaps it was her guilty conscience. She had so much to feel guilty about these days. Sam imagined her guilt as a physical thing, wrapping itself around her heart and squeezing like a cobra until all the warm fuzzies oozed out and only loneliness remained.

It was her fault Tobias was gone, spending his winter break away from his own family. Her fault that he'd gotten in trouble. Her fault that she'd disappointed Lydia and Paul. Her fault that she'd fallen in love, not only with Tobias, but with his entire family, when her own parents were being bathed and dressed and fed and rehabilitated by strangers.

Her fault that she was a bad daughter to *two* sets of parents.

The car ride to Mass on Sunday morning was one more reminder of what she'd done and how much she had to make up for. Where Sam normally squished into the middle seat between Tobias and Bear, there was now an empty space. She buckled herself into the seat behind Paul, and Bear felt so far away.

Sam noticed three things about the Scripture readings that day: pregnant ladies, the will of God, and a shepherd.

Over the weeks, she'd figured out that Christmas was about more than the Christmas morning gift exchange. Each Sunday of Advent, Father Bernard talked about preparing for the birth of Jesus, and Sam came to realize that Christmas was actually a huge birthday celebration for God's Son (who was also somehow God himself). So in the context of getting ready to celebrate a famous birth, the pregnant ladies kinda made sense.

Sam prayed Father Bernard's homily would be about the other two things.

$$\left\| \raisebox{0pt}{$\textstyle \natural$} \; \raisebox{0pt}{$\textstyle \downarrow$} \; \raisebox{0pt}{$\textstyle \flat$} \; \raisebox{0pt}{$\textstyle \downarrow$} \right\|$$

Father Bernard's Homily for the Fourth Sunday of Advent

My dear brothers and sisters in Christ:

Today we celebrate the Fourth Sunday of Advent, the <u>last</u> Sunday of Advent. Christmas is coming. <u>Christ</u> is coming.

You can feel Mary's eagerness today, can't you? "In those days Mary arose and went with <u>haste</u> into the hill country," Luke's Gospel tells us. "With <u>haste</u>."

And the child in Elizabeth's womb — John the Baptist, whose words for the last couple weeks have been preparing us to receive the Lord — he leaps for joy at the sound of Mary's greeting. He can't wait to meet his Messiah, his Lord, his King, his God, this shepherd of Israel — in the <u>flesh</u>!

And Elizabeth herself: "And why is this granted me, that the mother of my Lord should come to <u>me</u>?" In other words, "What have I ever done to deserve this blessing? How is it possible that God wants to meet little, unworthy <u>me</u> face-to-face, to dwell in my home, to favor me with his presence?"

And then those glorious words of Mary's Magnificat: "My soul <u>magnifies</u> the Lord, and my spirit <u>rejoices</u> in God my Savior... behold, henceforth all generations will call me blessed, for he who is mighty has done <u>great</u> things for me, and holy is his name."

If the excitement, the eagerness, the anticipation and joy with which Mary and John and Elizabeth await the Lord don't get you absolutely pumped for this coming Friday, you haven't been paying attention.

Why? Why are they so excited?

Listen again to our first reading, from the prophet Micah: this savior, this Messiah, this shepherd who is to be born of Mary "shall stand and feed his flock in the strength of the LORD, in the majesty of the name of the LORD his God... and this shall be peace."

A shepherd who brings peace. Who is peace. What a promise. And this is what they've been waiting for, this is what Mary and John and Elizabeth know is coming. They know that the child Mary carries in her womb is the fulfillment of this prophecy, that Mary's baby will be the Good Shepherd God promised to send — not just here in Micah, but by the other prophets as well, in Ezekiel and Jeremiah, and in the Psalms, including today's Psalm, Psalm 80 — the Good Shepherd who will rule Israel, and not just Israel, but as Micah says, "now he shall be great to the ends of the earth." God is sending someone to save everyone.

But he's not just sending anyone. He's sending his very own Son — in the flesh! As it says in our second reading today, from the Letter to the Hebrews, "when Christ came into the world, he said... 'a body hast thou prepared for me.'" And that you and I "have been sanctified through the offering of the body of Jesus Christ once for all." For all people, Christ came into the world so that he might offer his body to save us.

This, my brothers and sisters, this is God's will for us. Our salvation is God's will. Again from our second reading, Christ said, "Lo, I have come to do thy will." And Mary, in our Gospel acclamation today, says, "Behold, I am the handmaid of the Lord; let it be to me according to your word," according to your will.

When we submit ourselves to God's will, as Jesus and Mary show us, we submit ourselves to his mercy: "His mercy," Mary says, "is on those who fear him from generation to generation," and, "He has helped his servant Israel, in remembrance of his mercy."

Christ, the promised shepherd, is the very <u>embodiment</u> of God's <u>mercy</u>, and he wants to meet every single one of us — you and me — he wants to see you face-to-face and tell you that your sins are forgiven; he wants to touch you and heal you; he wants to give you his very <u>flesh</u> in the Eucharist that you might be one with him as he is one with the Father.

That, my brothers and sisters, that is why Mary and John and Elizabeth are so darn excited today. That's why you and I should be excited for Christmas. Not because of the presents or the music or the decorations or even the family and loved ones. We should be excited because Our Lord is coming to <u>rescue</u> us from our sins, from our guilt and dysfunction and unworthiness, from death and despair, to <u>shepherd</u> us into God's <u>mercy</u>, God's <u>peace</u>, to shepherd us into everlasting life with him.

All glory and honor be to our Lord Jesus Christ forever. Amen.

♩ ♪ ♩ |

It took Father Bernard no more than five minutes to deliver his homily.

In no more than five minutes, Sam's whole life changed.

She had prayed that Father Bernard would talk about God's will and the shepherd, and God had answered that prayer immediately. But more than that, Father Bernard seemed to address his words specifically to Sam. It was as if he'd seen inside her soul and aimed his message directly at the turmoil there.

How long had Sam been tortured by her guilt? Her unworthiness? Her dysfunction? Her despair that she would *never* be a good daughter? How long had she desired rescue from those things?

In a flash of sudden understanding, all the Mass readings and homilies Sam had heard and all the books she'd read clicked into place in her mind. All those facts had hovered in a disconnected jumble, and Sam had struggled to put them in an order and context that made sense. Now, somehow, she just… *got it.*

It was the same feeling she'd had when she recognized the words of the Requiems as the words of the Mass, as if some Truth beyond her comprehension had been unveiled to her. It was a Truth so magnificent, Sam couldn't even find words in her big brain to articulate it. But in some mysterious way, she *knew* with absolute certainty that everything the Howards had ever told her about God and the Church was true.

And it terrified her.

Did this mean she believed, really and truly, in God and Jesus and all the rest?

And if she did, really and truly, how could she ever stop going to Mass? What would her parents think? Would they let her be Catholic? Would they continue to let her go to church with the Howards when she eventually moved back home?

Sam didn't realize she was hyperventilating until she became lightheaded.

Too late, she realized she was passing out.

|𝄾 𝅗𝅥 ♪ ♩ |

Sam was only out for a minute, maybe two.

Someone had laid her flat on the pew. When she came around, everyone was standing for the Prayer of the Faithful. Lydia crouched next to her, brushing the hair from her forehead and waving a small, tattered prayer book like a fan. Someone handed Lydia a bottle of water, and she helped Sam to sip it.

"Can you sit up?" Lydia whispered.

Sam nodded. Just in time, she swung her legs over the edge of the pew and sat up. The congregation said, "Amen," to conclude the Prayer of the Faithful, and everyone sat. If Sam had still been lying down, Bear wouldn't have had room to sit.

Sam still felt lightheaded, but she continued to sip on the bottle of water.

"If you feel like you're gonna pass out again, put your head between your knees, okay?" Lydia whispered.

Sam nodded again. She felt embarrassed that she'd passed out in the middle of Mass. She focused on taking slow, deep breaths to keep it from happening again. As much as she wanted to concentrate on the rest of Mass, her mind kept wandering back to Father Bernard's homily and the series of thoughts that had preceded her syncope.

By the time the others got up to receive Communion, Sam found herself in an impossible dilemma: the one thing that promised to rescue her from her guilt was also the one thing that might possibly make her feel even guiltier. According to Father Bernard, Jesus promised to wipe away all the things that made her a bad daughter. But if Sam became a Catholic against her parents' wishes, wouldn't that make her an even worse daughter?

As Father Bernard said the final blessing at the end of Mass, Sam realized she knew what she had to do. It was Sunday, the day she visited her parents. Talking to her father about it was out of the question, but her mother...

Sam's stomach clenched with nerves.

She wished God had kept his revelations to himself. She wished she hadn't been convinced, that the veil hadn't been pulled aside. But no matter how hard Sam wished, she couldn't un-believe.

And she had to tell her mother.

♩ ♪ ♩

Her mom stared at her.

Sam thought maybe she hadn't understood.

"Did you hear me, Mom?" she asked. "I've been going to church with the Howards and praying, and I think it's real. I believe in it. All of it."

Her mother mumbled something unintelligible, and her faced scrunched up. Sam realized she was crying. But why? Because she was mad at Sam? Disappointed? Happy? Relieved?

"Mom," Sam entreated. "Please don't cry."

Her mother moaned pitifully, and a bubble of spittle popped between her lips.

Sam reached for her mother's hand, and her mother recoiled from her. Sam's heart spasmed painfully. Her mother turned away from her and wouldn't look at her.

Sam felt her own tears well up. Why would God do this to her? If he wanted her to believe in him so badly, why did he have to make it so difficult?

"Mom, I'm sorry," Sam said, sniffling loudly. "I don't know what to do. You and Dad never said one way or the other if you believed in God, and I didn't believe in him at first, but then I started praying. He doesn't always answer, but sometimes he does. He really does, Mom. And this morning... I don't even know how to explain what he did this morning, but you have to believe me, Mom. He's real. And now that I know he's real, I think I have to listen to him. I mean, he's *God*."

Her mother turned toward her again. She'd regained control of herself, but her face was all puffy and red and tear-stained. Sam handed her a tissue. Her mom still struggled mightily with her motor skills, but she managed to wipe the tissue across her nose. A strand of snot connected to her nose came away with it, and Sam tried really, really hard not to be disgusted.

Her mom closed her eyes, and a line that appeared between her eyebrows told Sam she concentrated very hard.

"Tham," she said slowly. Sam recognized it as her name. Her heart jolted hearing her mother say it for the first time since the accident.

Sam reached for her mother's hand again, and this time her mother didn't pull away. Sam squeezed.

"I'm here, Mom. I'm listening."

"Thawly," her mother breathed. Sam interpreted it as *Sorry*.

"What for, Mom?"

Her mom swallowed and breathed hard. The effort it took for her to concentrate and form almost-words was immense. Sam waited patiently.

"Um... ploudh... fff... ooo." Her mother opened her eyes and gazed intensely into Sam's eyes, as if she could communicate with a look all the words she couldn't speak.

But Sam understood her words, garbled as they were.

Her mother was proud of her.

The tears Sam held back earlier couldn't be stopped now. She crawled onto the bed beside her mother and snuggled close to her.

They cried together for a long time. Cried and talked and cried some more. They didn't stop until a nurse arrived to help Sam's mom take her nightly bath.

Before Sam got up, her mother pressed her mouth against Sam's hair. Her lips couldn't properly pucker, but Sam felt the kiss all the same, and she returned one on her mother's cheek.

"I love you, Mom."

Her mother nodded, and the nurse smiled sweetly at Sam as she left.

SIXTY-FIVE
𝄢

The week crawled by like cold honey for Tobias.

He loved his paternal grandparents and enjoyed their company, but Christmas Eve could not come soon enough.

His mother's parents lived in a different state, and he didn't get to see them as often. They tried to make the rounds once a year, visiting Tobias's mom and her four sisters, now all spread across the country with their own families, but he hadn't seen them since last spring.

His father's parents, though, always hosted Howard holiday gatherings and barbecues for birthdays and graduations and Baptisms and all sorts of other occasions. Tobias got along especially well with his Grandma Jo, and by Monday, she pried from him all the details he'd successfully kept from his parents: about his feelings for Sam, the friendships he'd lost and gained because of her, his doubts and fears and confusion. He even told Grandma Jo about Sam's date and the fact that she'd kissed him.

Grandma Jo was wonderfully understanding and never seemed surprised by anything he told her. That's what he appreciated most.

Tobias spent so much of his life around his mother and Bear, who constantly needled him and gave him a hard time about something or other. Feigning shock was one of their favorite go-to schticks to make light of things they thought Tobias took too seriously. Even if they meant it in good fun, it wore on him at times. He didn't enjoy the spotlight, and they had a knack for shining bright ones on the things that already made him most self-conscious.

But not Grandma Jo. She made all his secrets seem normal and boring and not worth dwelling on or pointing out to other people.

Still, Tobias could hardly wait for Christmas Eve, when all the Howards would come together at Grandma Jo and Grandpa El's again, including his parents and Bear and, of course, Sam. He didn't know if he and Sam were supposed to avoid each other when everyone else came for Christmas Eve, but he imagined he would feel better just seeing her.

And then Christmas Day… It would be a true holiday, like in the old war movies when both sides agreed to a ceasefire and celebrated together despite their differences. Not that he and Sam were enemies. Not even close. But they would be able to celebrate together despite their punishment.

Tobias had no doubt it would be his favorite Christmas yet.

SIXTY-SIX

♪

Sam could tell that Lydia was shocked when she told her. Almost as shocked as her own mother had been.

"Do you know what you're asking, Sam?" Lydia's eyebrows had disappeared behind her bangs. "I mean, what you're talking about — it's a one-and-done deal. You can't just change your mind later and be un-baptized."

"I know," Sam said firmly.

Her mother had actually been the one to suggest it. Sam thought it would be enough to say she believed, but somewhere in the middle of all the crying, her mother managed to make Sam understand that she needed to be baptized (her mother had to repeat the word *baptized* several times before Sam figured out what she was trying to say). She remembered reading about Baptism in Lydia's book on Catholic practices — what the water and words meant and the structure of the rite itself — but the necessity of the Sacrament hadn't truly sunk in until her mother insisted on it.

"And your parents? They're okay with this?" Lydia questioned.

Sam nodded. "It was my mom's idea." But then she looked at the ground. "My dad doesn't know, though. I'm still not sure how much he understands, or if he knows who I am."

Lydia's face softened and she exhaled a breath she had apparently been holding in for a while. "I'm not exactly sure how it'll work, Sam, but I'll talk to Father Bernard about it," she promised. "There's a program for kids your age who want to join the Church — it's called RCIC — but the parents are usually heavily involved in that process."

Sam shrugged. "Can't you and Paul be, like, substitute parents?"

Lydia laughed softly, but Sam also detected that she held back tears. "Sam," Lydia whispered. She shook her head, perhaps shaking away her tears, too. "Let me talk to Father Bernard. And then we'll figure out what our next step needs to be, okay?"

Sam nodded and smiled. "Thank you, Lydia."

Lydia drew her close and hugged her.

Sam hugged her back and thought how lucky she was to have *two* mothers who loved her so much.

|𝄽 𝅘𝅥𝅭 𝅘𝅥𝅮 𝅘𝅥 |

Bear seemed to miss the point that the time apart from Tobias was supposed to be a punishment for Sam.

He made every effort to keep her entertained, constantly asking her to play video games or cards or pool. He even offered to take her to see a movie until Lydia quashed the idea.

One evening as they played pool, though, a curious thought struck Sam: after all this time, she still didn't know Bear's real name. So she asked him.

Bear chuckled. "Ugh, I knew I couldn't avoid it forever. It's Lawrence."

"That's not so bad," Sam tried to tell him.

"Yeah, until they start calling you Larry," Bear replied, and Sam snickered. "That's how it got to be Bear. First it was Larry. Then Lar-Bear. Finally just Bear."

"It wasn't because you're so big?"

"I beg your pardon?" Bear stood up straight and sucked in his gut. Sam giggled. "I don't know what you're talking about. I'm nought but a dainty flower, Sam."

Bear couldn't keep his belly in any longer, and Sam laughed harder. But talking about Bear's past made her think of something else, and for some reason, Bear seemed the right person to ask.

He bent over and focused his gaze along his cue stick.

"Bear?"

"Yeah."

"How come no one ever talks about Jake?"

Sam had often wondered about the mysterious missing brother. She'd grown so close with all the other Howards, it seemed bizarre that there was one out there she'd never met. It seemed even stranger that no one ever mentioned him.

Bear straightened again. "What do you already know about Jake?"

Sam shrugged. "Just that he used to practice with his rock band in there." She jerked her head toward her music room. "He didn't come for Thanksgiving, and no one said anything."

Bear picked up the blue cue chalk and applied it to the tip of his cue stick. He applied more than necessary as he thought about his answer. "We haven't seen or heard from Jake since I was Tobias's age," he finally told her. "He got into some really bad stuff, started hanging out with the wrong crowd."

"Did your parents kick him out?" Sam asked incredulously. She wouldn't have suspected Paul and Lydia capable of something so heartless.

But Bear shook his head. "Didn't have to. He stole some of my mom's jewelry, stuff she'd inherited from her grandma, so he could sell it for drug money. When Mom and Dad called him out on it, he just walked out the door and never came back."

Sam didn't know how to respond. Bear was clearly sad about what had happened, but it was a long-ago sadness, something he'd let go of at some point.

"Is that why you were so mad at Tobias?"

"What?"

"When you picked us up from the party. It's the last thing I remember — you yelling at Tobias," Sam explained.

"Maybe," Bear said, more to himself than to her. "I guess those feelings were in there somewhere, but mostly I was just scared. You didn't look so good, you know."

Sam huffed. "Believe me, I *never* want to do that again. Ever."

Bear smiled. "Good. Otherwise I'll have to come all the way back from seminary to chew you out."

"Seminary?"

Bear nodded and grinned sheepishly. "Only Tobias knows."

"Knows what? What is seminary?"

"It's where guys go for formation to become priests."

Sam mentally added *seminary* to her list of Catholic things to read about. "You want to be a priest?"

"More importantly, I think God wants me to be a priest."

Again, Sam didn't know how to respond. Should she congratulate him? He seemed happy about it. "Cool."

Bear laughed. "Cool. Yes, it's cool. And terrifying." He took a deep breath and exhaled. "And humbling."

"I think you'll make the best priest ever," Sam said earnestly. "You'll have the funniest homilies."

Bear laughed again. "Hopefully, they actually help people grow in their faith, too."

Sam shrugged. "You and Lydia make me laugh all the time, and you helped me believe in God."

"Well, that's just"—Bear shook himself—"too serious for me. Let's keep playing. Get on with the game. Enough of this solemn talk."

Sam giggled. "It's your turn."

|𝄽 ♩. ♪ ♩ |

The rest of the week went by fairly quickly for Sam.

She had thought about Tobias during the week, of course, but he hadn't occupied her thoughts the way she'd expected. Instead, Sam spent all her time praying and studying and learning and thinking about God. She even started praying the family rosary with the Howards after dinner.

Upon her request, Lydia gave her even more books on Church-y stuff, and she blew through them with lightning speed. The more Sam read, the more she felt she had made the right decision.

With the big holiday coming up, Father Bernard didn't have time to meet with Lydia and Sam yet. At first, Lydia had thought to meet with him one-on-one, but when she explained the situation to him, Father Bernard insisted that Sam be present for the meeting as well. Sam felt both nervous and excited to find out how Father Bernard planned to handle her unique circumstances.

Though she'd heard the Howards talk about the Sacrament of Reconciliation before, she never thought much of it until that week. After she read one particular meditation on the Prodigal Son Parable, she felt convinced it was the one she most needed. The prospect of baring her faults and sins to Father Bernard made her uneasy, to say the least. If anything could get rid of all her guilt and failures as a daughter, though, it was that Sacrament.

But as with all the other Sacraments, Sam had to wait for Father Bernard to give the green light.

Christmas Eve practically snuck up on her.

Glory to God in the highest,
and on earth peace among men with whom he is pleased!

Luke 2:14

SIXTY-SEVEN
𝄢

Aunts and uncles and cousins started arriving at Grandma Jo and Grandpa El's midmorning.

Tobias was happy to see all of them, of course, but the anticipation of seeing his own family — and Sam — tortured him.

While he waited, he occupied himself playing basketball in the backyard with Bryce — it was an unseasonably warm day, and Tobias didn't need more than a light jacket. His grandparents had a large backyard with a lawn and a wide cement quad that served as the basketball court. An overgrown arboretum bordered one edge of the quad.

Bryce made an ill-advised shot that careened off the rim and straight into the arboretum.

"Oops." Bryce grimaced.

"Go get it," Tobias ordered him.

"No way, man," Bryce replied, holding up his hands and shaking his head. "You know how I feel about bugs."

"It's winter."

"Nope."

Tobias rolled his eyes and plunged into the thick snarl of dead branches and withered bushes. The branches snagged on his clothes and hair. An old spiderweb clung to his face, and he shivered despite himself. At last, he spotted the ball and retrieved it.

With his hand up to protect his face, Tobias emerged from the arboretum and bumped into a body.

She went sprawling backwards and landed on her rump with a look of surprise on her sweet face.

"Sam!"

Tobias let the basketball roll off his fingertips and bounce away as he rushed to help her up. He was horrified, but she was laughing. Tobias held out a hand and hauled Sam to her feet, the momentum of his pull bringing her close.

"Hello," Sam said, still giggling.

She was adorable.

"I love you," Tobias blurted. He hadn't planned to tell her like that, but he'd spent the week thinking about it and decided he was ready to say it.

Sam laughed in disbelief. "What?"

"I mean… hi," Tobias said. He felt his cheeks burning. "And I'm sorry I knocked you over."

Not knowing what else to do, he threw his arms around Sam, lifting her off her feet. She squealed and giggled and wrapped her small arms around his neck. After a good squeeze, Tobias let her down. He kept his hands at her waist, though, and she kept hers on his shoulders.

"Ugh, get a room, you two!" Bryce taunted.

Tobias ignored him. Truth be told, he wanted nothing more than to find a room where he could sit and talk with Sam with no one to bother them. Maybe even kiss her.

"I missed you," Sam murmured.

"I missed you, too."

SIXTY-EIGHT

♪

Sam and Tobias were inseparable all of Christmas Eve.

She hadn't realized how much she missed him until she saw him crawl all disheveled out of that silly arboretum. The dead leaves stuck to his shirt, the messy hair, the spiderweb on his face... Somehow all of it made him dearer to her than if he'd appeared perfectly perfect.

And then what he'd said! The first words out of his mouth, no less!

Tobias hadn't repeated it — yet — but Sam knew she hadn't misheard. He'd definitely said he *loved* her, and she would cherish that memory for the rest of her life.

Sam was eager to tell Tobias all about her week, but she wanted to choose the moment carefully. It wasn't the kind of conversation to have with so many other people around.

The moment came after they'd said their goodbyes to everyone else. They waited by the car to drive back to their own parish for Midnight Mass. Tobias's parents and Bear hadn't come out yet, so it was just the two of them.

"Guess what?" Sam said.

"What?"

Tobias looked at her with a kind of twinkle in his eye, and it suddenly struck her that he gazed at her the way Paul gazed at Lydia — the way she'd always dreamed someone would gaze at her — and all other thoughts flew out of her head. For the life of her, she couldn't remember what she'd been about to say.

"What?" Tobias chuckled and nudged her.

"I don't remember," she admitted, laughing.

"*You*?!" Tobias teased. "*You* don't remember? You remember everything!"

He was right. But Sam had to look away from his face before it came back to her.

"Oh, I remember," she said. "I'm going to become Catholic."

Tobias said nothing.

When his silence became unbearable, Sam looked up at his face again to see whether his speechlessness was a good thing or a bad thing. His mouth hung open — he was obviously surprised — but she couldn't read any deeper into his expression.

"So... what do you think?" she asked.

"I don't know. That's not what I expected you to say," Tobias answered, but then the corners of his mouth curved into a smile. "I didn't even know — I thought you didn't believe in God, even."

Sam shrugged. "I didn't, and then I did. I do."

She told him how it happened and included parts of the story she hadn't even told her mother or Lydia. It was difficult for her to find the right words, and it frustrated her trying to describe a concept so big and so sublime. Her words wouldn't fit around it or reach it.

But somehow, Tobias understood anyway. He hadn't understood about the Requiems, but he understood prayer and guilt and despair and mercy and Sacraments. He nodded along as she spoke, and she saw that her tale, though clumsily told, resonated with him.

"Sam, that's incredible," Tobias breathed when she finished. "You..." He licked his lips. "You inspire me."

Sam was taken aback. She scrunched her nose. "Really?"

Tobias swallowed and nodded. "Really."

He reached up and touched her face. Sam swore he would've kissed her if his parents and Bear hadn't walked out right at that moment.

"Sorry, sorry, sorry," Lydia apologized. "You know how I get going with Miranda sometimes. It's my fault. Let's go."

Everyone piled into the car.

Sam and Tobias held hands all the way to Mass.

|𝄽 𝅗𝅥 ♪ 𝅘𝅥 |

Midnight Mass
In darkness my soul lies
In darkness wretched humanity
Blind, cold
Wasting

With light the Savior comes
With light Blessed Divinity
Bright, warm
Illuminating

In flesh the Bridegroom caresses
In flesh Word of God
Real, true
Suffering

With love my soul revives
With love Beloved Redeemer
Soft, sweet
Awakening

|𝄾 ♩. ♪ ♩ |

Even though they'd all gone to bed well after 1 a.m., Sam was up with the sun. Before the sun, actually.

Her stomach buzzed with excitement, and Sam could hardly wait to go downstairs and watch the family open the presents she'd given them. She figured everyone else would sleep in, but unable to contain herself, she threw on her robe and snuck down to the living room to wait by the Christmas tree.

Sam was shocked to find that she was, in fact, the last one up.

Lydia and Paul snuggled on the loveseat, each with a cup of coffee in hand. Tobias sat on the floor with his own cup of coffee, and Bear rocked in an antique rocking chair.

"About time, geez!" Bear quipped as soon as he saw Sam.

"Merry Christmas, Sam," Lydia greeted with a smile. She raised her coffee cup in a kind of toast.

"Merry Christmas, Sam!" the other family members echoed.

"Merry Christmas," Sam returned, a little abashed at the attention.

Still a little unsure of what, if any, boundaries she and Tobias were supposed to have, she chose to sit on the floor next to Lydia's feet, with her back against the loveseat.

Tobias jumped up almost as soon as Sam was down and began rummaging through the presents under the tree. Not sure if there was an order to this business, she simply sat and watched him.

"How'd you sleep?" Lydia asked her.

"Not well at all," Sam answered honestly. Lydia laughed. "I've never been excited for Christmas morning before, but I could hardly sleep."

Bear chuckled. "That's normal. I think I heard Tobias sneak past my door around four."

"Shut up," Tobias griped, but he smiled when he said it.

"You'd think they would've outgrown it by now, but I guess some things never change," Lydia said and squeezed Paul's knee. He must have been up early, too. Suddenly, she snapped her fingers at Tobias. "Hey, don't forget the stockings."

"Oh, yeah!"

Tobias stopped rifling through the presents under the tree and went to the mantle where the stockings hung. Sam didn't come into this room often, and she only now noticed that Lydia had hung a stocking with *her* name on it. Tobias brought the stocking to her and passed out the others as well.

Sam glanced around, not quite knowing what to do. The others reached into their stockings and pulled out little goodies, so she copied them. She pulled out a pair of winter gloves (her old pair had been unravelling between the thumb and first finger), a small bag of chocolates, and a little bracelet with music-themed charms on it — a piano, eighth notes, a treble clef, and a trumpet. It touched her deeply.

"Who are these from?" Sam asked, wanting to thank the proper person.

Lydia winked. "Santa Claus, of course," she answered.

Sam laughed softly. "This is beautiful. Thank you."

She undid the clasp on the bracelet and set the chain on the back of her wrist. It slithered off almost immediately.

Lydia ran a hand over her hair. "You're welcome."

"Here, let me help you," Tobias offered.

He scooted over to her on his knees and took the bracelet from her. Sam held out her wrist and let him secure the clasp. Her skin tingled where Tobias's fingers brushed against her wrist.

"All right, get on with it," Bear complained.

Tobias grinned and went back to the presents under the tree. He tossed one to Bear, and Lydia gasped.

"Tobias!"

"Sorry," he muttered. "Is it breakable? I thought it was socks or something."

"In a box?"

Tobias shrugged.

Bear tore it open. It was a high-end men's watch.

"Whoa. Thanks, Mom and Dad."

"You're welcome," Lydia answered, still sounding a little peeved with Tobias.

Tobias handed a present each to Lydia and Paul and one to Sam and then settled into his own spot with the present Sam had given him. Instead of opening her own gift, Sam watched Tobias nervously.

He unwrapped the CD, and he smiled broadly. Tobias looked up and locked eyes with Sam. She felt her cheeks grow warm.

"Thank you, Sam," Tobias said. He nodded at the box in her lap. "Aren't you going to open mine?"

Sam hadn't even realized he'd handed her his own gift. "Yeah, of course."

Sam's fingers trembled, and it embarrassed her. It was just a silly gift, just like the one she'd given him. Why was she so nervous?

Sam ripped off the wrapping paper and slid her finger through the tape holding the box closed. Inside was another, smaller box. She laughed, thinking it was a joke. "Aw gee, a box. Just what I've always wanted."

"Keep going," Tobias urged her.

With one eyebrow raised, Sam opened the box and found yet another box inside of that one. All of them watched her now, not just Tobias, and her cheeks went from warm to hot. Brow furrowed now, she opened the third box.

Inside was an envelope.

"Open it," Tobias encouraged when she hesitated.

What kind of gift would be inside an envelope? Sam lifted the flap and saw the edge of familiar ticket stock. Her breath caught. She pulled out two tickets.

Box B3. The symphony. Playing Mozart's Requiem.

Goosebumps spread all over her arms and legs.

"You can take whoever you want, of course," Tobias said, "but I'd be happy to go with you if you can't find anyone else."

Sam was afraid to speak. Afraid she would start crying if she did.

"Do you like it?" Tobias asked.

Sam nodded vigorously.

"Very much."

SIXTY-NINE
𝄢

Bear took Tobias back to their grandparents' house late in the afternoon.

Tobias was loathe to leave, but he knew it was only fair that he serve the rest of his sentence.

He would be home for New Year's Eve, and he counted the hours. He secretly promised himself that, no matter what, he would absolutely, one hundred percent kiss Sam when the clock struck midnight on New Year's Eve. Tobias had been kicking himself for having wasted the opportunity at his grandparents' house, when they were alone at the car, but he'd been so sure his parents were right behind them.

Sam's reaction to his gift was exactly what he had hoped for. He knew his family's response when she talked about Requiems had disappointed her. Truthfully, Tobias only understood half of what she'd said that day. But since she had used his phone to search for the music, he had something to reference when he started planning his gifts. It was like a message from heaven when Tobias saw the flyer in the mail advertising upcoming symphony concerts. The second he saw the word "Requiem," he knew he'd found the perfect gift. And to top it all off — as if God had wrapped the present himself and put a great big bow on it — the concert was the same weekend as Sam's birthday.

Only, in order to convince his parents to spend that much money — they had a pretty tight budget buying for siblings — Tobias had agreed to give up a couple of his own gifts. Luckily, Sam hadn't noticed that he was short a few gifts from his parents. Trying to explain the reason would have embarrassed him.

As much as Tobias wanted to spend every second of Christmas Day with Sam, he knew he had to get his mom alone. During his time with Grandma Jo, he came to the conclusion that he needed to come clean with his mom and get the guidelines out in the open. Tobias could no longer hide his feelings for Sam, but he wanted to respect whatever boundaries his parents put in place. His opportunity came when Sam stepped away to try on some of the new clothes his parents gave her.

Tobias cornered his mom in the kitchen as she pulled the innards out of the turkey.

"Can I talk to you?"

"Of course. You can always talk to me, Tobias," she answered. "What's up?"

"Sam," Tobias said. His insides squirmed, but he was determined to be manly about this. "I love her."

His mom stopped with her hand still inside the turkey. "What kind of love are we talking about here?"

"I suspect you already know," Tobias replied. He swallowed. "I want her to be my girlfriend."

His mom nodded and pulled her hand out of the turkey. She turned to him, and Tobias found the goop on her hand distracting. "Is that what she wants?"

Tobias nodded. "But I don't want to do anything… inappropriate," he stated, trying to sound as mature as possible. "And I don't want to sneak around behind your back. I want to be honest and out in the open, but… I need to know what the guidelines are."

His mom nodded again and pursed her lips thoughtfully. Tobias watched the goop drip from her hand to the counter. "Your father and I will discuss it while you're gone and let you know what we've decided when you come back for New Year's. Deal?"

"Deal."

Then his mom winked and smiled, and Tobias knew he had an ally.

SEVENTY

♎

Sam hated to see Tobias leave again, and she willed the week they'd be apart to pass quickly.

After Bear and Tobias left, Lydia took Sam to see her own parents.

Sam spent five minutes with her father. She had begun to suspect that he did indeed recognize her, but that he didn't *want* to see her. What had once seemed to Sam a look of lost-ness had subtly and gradually shifted each time she went. Now she saw something more like resentment and antipathy. Though why he should dislike her so much, she couldn't understand.

Unless he suspected how she felt about the Howard family. Maybe he envied the Howards because Sam loved them, and they loved her. Maybe to her father, that made her disloyal.

Whatever the reason for the dark look he gave her when she entered the room, Sam was not eager to linger under that gaze. So she stayed just long enough to wish her father *Happy Holidays* (she'd never once heard him say *Merry Christmas* and she feared, truly, for the first time since deciding to join the Catholic Church, what his reaction would be when he found out).

Sam spent a good hour with her mother, though, and decided this time to invite Lydia into the room with her. It was only then, seeing these two mothers together, that Sam wondered how Lydia and Paul had managed to keep custody of her. So much of what happened around the time of the accident seemed a blur, but there must have been some official, formal arrangement made, some legal means by which Lydia and Paul had taken responsibility for Sam. How did they do it while her parents were both comatose and incapable of agreeing

267

to or signing anything?

It bothered Sam so much that she asked Lydia on the way back to the Howard home.

"Well," Lydia started, "it's called kinship care. Since you have no other family that you know of, we applied to the court to be kinship caregivers for you until your parents are well enough to resume parental responsibilities."

"The court?"

"Yes," Lydia replied. "We spoke with a county judge and had our lawyer go over all the options with us."

"Your lawyer?"

"Mm-hm," Lydia answered. "Why do you ask?"

"Lawyers are expensive, aren't they?"

"They can be."

"And all the food and clothes and Christmas presents you've given me."

"What about them?"

Sam shrugged. "I just never really connected all the dots before. How much trouble I've put you all through."

"Samantha Ingram." Lydia gave her the side-eye. "Never, ever think like that."

"What about my parents?" Sam asked, ignoring Lydia's chastisement. "My mom, at least. She still doesn't talk very well, but she thinks just fine. Does she know about... kinship care? Now that she's awake, would she be able to — I don't know — veto or something?"

Lydia smiled weakly. "She could, but she didn't."

"What do you mean, she didn't?"

"I spoke with your mother several weeks ago, Sam," Lydia explained. "A very nice, long chat. While you were at school one day. You're right that things changed when she came out of her coma. It was no longer the court's decision, but hers — whether you could continue to stay with us. And actually, before that, when your father came out of his coma, Paul tried talking to him, but he was not responsive."

Sam's heart jammed in her throat. That's why her father hated her, she was sure of it. He *knew* another family wanted her, and he was angry that he couldn't do anything to stop it.

"But your mother," Lydia continued, "your mother was very grateful for what we'd already been doing for you and agreed to let us continue until she's healthy enough to go home. In fact, she signed — er, had a proxy sign for her — a Power of Attorney granting us a little more authority to make important decisions about your care."

Sam frowned, absorbing everything Lydia explained. On the one hand, she felt grateful that the adults had worked everything out (except for her father — he seemed like a bit of a wild card, and it worried her). But on the other hand, she felt a little hurt that they'd done it all behind her back. Or perhaps it was her guilt that hurt — guilt that she'd been too preoccupied with Tobias and school and her rollercoaster emotions to even consider such an important matter before now.

"Do you understand, Sam?" Lydia asked. "Are you worried about something?"

Sam shook her head. Something about the whole thing *did* bother her, but she couldn't articulate it just yet.

"I was just curious."

O that you would kiss me with the kisses of your mouth!

Song of Solomon 1:2

SEVENTY-ONE
𝄢:

It was New Year's Eve, and Tobias — the boy who was always running late — was packed and ready to go an hour before Bear arrived to take him home.

The week between Christmas and New Year's passed even more slowly than the week before, and Tobias thought he might lose his mind if he had to stay one more day. Not only was he eager to see Sam again. He was anxious to hear about whatever arrangement his parents had decided suitable for him and Sam to date each other.

They arrived home in the late afternoon. Tobias suddenly felt nervous. Should he seek out Sam first? Or his mom?

As it turned out, his mom wasn't even home. She was out grocery shopping. Tobias could hear his dad running the wet/dry vacuum out in the garage — he must be reorganizing again — but the rest of the house was quiet.

Where was Sam?

Leaving his duffle at the landing, Tobias ventured down to the basement. Sure enough, he could hear, just faintly through the music room door, Sam playing her trumpet. He smiled and knocked loudly to make sure she heard.

The door jerked open.

Sam's face lit up, and Tobias didn't wait until midnight.

He bent down and kissed her.

SEVENTY-TWO

♪

Somehow, she'd been ready for it.

Some instinct, something in Sam's gut told her Tobias would kiss her the next time they saw each other. And it was every bit as marvelous as she'd imagined it would be.

The first one was brief, shy, unsure.

But then came the second one. More confident, a little longer, a little sweeter.

And the third. Brief again, but full of purpose.

Tobias pulled back a little and grinned. "I meant to wait until midnight."

Sam wrapped her arms around his waist and hugged him close, resting her cheek against his chest.

"I'm glad you didn't."

WINTER

Requiem æternam dona eis, Domine
Et lux perpetua luceat eis
Te decet hymnus, Deus, in Sion
Et tibi reddetur votum in Ierusalem
Exaudi orationem meam
Ad te omnis caro veniet

SEVENTY-THREE

♪

Sam turned thirteen on January 15, a Friday.

Her mom had improved significantly in the last two weeks, and the doctors were confident she would be able to go home by the end of February. After that, she would still require some in-home care for a couple months. There was a great deal of discussion about whether Sam should go home when her mother was discharged from the hospital or stay with the Howards until she no longer needed in-home care.

Sam herself felt torn. Part of her wanted to stay with the Howards until her mom could stand on her own two feet. Sam didn't feel ready to take on the responsibilities that would be required of her if she moved back in with her mom sooner than that. But the other part of her desperately wanted to go home so that she and Tobias could start acting like a real couple once and for all.

Although Lydia and Paul expressed support for Tobias and Sam's relationship in general, their rules were shockingly restrictive. Whenever they were at the house, there was to be no kissing, no cuddling, no holding hands, no being in a room alone together.

Sam knew they just wanted to be cautious — to help her and Tobias *avoid the near occasion of sin*, as Tobias had once put it — but in the last two weeks, following the rules had bordered on impossible. Six times Tobias and Sam found themselves alone in a room together without meaning to be, and then they'd bicker about which one of them should have to leave the room.

At least Sam and Tobias had their walks to and from school. They could hold hands and kiss all they wanted in those six short blocks.

But the after-practice walks from school to the house started to take noticeably longer. Noticeable to Lydia anyway. She hadn't said anything about it yet, but Sam could see that suspicious look in her eye each time she and Tobias walked in the door just a little bit later than they had the day before.

Sam's father had also made rapid strides in the last few weeks — physically, anyway. He had been moved to the rehabilitation center where her mother was, but his rehab focused more on regaining strength than motor skills like her mom.

When Sam visited him after he first transferred to the rehab center, she expected that his cognitive and verbal skills would have improved as well. Perhaps they had. Nevertheless, as usual, he said nothing to Sam, merely watched her.

Ignoring the unsettled feeling it gave her, Sam spent more time with him during that first rehab center visit than she normally did, telling him many of the things she'd hesitated to communicate over the past months. She did not, however, tell him about her meetings with Father Bernard — she still wasn't prepared for whatever his reaction might be to the news that she planned to join the Catholic Church, with her mother's blessing no less.

Sam had met with Father Bernard three times already. At their first meeting, Father Bernard was reluctant to accept Sam into the RCIC program while her parents were incapacitated. But Sam managed to persuade him that she was old enough to make the decision for herself and that she was in no way being coerced or unduly influenced by the Howard family.

She described as much of her conversion experience — all the little moments and epiphanies that led up to Father Bernard's own homily on the Fourth Sunday of Advent — as she was able to articulate. Using terms like *age of reason* and *catechumen* and *Sacraments of Initiation*, Sam demonstrated the depth of her understanding and her eagerness to take the next step in the process.

By the end of their second meeting, Father Bernard agreed to receive Sam into the Church at the coming Easter Vigil. She'd read and studied enough on her own, he said, and shown such a remarkable gift for remembering and comprehending what she'd read, that he deemed it unnecessary to make her wait and complete the entire RCIC program next year.

Sam was overjoyed.

| ♩. ♪ ♩ |

Because her parents had improved so much, Sam wanted to celebrate her thirteenth birthday at the rehab center.

The staff were very understanding and enthusiastic about the idea and offered a small community room for the occasion.

While Sam and Tobias and Bear were at school, Lydia and Paul decorated the community room with streamers and balloons. Bear picked Tobias and Sam up after basketball practice, and they stopped by the grocery store to pick up the cake and a sandwich platter Lydia had ordered earlier in the week. Tobias teased Sam all the way to the rehab center about not peeking at the cake.

"It's bad luck," Tobias claimed.

"You're a liar," Sam shot back, grinning.

"I'm serious," Tobias insisted, feigning a somber look. "You won't get any of your birthday wishes if you look."

"That's not how it goes," Sam retorted, narrowing her eyes at him. "You don't get your birthday wish if you don't blow out all the candles."

"Or if you tell someone what the wish is," Bear chimed in.

"Or if you look at the cake," Tobias added.

"Stop it!" Sam giggled.

When they arrived, Sam's mom had already been wheeled into the community room, and Lydia and Paul waited there, too. But her father was nowhere in sight. She tried not to feel the sting of disappointment.

Sam wondered if her father and mother had even seen each other since the accident. It hadn't occurred to her to ask her mother before now. Both of her parents stayed in the same building, but perhaps her father wanted to see her mother as much as he wanted to see Sam — that is, not at all.

The mood was festive despite Sam's missing father. Sam's mom and Lydia got along quite well. Most people would have been uncomfortable interacting with someone who drooled when she spoke and couldn't use her fingers properly, but Lydia seemed completely at ease around Sam's mom. She managed to offer help without ever sounding condescending or making things awkward. It was that gift Lydia had — that gift of making everyone around her feel comfortable and important and loved.

When Sam finally got a look at the cake, she saw that it had been meticulously decorated with two staves of music. Sam recognized it immediately as the opening bars of her favorite Mozart piano sonata. She played it often at the house, but she couldn't recall anyone ever having asked her the name of the piece. She was sure none of them had ever been familiar with it before she played it for them.

But, Sam had learned time and again, that's just how the Howards were — thoughtful and sincere and a little bit sneaky.

The presents they gave her were the same way. Bear gave her a book of sheet music for Tchaikovsky's *The Seasons*; Lydia and Paul gave her a necklace with a St. Cecilia medal (she was the patron saint of music and the one Sam planned to choose as her Confirmation saint); and Tobias gave her a lovely music box that played Beethoven's *Moonlight Sonata*.

"Remember?" Tobias prompted. "It was one of the first pieces I ever heard you play."

Of course, Sam remembered. And she loved that he remembered, too.

Paul pulled out a huge box from behind the door. "This is from your mother, Sam."

Sam looked at her mom, who nodded and smiled crookedly.

It was an electronic keyboard.

"So you can come here and play for me," her mom enunciated slowly, the words still slurred and difficult to understand.

Sam went to her mother and hugged her. They were both a little teary-eyed, and Sam heard Lydia sniffle behind them, too.

It amazed Sam that she felt closer to her mother now than she ever had in her life. They only saw each other once or twice a week, and her mother could barely even speak, yet their bond had deepened in some inexplicable way. And Sam was grateful.

"Play something now, Sam," Tobias suggested.

"Yeah, something out of your new book!" Bear agreed.

Paul set up the the keyboard, and Sam opened her new Tchaikovsky book to her favorite of the twelve pieces, *June*. She could memorize anything, but sight-reading was a different story. Luckily, she'd already figured out some of it by ear long ago. Sam took a moment to let the notes settle into place in her big brains before she set the music book on the rack.

She took a deep breath and played.

It was worse than imperfect. It was terrible, actually.

But she had the nicest audience in the world, and they applauded uproariously when she finished.

Sam wished her father had been there to hear it.

SEVENTY-FOUR
𝄢

Tobias never truly expected Sam to ask anyone else besides him to use the second ticket for the Requiem concert. He was right.

Tobias was honestly excited to hear the symphony live again, but mostly he couldn't wait to have a real date night with Sam. His parents arranged to have their own date night at the same time. They would go to the restaurant across the street for a romantic dinner while Tobias and Sam were at the concert.

Last time they'd gone to a concert together, they dressed in silly Halloween costumes. Sam made an adorable squirrel, but tonight she wore a lovely dress that transformed her from a cute little girl into a beautiful young woman. Tobias knew as soon as he saw her pacing by the front door that he would have a very hard time concentrating on the music.

"Come on, your parents are already in the car," Sam said, grabbing his hand and dragging him out the door.

Tobias wanted to tell her how gorgeous she looked, but his tongue wouldn't cooperate. So he just grinned at her, and she grinned back. They spent the entire car ride to the concert hall grinning at each other like idiots.

His dad parked in a parking garage a block away from both the concert hall and the restaurant. The foursome walked to the front entrance of the concert hall together, and his parents saw Tobias and Sam safely inside the building before turning to cross the street to their own destination. Before they'd parted, Tobias's mom had fussed like a hen, reminding them for the thousandth time to text as soon as the concert was over and to meet them in that exact same spot.

284

As soon as his parents' backs were turned, Tobias laced his fingers through Sam's. She squeezed and smiled at him. That smile… It made his heart light up like that chandelier Sam admired so much.

Tobias led Sam to where an usher scanned tickets. He felt like a grown-up taking the tickets out of the inside pocket of his suit jacket and handing them over. They wove through the milling crowd, up the stairs to the balcony, and through the door that led to their box seats. It was the same box they'd sat in at the Halloween concert, and Tobias hoped Sam noticed.

Of course, she would — she remembered *everything*. But when they got there, Sam didn't say anything.

"Do you recognize it?" Tobias asked as they sat down.

"Recognize what?"

"The box."

Sam glanced around. "You mean because it's the same one we sat in last time? I knew it would be when I saw the tickets. Box B3."

Tobias was both amazed and disappointed that she'd figured it out earlier.

But then Sam smiled. "You thought of everything," she said. "It's the best gift I've ever been given, Tobias. Truly."

Tobias's chest squeezed and his heart raced. He wanted to kiss her, but he was too shy. Sneaking kisses in the alley was one thing. Tobias didn't yet feel experienced or confident enough to kiss her in front of other people.

The lights dimmed, that beautiful chandelier rose into the ceiling, and Sam turned back toward the stage. In the dark, Tobias saw his chance.

He leaned forward and whispered in Sam's ear, "Happy birthday, Sam."

He meant to kiss her on the cheek, but she turned her face, and the kiss landed awkwardly on the corner of her mouth. Sam snorted and giggled, but Tobias felt horribly embarrassed. As the audience clapped for the concertmaster coming on stage, Sam faced him and, grabbing the back of his head, drew him in for a real kiss.

It was their best one yet.

"Thank you," Sam whispered when she pulled away.

Then she turned back toward the stage and joined the applause for the conductor.

SEVENTY-FIVE

𝄞

The first half of the concert featured overtures from three of Mozart's operas: *Le nozze di Figaro, Die Zauberflöte,* and *Don Giovanni.*

The music transported Sam to a transcendent plane of existence, as it always did. The sound of the orchestra filled her lungs and flowed through her veins and flooded her soul.

For some strange reason during *Don Giovanni,* however, it dawned on Sam that she'd never actually told her mother about her and Tobias. Her mom probably figured out long ago that Sam had a crush on the handsome boy across the street, but in all the months since the accident, Sam had never dwelt particularly on her relationship with Tobias when she talked to her mother. Now that they were a real couple, Sam decided it was time to take Tobias with her on some of her Sunday visits — maybe not every week, but sometimes at least. Starting tomorrow.

At intermission, Sam shared her idea with Tobias.

"Will you come with me tomorrow when I go to visit my mom?" she asked.

Tobias seemed surprised. "Sure, if you want me to," he replied.

"I just think the two of you should get to know each other better. I mean, I know your family *really* well, but you've never really spent much time with my parents," Sam explained. "Now that we're... you know..."

Tobias grinned. "Yeah, I know," he said. "Now that I'm your boyfriend, your mom's gotta look me over, make sure I'm good enough for ya."

"It's not like that," Sam protested. Tobias grinned wider, and Sam realized he was joking. She smacked his knee with the back of her hand.

Sam couldn't believe she'd ever thought Tobias was the serious one. The closer they'd grown, the more often he cracked jokes, and she had learned to treasure them as something only those closest to him had the privilege of hearing.

"Hey, I can't blame her," Tobias said. His smile faded, and he looked down sheepishly. "I know I'm not."

"Not what?"

"Good enough for you."

"Tobias," Sam said sternly, and he looked back up at her. "If one of us isn't good enough for the other, it's obviously me." He started to object, but she charged onward. "Think about it. Before me, did you ever get in fights or get drunk?"

Tobias opened his mouth and shut it again. "Well, no, but—"

"See? I've corrupted you," Sam declared.

"Oh, and you were getting drunk before me?" Tobias shot back.

Sam laughed. "No."

"So maybe I'm the one who corrupted you."

"Yeah, but you made up for it by having parents who take me to church every Sunday," Sam returned.

Tobias snorted. "So you're saying the only thing that makes me worthy of you is something I can't even take credit for?"

"No," Sam replied seriously. "I'm saying that you and your family are the best thing that's ever happened to me. If that's not good enough for my mom, nothing ever will be."

Her statement apparently caught Tobias off guard. He didn't respond for a long time.

Finally, Tobias nodded and said, simply, "I'd love to go with you tomorrow."

SEVENTY-SIX

𝄢

Tobias hoped Sam didn't ask him what he thought of the concert afterward.

He'd enjoyed the Halloween concert, but it must have been because he recognized most of the music. Tonight he didn't recognize anything they played (he remembered Sam showing him one of the songs from the Requiem, but hearing it once wasn't enough to make it stick, apparently).

It was clear that Sam relished the music, though, and that's all that mattered. He delighted in her delight. Even if the music didn't interest him, Tobias felt as if he could spend the rest of his life just watching Sam's face as she listened.

When the concert ended, Tobias texted his mom, but they waited for the people bottlenecked at the exit to thin out before leaving their box. As they waited, Tobias put an arm around Sam's waist, shyly at first, but tightening his grip when she leaned into him. He wasn't ready for their date night to end.

"I love you, Sam," Tobias said.

It was the first time he'd said it since he'd stupidly blurted it out as a greeting on Christmas Eve.

She looked up into his face. "I love you, too."

Screw all the people around them. This was their date night, a precious opportunity, and Tobias wasn't going to waste it. He bent down and kissed her. She kissed back. It sent thrills through his entire being. They didn't come up for air until Tobias felt his phone vibrate in his pocket.

A text message from his mom.

Where are you?

Tobias felt his cheeks burning. He cleared his throat and moved his hand from Sam's waist to intertwine their fingers. "They're waiting for us."

Sam grinned and allowed him to lead her out of the hall.

SEVENTY-SEVEN

𝄞

Sam stopped short at the doors, dragging Tobias to a halt.

She could see Lydia and Paul standing outside, and she could see Lydia's face. Something was wrong. Horribly wrong.

Sam flashed back to that moment at Tobias's birthday party when, having just answered the door, Paul whispered in Lydia's ear, and Lydia looked straight at Sam.

Suddenly, all Sam wanted was to turn around and run back to the box seats and pretend the concert hadn't ended yet. She imagined her life playing like a scratched DVD, and she wished these next moments could be the part that got skipped over.

Tobias looked from her to his parents standing outside. He must have seen it in Lydia's face, too, because he seemed to deflate next to Sam. He led her slowly out the doors.

"Sam," Lydia started, but that's all she got out before her chin quivered and tears spilled through her eyelashes.

She didn't have to say more. Sam knew.

Her mother was dead.

Is it nothing to you, all you who pass by?
Look and see
if there is any sorrow like my sorrow
which was brought upon me,
which the LORD inflicted
on the day of his fierce anger.

Lamentations 1:12

SEVENTY-EIGHT

⚓

A pulmonary embolism.

Explaining to a thirteen-year-old girl that her mother died of a pulmonary embolism was the hardest thing Lydia had ever done. Paul offered to be the one who delivered the news, and Lydia probably should have let him. But for some reason, she *needed* to be the one to tell Sam.

Because Renee had given them Power of Attorney, Lydia had been the one the doctor called when it happened. She and Paul had just ordered dessert. Lydia had been so shocked, so devastated, that she'd completely forgotten to ask about Sam's father.

Did John know? Had they told him? And if they had, did he understand? She didn't think of these questions until she lay in Sam's bed much later that night.

Sam was inconsolable. Understandably so. Lydia cradled her and rocked her and soothed her until she cried herself to sleep in her arms.

But Lydia couldn't sleep. She grieved. Her heart ached for Sam, but Renee had become a friend in the last several weeks, and Lydia grieved her own loss, too.

The questions about Sam's father swirled in her mind. The custody situation had already been so complicated. Now that Renee was gone...

And what about the funeral? As Sam's kinship caregivers, would she and Paul be responsible for planning the funeral? Were they supposed to contact anyone else? Did Renee have a will? What about life insurance and bank accounts? Was John in any kind of mental shape to help them deal with this mess?

But Lydia couldn't think about any of that just now. The grief was too raw, the pain too sharp to think clearly.

She should remember to tell Paul about her questions in the morning, though. Let him think it through. Let him come up with all the answers. Lydia was so tired of leading the charge. The burden was too much this time. But Paul would take care of it. He would. All she had to do was ask him.

In the morning.

SEVENTY-NINE
𝄢:

Tobias felt young.

So blasted young. Too young. Young and inadequate.

Earlier in the night, he'd felt so grown-up and mature, taking his beloved to a symphony concert, holding the tickets in his jacket's inside pocket, kissing her in front of all those people.

But this… Tobias was too young to deal with this.

He didn't know what to say or do for Sam, what she needed from him, how to comfort her. Adults always seemed to know what to do when someone else lost a loved one — they had the right words, had an instinct for when to offer a hug or a touch on the shoulder.

But Tobias had just stood there like an idiot, gaping, frozen, paralyzed, speechless.

As he lay on top of his covers that night, their conversation at intermission came back to him, mocking him, haunting him. *You and your family are the best thing that's ever happened to me. If that's not good enough for my mom, nothing ever will be… I know your family really well, but you've never really spent much time with my parents.*

And now Tobias would never get the chance to know Sam's mother. She was gone. Forever.

Tobias tried to put himself in Sam's shoes. It seemed so horribly unfair. She didn't have much family to begin with. Now half of it had been ripped away forever, and the other half didn't even recognize her.

It made his own inadequacy all the more painful and shameful. Sam would count on Tobias for comfort, for consolation, for *something*, and he would fail her. He just knew it. Now, when she needed him most, he was at a complete loss what to do, what was expected of him.

Tobias felt so young.
Too young.

EIGHTY

𝄞

How could God do this to her?

Sam didn't understand. Had she done something wrong? Something to displease him?

Ever since her epiphany on the Fourth Sunday of Advent, Sam had felt her guilt less keenly. It hadn't gone away exactly, but it had sort of moved to the background.

Now it eclipsed everything else.

When she awoke the morning after her mother's death, Sam wanted nothing to do with the Howards. She didn't deserve their compassion, their kindness, their love. She didn't deserve it, and she didn't want it.

Her heart had been a traitor for too long, loving a family that wasn't her own. Her mother had deserved better than that. Her mother had deserved her whole heart, but Sam hadn't given her that. No, she had given her heart to the Howards.

It had to stop. Now. Before her father was taken from her, too.

Sam fell asleep in Lydia's arms but awoke alone. Eventually, someone came to knock on her door — no doubt to tell her it was time to leave for Mass — but Sam ignored it. Still in bed and facing the window opposite the door, she heard the door open behind her. She pretended to be asleep so whoever it was would just leave her alone. And they did. The door clicked shut a moment later, and footsteps retreated toward the stairs.

If God still thought she was becoming Catholic after this, he was sorely mistaken. He couldn't just destroy her life and then expect her to join his religion. No way.

Determined now to avoid all of the Howards as much as possible,

Sam thought she should sneak downstairs and grab something for breakfast before they returned from Mass. That way she wouldn't starve when she refused to come down for brunch later.

Sam made it to the pantry before she realized she wasn't alone.

Paul sat at the breakfast table drinking coffee.

"Everyone else is at Mass," he told her, as if she didn't know. "We thought you might need a little extra rest, though. You can go to Mass with me this evening, if you'd like." He paused. "How are you feeling, Sam?"

Sam clenched her jaw and refused to look him in the eye. She didn't want to answer him. She was mad that he hadn't left with the others, that her plans for solitude had already been ruined.

"I understand if you're not ready to talk. That's okay," Paul said gently. She hated him for being so nice. "And if you're not ready to see anyone else, that's okay, too. We'll still be here whenever you *are* ready. But for now, just pretend I'm not here."

She did.

Sam poured herself a bowl of cereal and took it back to her room, acting the whole time as if Paul didn't even exist.

𝄽 ♩ ♪ ♩ 𝄂

Sam did not go to Mass with Paul that evening.

In fact, she didn't leave her room again for the rest of the day even though her stomach started rumbling again by early afternoon.

Late in the evening, close to her normal bedtime, there was a knock on her door. Sam sat on the floor, her back against her bed and facing the window. Anyone at the door wouldn't be able to see her without coming further into the room.

When Sam didn't answer, the door opened.

"Sam?" It was Lydia.

Sam heard her soft footfalls and then felt the bed depress behind her.

"I brought you a plate of dinner in case you're hungry. I know you haven't eaten much today."

Sam didn't respond.

"I'll just leave it here on your nightstand."

Sam heard the scrape of the plate on wood as Lydia set it on the nightstand, but Lydia didn't leave just yet.

"Sam, I know you're in a lot of pain," Lydia said quietly. "And there's nothing I can do to take that pain away. It's okay to take time for yourself, but don't forget that, outside of this room, there are people who love you very much, and we will do whatever we can to help you."

Lydia was silent, giving Sam a chance to respond. But Sam didn't want to, so she didn't.

Finally, Lydia walked out and closed the door softly behind her.

EIGHTY-ONE

𝄢

Tobias waited in his bedroom doorway for his mother to emerge from Sam's room.

He worried about Sam, and he felt so helpless. As soon as Sam's door opened and his mother came out, Tobias approached.

"How is she?" he whispered.

His mom sighed and shook her head. "She wouldn't talk to me, but I think she just needs some time."

Tobias could see that his mom put up a brave front, that Sam's refusal to speak to her had hurt her feelings. He knew how she felt. He hoped, despite feeling wholly inadequate for the task, that Sam would ask for him or seek him out for comfort. It was selfish, perhaps, but it disappointed him that she wanted to be alone.

Tobias hugged his mom, knowing they both needed it, and she squeezed back. He felt her shudder with the tears she'd been holding in all day.

"I was supposed to go see her mom with her today," Tobias whispered, feeling his own eyes fill with tears. He couldn't remember the last time he'd cried. It made him feel like a little boy. "She wanted us to get to know each other better."

His mom squeezed harder, and she rubbed his back. "Oh, honey, I'm so sorry," she said hoarsely. "I'm so, so sorry."

"Me, too."

Therefore do not pronounce judgment before the time,
before the Lord comes,
who will bring to light the things now hidden in darkness
and will disclose the purposes of the heart.
Then every man will receive his commendation from God.

1 Corinthians 4:5

EIGHTY-TWO

♪

Sam didn't go to school at all that week.

She couldn't shake the feeling that she now lived someone else's life, that Samantha Josephine Ingram had somehow ceased to exist. None of the things that had once occupied her mind or entertained her or made her happy held any interest for her. Not her trumpet or her piano. Not reading about the Church. Not even Tobias.

The world moved around her — funeral plans were made; flowers and condolences poured in from Sam's teachers and Paul and Lydia's family members; Tobias played his last basketball games of the season; and Lydia spent a great deal of time with Ms. Helton, the social worker who had been her mother's case manager. She still was the case manager for her father.

Sam remembered meeting Ms. Helton shortly after the accident, but she only now realized how much of her parents' care had fallen on Lydia's shoulders from the very beginning. Lydia had carried the burden so effortlessly, never letting on how much she did for Sam's family. She worked with Ms. Helton from the get-go to ensure that the Ingrams' bills were being paid and paperwork was in order and appropriate care was being delivered.

Sam knew she should be grateful for everything Lydia had done for her family, especially since she had never once sought credit for her efforts. But all Sam could feel was strangling, suffocating guilt. All she could think about was how unaware she'd been, how little interest she'd taken in her parents' care, and how things that should have been *her* responsibility had fallen on someone else.

Sam lost track of the days, but on one of them — a day when Tobias and Bear were at school and Paul was at work and Lydia was meeting with the funeral director or Ms. Helton or someone else — she walked across the street and unlocked the door of her parents' house.

It was dark and cold and quiet.

No one had been inside this house since they'd moved the piano in early November. Sam shut the door silently behind her and tiptoed toward the hallway. It felt wrong to disturb the stillness here, as if she might awaken some ghost or monster if she made too much noise.

Her destination was her mother's hobby room.

Since the accident, it had often crossed Sam's mind to come here and find out, once and for all, what that file cabinet contained. But every time, she convinced herself it would be an invasion of her mother's privacy. Now that her mother was gone, Sam *needed* to know what was in that cabinet. Whatever secret the cabinet held was a piece of her mother's life that Sam had never been allowed to see, and she was desperate to find and hold onto anything her mother had considered so precious.

When she opened the door to the hobby room, the smell overwhelmed her. The smell of her mother.

Sam choked back tears, not ready to let them have their way with her again. Closing her eyes, she inhaled deeply and breathed it in, that smell, and let it soak into her being.

She crossed the room to the file cabinet.

It was locked, and she had no idea where to even look for the key. Knowing it would be locked, though, she'd had the forethought to find a crowbar among Paul's tools in the garage and didn't think he'd mind if she borrowed it. She reasoned that she had every right to break into this file cabinet. Whatever was inside had belonged to her mother. Maybe it belonged to her father now — she didn't know how those things worked — but why shouldn't she have as much right to it as he did? It wasn't like he was in any shape to care anyway.

The cabinet had two deep drawers, one on top of the other. Sam wasn't quite tall enough to get the right leverage on the top drawer, so she jammed the crowbar into the seam at the top of the bottom drawer. Prying it open was harder than she thought it would be. But finally, with a loud metallic *bang!*, the lock snapped and the drawer slid out.

Sam set the crowbar aside.

There were several file folders neatly organized inside, each containing a ream of paper. Sam pulled the first folder out and opened it. The top sheet looked like some kind of title page for a novel: *A*

Summer of Passion by R.R. Ingram. Sam flipped to a page somewhere in the middle, and sure enough, it was a manuscript. And what Sam read made her eyes go wide and her cheeks blush. She slammed the folder shut and set it down, more than a little uncomfortable thinking of her own mother writing such things.

Sam pulled out a second file folder and opened to the title page. Another manuscript, this one titled *Forbidden Fruit by R.R. Ingram.* Sam didn't bother to look further, suspecting whatever she found would only make her more uncomfortable.

Her mother's secret hobby had been writing steamy romance novels? It was not at all what Sam had expected or hoped to find. She had hoped to find something that would make her feel close to her mom again, but now she just felt awkward.

Maybe the top drawer would have something else.

Sam tugged on it — it had come loose when she broke the lock on the bottom drawer — but it jammed partway out. She pulled harder and only managed to tip the entire cabinet forward. Thinking perhaps the tracks were dented or crooked, she bent down to look at the underside of the drawer. But it wasn't damaged tracks that caused the drawer to stick; there was something taped to the underside of the drawer.

A small, wooden trinket box.

Sam ripped it loose from the tape. She ran her fingertips over the intricate carving on the lid, a carving of mountains and pine trees. This is what she had hoped for, but now that she had it, she was scared to open it. What if she found out something else about her mother that she didn't want to know? Steeling herself, Sam snapped open the clasp and lifted the lid.

Her breath caught.

A blue crystal rosary. The crucifix and medal and chain links looked old and tarnished, but the crystal beads were still sharp and shiny.

Tucked under the rosary was a folded piece of paper. With shaking fingers, Sam gently pushed the rosary aside and pulled the paper free.

She unfolded it, and everything changed.

|﹖ ♩ ♪ ♩ |

For Samantha, if I should die before I'm brave enough to tell you

My dear Daughter,

I have so much to tell you, I don't quite know where to begin. We've hidden many things from you, and part of me still understands why. But the other part of me hopes that I have the courage to tell you these things face-to-face and that you'll never have to read about them here. If you are reading these words, it is because my cowardice won out, and for that, I am deeply sorry.

Before I tell you any of the things we've kept from you, let me first tell you something I hope I never kept from you — I love you. If I have made mistakes and been a poor mother, it is because I am a flawed person. It was never because I didn't love you. If, when you read this, there are things I did for which I didn't have a chance to beg forgiveness, I beg it now. You are my heart, dear Daughter, and I regret all the ways my actions may have hurt you in the past and the ways they may continue to hurt you for years to come.

I grew up in a big family. You never knew that. As far as I know, my parents and my three siblings are still alive. The last time I saw them, my parents were still living in the house I grew up in, in a small farming community in Eastern Colorado. My siblings and their spouses and children lived near them. My maiden name is Emory, if you ever care to look them up. The rosary in this box belonged to my mother, and her mother before her. I'm not even certain why I kept it, but it seems right to pass it on to you.

I met your father when I was a freshman in college. As you know, he is several years older than I. We met at a bar I used to go to with my girlfriends. He was a businessman — at least, that's all I thought he was at the time. We fell in love quickly, and before I knew it, we were married and moving to another state.

We had moved three times and been married four years before I found out the truth. By then, blind and naive as I was, I had allowed your father to isolate me from everyone and everything I had known before, and I was too ashamed (and still am) to reconnect with my family. They tried to warn me, you see, but I was headstrong and so madly in love. I left your grandparents on very bad terms.

I was also, by the time I learned what your father was really up to, pregnant with our first child. Yes, my Daughter, this is indeed a very difficult truth to reveal. You have an older sister out there somewhere. I don't even know her name. We were in such an impossible situation at the time, we gave her up for adoption (your father didn't even want me to carry the child to term, but in that, at least, I stood up to him).

You must be wondering what was so terrible that I had to leave my family behind and give up my first-born daughter. I'm still hopelessly in love with your father, Samantha, but he is not a good man. He is and always has been involved with drug trafficking and other smuggling activities. Even if I knew all the details of his work, I think I would spare you having to read them. Suffice it to say, it is dangerous to linger too long in any one location and to make too many friends, which is why we've lived the way we have your whole life. It hasn't been fair to you, I know, and I am so very sorry.

If I've kept you at arm's length, my dear Daughter, it's been to protect you. I am weak and fragile. Hiding the truth always seemed the best way to keep you safe, and I knew if I allowed myself to get too close to you, I risked bringing you too close to danger. This I regret most of all, as I think we could be great friends if we ever have the chance.

Do not judge me too harshly, sweet Daughter. My mistakes are many and grave, but they were made honestly. Remember that your poor mother loved you and wanted only to protect you.

With all the love in my heart,

Your Mother

𝄆 ♩ ♪ ♩ 𝄇

Sam reread the entire letter twice more.

The revelations she read there stunned her. But in some strange way, she felt lighter. Her family history was ugly, marred by lies and crimes and — though her mother didn't say it explicitly, Sam suspected — abuse. Why, then, did she feel some burden lift?

Perhaps it was nothing more than simply knowing the truth — or at least much more of the truth than she had known before.

Or perhaps it was the fact that she had more family out there somewhere — and she fully intended to look up her grandparents, as her mother suggested, and even though she didn't know how to begin such a search, she wanted to find her sister, too.

Or perhaps it was some sense of closure, the final goodbye she'd been robbed of.

Or perhaps it was the validation that she'd been right to mistrust her father all this time.

Sam lost track of time sitting on the floor among the steamy romance novels, the broken drawer, and the trinket box with its precious treasures. Before she knew it, the sun had gone down, and she was left in darkness.

Sam's only prayers since her mother's death had been accusations hurled at God for letting her mother die just when they started to grow close. But now, she prayed the way she had grown accustomed to praying before — telling God *all* her thoughts and hurts and sorrows and confusion.

And guilt.

She cried.

She clutched the rosary and the letter to her chest and curled up in a ball on the floor and cried.

EIGHTY-THREE
𝄢

Sam was missing.

One by one, they'd all arrived home, and Sam wasn't with any of them. No one knew where she was. And it was well after dark.

Tobias's dad took the family car to look for her, and Bear took his own car to do the same. His mom took a flashlight and started knocking on neighbor's doors. Tobias took a flashlight, too, and walked the six blocks between home and school, looking in all the secret places they'd stopped to share a kiss in the past few weeks.

Tobias didn't find Sam in any of their special places, and as he turned back toward home, he prayed. He'd been praying all along, of course, but now he prayed with a kind of urgency he'd never known in his life. The thought of losing Sam made him sick to his stomach. The way she'd acted all week…

She wouldn't hurt herself, would she?

Tobias remembered how his mom frequently prayed for Saint Anthony's intercession when something was lost and couldn't be found. Tobias pleaded with Saint Anthony to help him find Sam.

Not thirty seconds after he finished his prayer, a strange thought occurred to Tobias. An idea. It seemed implausible — Sam *never* wanted to go there, had told him, in fact, that it creeped her out.

But something in his gut told him to try it anyway.

EIGHTY-FOUR

𝄞

From where she lay on the floor, Sam heard the front door open.

She bolted to her feet, and her heart raced. Someone was breaking into the house. Sam didn't know what to do. Should she look for a weapon? Hide? Scream for help?

After several long moments of terror-filled silence, a voice called out.

"Sam?"

Tobias.

Sam wept with relief. He must have heard her because footsteps raced toward the hobby room, and he appeared in the doorway a second later. He strode across the room and pulled her into a tight hug.

"Oh, Sam," Tobias breathed. "I was so scared. I didn't know where you were. Are you okay? Everyone's looking for you."

Sam couldn't answer through all the powerful emotions jerking tears from her eyes. All she could do was bury her face in Tobias's shoulder and sob.

Tobias rubbed her back soothingly until she calmed down enough to lift her face.

"Are you okay?" Tobias asked again.

Sam didn't know if she was okay. She was and wasn't at the same time.

"I'm safe anyway," she answered with a sniffle. "You should probably tell your parents."

"Oh, yeah."

Tobias fished his phone out of his pocket with one hand, continuing to hug her with the other. Like he never wanted to let her go again. She

311

would be okay with that. He used his thumb to type out a quick message and hit send before pocketing his phone and wrapping her up in a full hug again.

Sam finally felt in control enough to return the hug, but all the crying had sapped her strength. She clung weakly to him, the rosary and letter still clutched in one hand, and he rested his chin on the top of her head.

"What happened here?" Tobias asked.

Sam glanced around at the broken drawer and the scattered files. "My mom called this her hobby room, but I never knew what she did in here all the time. I wanted to know."

"Oh," Tobias said. "So what did she do in here?"

Instead of answering him — she felt too embarrassed to tell him that her mother spent all her time escaping into romance novels — Sam handed Tobias the letter.

"I found this."

It was too dark for Tobias to read it. The only light in the room came from the streetlights through the window. But he took it from her and examined it.

"What is it?"

"Answers."

EIGHTY-FIVE

$\oint$

After Sam showed her mother's letter to Lydia and Paul, they immediately started the process to obtain permanent guardianship over her.

Sam gave her testimony to a judge, which seemed silly to her since she didn't know anything more than what was in the letter. Nevertheless, the lawyers claimed it was important that the judge hear from her before he would grant an order officially and permanently removing her from her father's custody should he ever recover.

It looked as if they were all in for a long and tedious process until one day in late February, her father checked himself out of the rehabilitation facility and disappeared. Ms. Helton and the doctors claimed that, all the way up to the end, he never uttered a word to anyone, but he had recovered his strength and completed his physical therapy.

He left a note.

> *Don't bother to look for me. I don't want to be found. I hereby release whatever rights and responsibilities I ever had as Samantha Josephine Ingram's father. The Howards can have her.*

It was short and devastating, and it inflicted a wound in Sam's heart that was somehow worse than the one she carried for her mother's death.

Sam realized now that, even before the accident — all her life, really — she'd felt like a disappointment to her parents. Somewhere along the way, the thought snuck into her mind that her parents were so distant because she had done something wrong, because she was a bad daughter. That thought had burrowed deep, and her father's cold abandonment did little to refute that long-held notion.

The revelations in the letter helped Sam to feel less guilty about everything, but her father's rejection still cut deeply. She could rationalize that her father's poor treatment of her wasn't about her being a bad daughter so much as his being a terrible person. Her emotions weren't rational, though.

It wasn't until she made her first Confession with Father Bernard that Sam felt truly purged of the weight she'd carried around for so many months. No, not months. Years. Father Bernard helped Sam to see that she didn't need to feel guilty for some of the things she confessed; and the things she rightfully felt guilty about were forgiven, totally and forever, because she'd confessed them and received absolution. Her guilt had been a many-armed monster holding her head under water for as long as she could remember, and walking out of the confessional felt like breathing freely for the first time.

Lydia and Paul helped Sam find contact information for her Emory relatives, and she exchanged several emails and phone calls with them. Lydia promised to take her to visit them in the summertime.

Soon after they applied to be her permanent legal guardians, Lydia and Paul sat Sam and Tobias down for a very serious conversation. Tobias's parents warned them that they had better think long and hard before they continued to date because things could get very uncomfortable and painful should they eventually break up. Legal guardianship meant Sam was there to stay, whether she and Tobias remained together or not.

Ultimately, though, Lydia and Paul said they would not forbid them from being together. After much discussion, Sam and Tobias agreed that it was worth the risk. They still were not allowed to hold hands or cuddle or kiss in the house.

As serious as the entire custody situation was, Sam found trivial pleasure in being considered Lydia and Paul's *ward*. It made her feel like a character in one of her favorite British novels, which took some of the sting out of being unwanted by her father.

At the Easter Vigil, Sam received the Sacraments of Baptism, Confirmation, and her first Communion.

She'd never felt so peaceful and loved in her entire life.

THE WEDDING

Do not be afraid, for she was destined for you from eternity.

Tobit 6:17

$

Somehow, despite all the other responsibilities that had been piled on her plate, Lydia managed to help Liz plan an April wedding.

It was Sam's first wedding, and it was just as romantic and lovely as she'd always imagined weddings should be. Liz and Micah (or Buzz Cut, as Tobias called him when Sam was the only one listening) both looked beautiful and happy.

There was something especially mysterious and wonderful about a wedding Mass — the joining together of a bride and groom within a liturgy that joined Christ the Bridegroom and his Bride, the Church — and Sam couldn't help but fantasize about standing there before the altar with Tobias one day.

The reception was modest but loads of fun.

Sam met Lydia's side of the family for the first time. They were different than Paul's family, more boisterous and hilarious (Lydia, it turned out, was the quiet one in her family), and Sam adored each and every one of them.

Paul's family members, meanwhile, were impressed that she remembered all of their names and how they were all related. She had memorized those things at Thanksgiving, of course.

Sam learned how to do dances that, apparently, were danced at every wedding. They were ridiculous dances, and she giggled the whole time.

Not surprisingly, Tobias was an exceptional dancer. He was graceful and athletic, just like he was on the basketball court, but Sam was unprepared for his enthusiasm for dancing. She had assumed that Tobias would be a quiet dancer because he was a quiet person, but he turned into a completely different guy on the dance floor. Tobias had a natural sense of rhythm, and he wasn't shy about showing off his moves.

The slow dances, of course, were Sam's favorite.

At first, Tobias seemed self-conscious about holding her too close with so many eyes around them. But by the second love song, he loosened up and wrapped his arms around her the way he did when they snuck time together in the six blocks between school and home. Sam never felt quite so safe and secure as she did when Tobias held her this way.

A sudden thought occurred to Sam, and she pulled away to look up into Tobias's face. "Will you still walk me to school next year?"

Tobias raised his eyebrows in surprise.

"The junior high school is on the way to the high school, and I could just go early since your classes start before mine, and you could wait for me after school," she rushed to explain, preempting what she thought he would say about it being impractical. But before Tobias could even respond, another horrible thought occurred to her. "Will you still want to date me when you're in high school?"

Tobias guffawed. "What?! Why would you even ask that?"

Sam shrugged. "You won't be embarrassed dating a girl who's still in junior high? I mean, I'm not even a cool junior high girl. I'm a weird, brainy junior high girl who listens to classical music and wears crazy socks and has no friends or family."

"Well, when you put it that way."

Sam's jaw dropped, and Tobias chuckled.

"It's not funny, Tobias," Sam complained. "I'm being serious. What if you — I don't know — outgrow me?"

Tobias furrowed his brow and grew thoughtful. "Remember that night at the symphony, when we argued about being good enough for each other?"

How could she forget? It was the same night her mother died.

Sam nodded.

"Well," Tobias said, "I still don't know about *good enough*, but I do think God made us *for* each other. And I don't think I'll ever outgrow that."

Sam felt like someone had filled her veins with champagne, all tingly and effervescent. She stood on her toes and kissed Tobias.

Maybe what Tobias said was crazy. They were only thirteen and fourteen years old. Kids. But Sam heard the conviction in his voice and felt the truth of his words in her soul. Whatever future lay in front of her, something — a little whisper in her heart — told her that she would face it with Tobias next to her. And not just Tobias, but all the Howards. And not just the Howards, but a whole community, her new brothers and sisters in faith.

At long last, Sam knew she was *home*.

Author's Notes

Note 1: A very odd thing happens to writers, and non-writers look at us like we're nuts when we tell them about this thing. Perhaps we are nuts. But it's a real thing. It's the thing that happens when the characters start to write the story instead of the writer. That thing happened more in this novel than in anything else I've ever written.

I spent a long time getting to know Sam and Tobias in my imagination before I sat down to write about them, and I imagined literally hundreds of scenes that never made it into a single draft. Instead, when I sat down to write, Sam and Tobias did their own thing. The only scene they agreed I could keep was the fight scene with Jason — it was, after all, the very first scene I imagined and the reason Sam and Tobias began to live in my brain in the first place. Even though I started with a rough outline and the basic premise — that Sam's parents were in an accident that forced her to move in with Tobias's family — the characters truly dictated the vast majority of the story themselves. I was simply their fingers on the keyboard.

Crazy, right?

But it's true. I can show you the beat board. Sam's parents were supposed to recover — both of them — and she was supposed to move back home. She was not supposed to become Catholic for many more years. Tobias and Sam's first kiss was supposed to be the day she moved out, and he was supposed to be the one to make the first move. Tobias wasn't even supposed to have his own chapters — I intended to tell the entire thing from Sam's perspective, but Tobias wouldn't let me.

As crazy as it sounds, this thing — where the characters write the story — is one of the greatest thrills of writing. If I may say so, Sam and Tobias made their story way better than the one I had in my head.

So whether you enjoyed this book or hated it, you can blame Sam and Tobias.

Note 2: All the Scripture verses quoted in this book come from the Catholic Revised Standard Version translation, even those used in Father Bernard's homily. All you hardcore Catholics out there know the readings we actually hear at Mass don't come from the Catholic RSV translation, and in real life Father Bernard would be quoting a different translation. But there are complicated copyright issues with the translation we hear at Mass, so Father Bernard is stuck quoting the Catholic RSV (arguably a better translation anyway).

Acknowledgments

On the day this is published, it will have been almost exactly five years that my paternal grandfather, Howard "Koko" Stone, passed away. My paternal grandmother, Josephine Ann Stone, passed two and a half years later. Their names are not all they've lent me for this work. Thank you, Grandpa Koko and Grandma JoAnn, for the gifts of family and faith that you handed on to so many of us.

I also owe special thanks to my parents. Of course, it's impossible to list everything they've given me; but for the purposes of this book, I want to thank them most especially for taking me and my sister to symphony concerts as kids (I still go to symphony concerts with my parents when there's not a stupid virus ruining everything). Mom and Dad, you instilled in me a passion for orchestral music, and music in general, that has enriched my life beyond measure. Thank you.

Huge thanks to my beta readers: Sarah, Jody, Denise, and Kristen. You probably didn't know what you were getting yourself into when I asked you to beta read, but I can't thank you enough. You are amazing women.

I picked a lot of brains to help me shape the details that make Sam and Tobias's experiences as authentic as possible. I asked a lot of people about their first crushes, their first kisses, their first parties... thank you to all who put up with my questions and gave me your insights into some of growing up's biggest moments.

Thank you to my incredible cover designer, Bilal Abiyhasa. You knocked it out of the park again, Abi, and I can't wait to finish another book just so I can see what beautiful cover you come up with next.

Thank you, as always, to all the family members, friends, and colleagues who have read my stuff, given me notes, and cheered me on over the years. Your generosity and love humble me.

And thank you, readers, for sticking it out to the end of my very first novel. A work means nothing without a soul to comprehend it. You, dear reader, give my work meaning.

Above all, I must give all thanks and praise to Christ, my Divine Spouse. I am nothing without Him: "Whom have I in heaven but Thee? And there is nothing upon earth that I desire besides Thee. My flesh and my heart may fail, but God is the strength of my heart and my portion for ever" (Ps 73:25-26).

About the Author

Tara started writing fiction when she was in first grade, but she didn't discover the thrill of screenwriting until she studied Communications Media at John Paul the Great Catholic University. Screenplays are her favorite way to tell stories.

Tara resides in Colorado, and in 2016, she became a Consecrated Virgin Living in the World in the Diocese of Colorado Springs. In addition to making things up and writing them down, Tara enjoys praying, hiking (definitely not running), going to the symphony (especially movies at the symphony), discovering new craft brews, and spending time with family and friends.

CPSIA information can be obtained
at www.ICGtesting.com
Printed in the USA
LVHW030145191120
672132LV00003B/64